A Tale of mystery, greed, revenge and murder that will keep you wondering what will happen next.

I'm Going to Kill That Cat

by

F. Della Notte

ISBN: 13: 978-0692961285
ISBN-10: 0692961283

Contents

Acknowledgements

1 Prelude to a Crime

Fat Tuesday: The Last Day before Lent

2 All's Right with the World...but Only for One Minute

3 The Nemesis

4 Running the Gauntlet

5 The Housekeeper Saga

6 You Can't Choose Your Relatives

7 Hemmed In

8 "...And sweet revenge grows harsh."

Shakespeare

Ash Wednesday: First Day of the Solemn Season of Fasting and Prayer: Lent

9 More Than Ash Wednesday Traffic

10 Where Is LaLa?

11 You Didn't Walk in Her Shoes

12 In The Crosshairs

13 Who Is in Charge?

Friday: Two Days after Ash Wednesday

14 Resetting Boundaries

15 That Damned Woman

Saturday: Three Days after Ash Wednesday

16 The Aftermath

Sunday: The First Full Week of Lent

17 Potluck

Monday: The First Full Week of Lent

18 It's an Insane Asylum

19 Stop Before You Get to the Knuckle

20 The Watcher

21 Dead Velma

22 Things Will Look Better Tomorrow

23 She's the Problem

Tuesday: The First Full Week of Lent

24 Not the Same

25 You're the Housekeeper

26 Thirty Thousand Pieces of Silver

Wednesday: The First Full Week of Lent

27 Another Piece of the Puzzle

28 A Mother Found, a Mother Lost

29 A Fragile Truce

30 Let's Help Them Close This Case

Thursday: The First Full Week of Lent

31 The Note

32 A Terrible Accident

33 I Just Wanted to Kill the Cat

34 Is He Catholic?

35 Cry Later

36 Someone Really Wanted Her Dead

37 Lent: A Time for Spiritual Growth and Renewal, but First...

Friday: The First Full Week of Lent

38 No Time for Murder

Saturday: The First Full Week of Lent

39 This Isn't Opera

40 The Constitution of a Horse

Sunday: The Second Week of Lent

41 Something's Gotta Change

42 I Feel It in My Bones

Monday: The Second Week of Lent

43 Naughty Cat

44 The Situation is Fluid

45 Monster

46 The Dead Can't Hurt You

47 Working Together

Tuesday: The Second Week of Lent

48 Time's Up

49 Rammed

50 Oh What a Tangled Web We Weave...

Thursday: The Second Week of Lent

51 Tying up Loose Ends

52 "In a Cat's Eyes, All Things Belong to the Cat.

ACKNOWLEDGEMENTS

Kudos to Hummingbird Web Designs
Valery Grey for my beautiful cover art
Nancy Verdi for my exciting webpages

Special Thanks to Justine Nimmo for her editing
and keen eye keeping storylines and facts consistent.

1

Prelude to a Crime

On his knees, the agony in his shoulders increased with every pull. Fear and searing pain made sweat pour out of him. His arms were being yanked out of their sockets. He pleaded, "Snake, please. I swear. Give me two months and I will pay you back every cent with interest."

Snake nodded to his enforcers. They pulled his arms up higher behind his back and twisted.

"Ahhh." He was powerless to control the scream that burst from his throat. His eyes rolled up in his head. On the verge of passing out, the pressure on his arms suddenly stopped. He stayed conscious, but his shoulders throbbed; his arms remained behind him so that the threat of another yank was real.

"How you gonna do dat?" Snake asked, walking around waving his Glock. He knelt down and set the gun against his victim's left temple. Snake and his associates smelled the mess made by the man's watery bowels. He cried out again in fear and shame. Snake pushed the gun hard against his head. "Asked you a question, fool. How you gonna do dat?"

"I'm going to get the money. You'll see. I'll come through."

Snake stood up and held his hand over his nostrils to reduce the sour odor of feces and fear. "A month. I give ya one month from today, then you die slow and hard. Now, here's the list of what I want. You want to stay alive, you bring it." Snake nodded again, and the victim's arms were released causing new sensations of pain as they dropped to his sides. One of Snake's enforcers thrust the paper into his hands.

Perspiration ran off his head and into his eyes like water. He couldn't see through the salty fluid that blurred his vision. He rubbed his eyes and gulped when he looked at the list, but he was too terrified to object. "Yes, anything you say." The two men standing behind him shoved him face-first into the dirt.

"You get me what's on this list, hear?" Snake said, tapping his long fingernail on the top of the paper. "And remember. One month for the money or you die."

By way of an answer, he lifted his head and nodded, then dropped his face back into the earth.

An engine raced. Car doors slammed. "Bury your mess, man, cuz animals will smell you. They be here soon." He heard laughter as the car sped away, kicking up gravel and stones, leaving him lying on the side of a dirt road in the dark.

***

The bedside clock read 5:00 a.m. She hit the button. Awake, she didn't need the alarm to go off. It was time to get up, dressed, and off to work. She'd slept fitfully all night, aware that he hadn't come back. "Hope they didn't kill the damned fool," she muttered, "I need him alive."

Dressed and ready to leave, she walked out of the bedroom when the front door opened and he stumbled in looking like a nightmare and bringing a stink beyond that of a feral jungle animal. She gagged. Breathless from the putrid odor, she asked, "What happened?" Pinching her nostrils, she stepped back, away from the heap of stinking humanity that fell to his knees on the floor, not wanting her clean shoes to touch anything foul. Her voice sounded tinny in her ears, but she didn't let go of her nose.

He doubled over, holding his stomach. "They're going to kill me if I don't pay it all back in a month," he cried.

She looked at him lying there in his own stench, sobbing like a child. Pathetic, she thought. Disgust alternated with satisfaction.

"You'd better call the office and tell them you have a stomach virus. Get yourself and this floor cleaned up. When I get back, we'll make plans." She stepped over him and headed out the door. "I warned you months ago," she said over her shoulder. "Now you have no choice...or you can just give yourself up to them and die." She slammed the door behind her.

A sliver of pity threaded its way into her head while she waited for the elevator. He was a pretty good guy, everything considered. When it's done, maybe I'll stick around and help him get over his addiction, she thought. Then again...

Fat Tuesday
Day Before Ash Wednesday

2

All's Right with the World...But Only for One Minute

Father Melvyn careened out the back of the rectory letting the door bang shut behind him. He knew it annoyed his trusted housekeeper and assistant, Mrs. B., and he imagined her wince when it slammed. Get that door fixed before she kills you, he scolded himself. Occupied with the day's schedule, he skipped down the steps. Across the main parking lot of Saint Francis de Sales Church he walked at his usual pace, which was just short of a jog.

A big man, and in spite of the weight he'd gained since Mrs. B. took over running the rectory, he moved his six-foot-plus frame with the unexpected grace of a large jungle cat.

The March breeze blew his normally unruly hair back from a high forehead revealing gray strands woven into the red-gold color. Wire-rimmed glasses perched on a straight nose did nothing to diminish the powerful intelligence of his piercing brown eyes, shaded by long red-blond lashes.

A bushy moustache the same color as his hair occupied the space between the end of his nose and the top of a full lip.

In his youth, his full face, strong features, and deep, soulful eyes made him a target for many young women. Even after taking vows, women, young and not so young, thought it a waste of wonderful manhood that Melvyn Kronkey was married to his church instead of being married in it.

His calling to serve God, his willingness to endure the celibate life, and his ability to stay focused kept him unfazed by female attention; he'd mastered the art of keeping a virtual wall around himself. A neon sign couldn't have been more explicit: *Not Interested*. It wasn't that he didn't like women. He did. The different perspectives they brought to any situation intrigued him, and having a keen sense of things pleasing to the eye, including the opposite sex, he developed a personal credo: *Look but Don't Touch*. He was fully devoted to his one passion: God.

Walking toward the front parking field to meet Rafael the gardener, the pastor of Saint Francis checked his wristwatch. Rafael was always prompt and Father Melvyn needed the gardener's help today.

Several parishioners complained to him that tree branches hanging across the driveway, and overgrown shrubs at the entrance at Cobble Drive scratched their cars. He decided to have Rafael cut them back before tomorrow's heavy traffic. Ash Wednesday services were always well attended, and Lent should not begin with more complaints.

Father Melvyn looked up into the clear blue sky. Puffy clouds pushed by the wind glided from east to west. He felt good. "God's in his heaven and all is right with the world." He almost sang the phrase. The big man drew a deep breath and felt a moment of peace...but only a moment.

Shrieks and screams erupted on the sidewalk from in front of the Church entrance on Cobble Drive. "Help, help." A battery of barking, woofing, yowling, and dogs' nails scratching on concrete accompanied the woman's screams. The cacophony sounded like a pack of hungry wolves, followed by a higher-pitched animal scream and screeching tires.

"What in God's name?" Father Melvyn wondered aloud before he propelled his large frame forward. His progress was cut off by the gardener's truck that pulled into the driveway and stopped short.

Rafael, flung open the cab door, jumped out, and ran toward the yelling. Father Melvyn froze for a nanosecond and then launched himself forward to find the source of the uproar. Lurching around the truck, he saw a woman on the ground, cursing like a sailor. He rolled his eyes. "Oh God. Of all people," he muttered.

Rafael reached her and was trying to get the leashes out of her hand, which increased the dogs' fierce barking.

Father Melvyn ran the last few feet. "Martha, are you hurt? What happened?" he shouted.

"I'm going to kill that cat. I wish it would get hit by a car, along with the witch who owns it. Wish they'd both get hit by a car," she sobbed, twisting and turning on the ground, trying to hold onto the dogs. Father Melvyn grabbed the leashes to help Rafael.

"Shush," he ordered. Martha Magswelle's dogs, Barklay and Smitty, knew Father Melvyn. They sat down at his command and whimpered as if to say, "Don't be mad at us, we're the good guys." The dogs and Martha quieted, and he thought things were coming under control until another female voice spoke from behind him.

3
The Nemesis

"I was sweeping my porch and saw you fall. Are you Okay? What happened?" Velma Scooterman-Maxwell asked. Her eyes contradicted the silky concern in her voice. Broom in hand, Velma looked down at Martha.

At the sound of Velma's voice, LaLa, her cat and the villain in the morning's drama, flew out from under a shrub. Ears pinned flat against her head, LaLa gave a loud, gulping meow and jumped into Velma's arms, amid the dogs' renewed barking and Martha's scream. "That damned cat made me fall again."

Father Melvyn and Rafael helped Martha to her feet. Her hand was red; the flesh swelling from the leashes pulled tight around her palm. "Let me take the dogs," Father Melvyn said to the irate and disheveled woman.

"It's Okay, LaLa," Velma crooned to her pet.

Looking at Velma, Father Melvyn mouthed the words, "It would be best if you take LaLa home." Velma nodded.

Before turning her well-coiffed head in the direction of her house she said, "Father Melvyn, my nephew Jeffrey asked me to tell you how much he enjoyed our dinner last Sunday. He said we should do it more often." Her announcement brought another infuriated outburst from Martha.

"Why don't you fly away on that broom and take your stinking cat. One of these days, I'm going to kill that thing," Martha shrieked as she steadied herself on Father Melvyn's arm. The immediate change in Velma's demeanor chilled the air. Father Melvyn and Rafael froze in place. The look in Velma's eyes sent a shiver up Father Melvyn's spine.

"If you try to hurt my cat, you'll be sorry...very, very sorry." Although whispered, the threat was as cold and dangerous as the iceberg that sank the *Titanic*. Velma turned, crossed the street with LaLa and went home.

From the corner of his eye Father Melvyn noticed that Rafael had stepped back and away from the frightful women. Can hardly blame him, Father Melvyn thought.

"She threatened me. Did you hear her?" Martha was on the brink of total hysteria. "She threatened me." Her voice rose and sounded brittle in the priest's ears.

"Calm down, Martha," Father Melvyn used his most soothing tone when all he really wanted to do was shake her. Martha was on her feet, but the dogs were restless, agitated. Afraid she wouldn't be able to control them, Father Melvyn held onto the leashes.

Frantically smoothing her dress down over her scraped legs, Martha sobbed, "I know. Isn't Velma wonderful? Isn't Velma terrific?"

Father Melvyn didn't answer. With one hand, he kept a firm grip on Martha's arm and with the other he held the dogs' leashes. "I'll be right back," he said to the gardener.

"No problem Father. Take your time." Rafael mopped his brow with a handkerchief and mumbled, "Dios mio, these women are crazy."

Father Melvyn's smile at the gardener's words was followed by a sigh of relief when he saw that Martha could put weight on the ankle that was healing from the break she'd suffered a few months earlier when she accidentally stepped on LaLa's tail. He remembered the uproar it caused.

LaLa had decided to stalk her prey onto Martha's property. Martha hadn't noticed the cat's tail sticking out of the shrubs; she accidentally stepped on it. The cat gave out a screaming yowl and bolted, throwing Martha off balance; she fell and broke her ankle.

"Weren't you to see the doctor yesterday? What did she say about your ankle?" Father Melvyn asked.

Martha harrumphed. "Mrs. B. talks too much. She tells you everything, doesn't she? Yes, I saw the doctor, and she told me to use my walker."

"No need to be unkind, my dear," the priest said. "Why would you try walking the dogs without your walker when you're still unsteady?"

"It gets in my way, and I can't have the dogs peeing in the house, now can I?"

You could let them out in the yard, he thought, but kept that to himself. Instead, he turned her toward her little house across Carpenter Street. "I'm meeting with Ms. Jenkins the school principal today. Why don't I ask her to get one of her students to come and walk the dogs? Yes?"

Martha stopped walking, turned, and looked at him. "Why that would be lovely, Father. Thank you." She sounded surprised.

Traffic was light, and they crossed Carpenter Street easily. Thank you, Lord, Father Melvyn thought. He was anxious to get Martha safely into her house and back to Rafael.

When Martha opened the front door, Father Melvyn released the dogs. "My dear, you should sit down and rest. If you need anything, call the rectory. Mrs. B. will help you."

"Thank you, Father," she said and stepped over the threshold. Placing her hand on the doorknob, she looked Father Melvyn square in the eyes. "I hate Velma. You think you know her, but you don't."

***

After closing the door in Father Melvyn's face, Martha went to the kitchen with her dogs. "Come on," she said affectionately. "I'll get you fresh water. You're panting from running after that cat." As Barklay and Smitty lapped up the water in their bowls, Martha felt the burning in her skinned knees for the first time. Reaching into a kitchen cabinet, she pulled out the first-aid kit to clean and cover her scrapes. "Ugh. I'm stiff already."

Barklay and Smitty emptied their water bowls while Martha treated her injuries. Tired from the morning's chaos, the dogs curled up on the shabby, old, multicolored rope rugs Martha had made for them. The strands of dock rope pushing through the fabric covering made her realize she needed to make new ones even if the dogs didn't seem to mind. "New beds for you by next Christmas," she said to her pets. Even though I make them myself, the materials cost money I can't afford to spend right now, she mused.

The thought of money brought Velma and her cat to mind. Bet LaLa sleeps on silks and satins. Martha hated the feelings of bitterness she couldn't hold back. That woman cost me so much in my life. As if they could read her thoughts, Barklay and Smitty huffed and groaned before closing their eyes.

"Exhausted from chasing LaLa? Oh, you really are naughty," she said, smiling at her precious pets. She reached over and stroked their heads. "You mustn't run after her that way. She doesn't want to play with you. Velma probably taught her to tease you." Martha checked the time. Her thoughts turned elsewhere and her heart skipped the in anticipation. He'd be here soon.

***

Crossing back to her side of the street, Velma held LaLa in her arms the way Mrs. B. showed her one day when LaLa, in typical cat fashion, ignored Velma's calls and ran up onto the porch of Saint Francis's rectory. Mrs. B. easily gathered the cat in her arms. When Velma caught up, Mrs. B. showed her how to hold LaLa so that the cat was comfortable and secure.

LaLa purred and rubbed her head under Velma's chin; Velma felt the love and appreciation. "Come now. That stupid woman doesn't want to kill you. She wants to kill me, but she doesn't dare." Velma's eyes narrowed at the thought of Martha. She is weak and powerless. If she thinks after all these years she's going to shove her dirty little secret under my nose and embarrass me, or worse, blackmail me, she'd better think again.

Standing inside her front door, still holding the cat, Velma murmured. "I think we'll have to take some steps to ensure that Martha stays away from both of us. I'll give it some thought. She'll be sorry. I'll make her pathetic little life even more miserable. Why the hell doesn't she sell that rundown house and get out of Austin?"

The stress of her thoughts prompted the old anger which triggered a burst of adrenaline. Velma's muscles constricted, tightening her grip on the cat; LaLa began to wriggle then jumped down. Velma's thoughts returned to her precious LaLa. "I think you've been out enough for today," she said and locked the cat portal in the front door then looked around.

She always felt a surge of satisfaction as she eyed the living room. Mentally, she ticked off the qualities of the furniture and accessories: silk drapes, designer couches and end tables, and her treasured tea set on the coffee table. Everything looked even more luxurious on top of the new, engineered wood floors. She'd replaced the wall-to-wall carpet months ago.

Looking at her reflection in one of the gilt mirrors hanging on either side of the fireplace, she compared her reflection to her portrait above the mantle, where Charles's portrait hung until his death. She'd removed it and replaced it with her own, painted by one of Austin's leading portraitists.

Turning from side to side, she preened, examined the skin around her eyes, and patted her hair. I've aged well with a little help, of course, she thought. Actually, I look better now than when I was young. Mother Nature was never kind to me and now, thanks to darling Charles, I can afford to change her designs any time I want.

The money she'd inherited from her parents was nice, but it was Charles's fortune that allowed her every luxury and service she desired. Velma wasn't dishonest or shy about admitting that she spent lavishly on beauty products. "What's the point of having it if you don't use it," she was fond of saying.

Sitting down with her calendar and notebook, Velma scanned the dates. I think a lovely party for the parish council would be appropriate in May, before the Memorial Day weekend, before the school year ends, and before people go away on vacation. She made some notes. I'll speak to Father Melvyn about it.

She looked at the clock. I wonder if scruffy old Martha will go to the noon mass after her little hissy fit on the sidewalk, she thought. Velma called to her headstrong cat: "Come here, LaLa. Have your treat before I leave."

4
Running the Gauntlet

Exasperated by Martha's behavior, Father Melvyn shook his head. On the short walk back to Saint Francis, where Rafael waited, the escalating animosity between Velma and Martha troubled him. He mulled over what he knew of these two women.

Neither had children or family living close by; one was widowed and the other had never married. They should be friends, not enemies, but he was aware of glaring differences.

Poor Martha, Father Melvyn thought. He knew she struggled to make ends meet, supporting herself on her social security checks. She'd never married and had no children. Her one brother, Jeremy, lived in San Marcos and didn't seem to visit often. Whenever Father Melvyn asked about him, Martha was always vague. Father Melvyn didn't think they had much of a relationship.

"He tries to help me, when he can; he does have a family to support you know," was Martha's usual terse answer. Father Melvyn remembered the one time he'd invited Martha to bring Jeremy to meet him after mass. He was dumbstruck by her answer.

"No, Father. Jeremy isn't even a CEO."

"CEO?" he asked.

"Christmas and Easter only. Jeremy is a WFO, weddings and funerals only." Father Melvyn shook off the memory. He never asked again.

In contrast, Velma's nephew, a doctor from Dallas, visited regularly, and always came to mass with his aunt. Father Melvyn's mouth automatically turned down at the thought of Jeffrey Scooterman. He reminds me of a peacock, Father Melvyn thought. Strutting around with his tail fanned out saying, *Look at me.* He preens and struts, basking in the praise showered on his aunt.

Then there was Velma's beautiful home compared to Martha's little cottage, which was well-kept, if shabby from age. Like its owner, it was once pretty, until wear and tear became visible, like the ravages of age and stress that etched deep lines in Martha's face, even though there was still evidence of a pretty woman under the surface. And unlike Velma who admittedly spent lots of money on cosmetics, creams, and hairdressers, Martha barely spent money to get a professional haircut, let alone beauty-enhancing cosmetics.

Father Melvyn sighed. Martha's opinion of Velma was well known to everyone in the parish. At least once, they'd heard Martha's nickname for her: Velma Fabulous. "Isn't Velma-Fabulous great; isn't Velma-Fabulous wonderful," Martha often snarled.

A patroness of Saint Francis de Sales, Velma often hosted parties and fund-raisers for the church and her need for recognition was well-known. Invited guests were aware that compliments on her beautifully furnished home were part of the price to be invited. "A price worth paying," the president of the parish council often said to Father Melvyn, in light of the frequent and generous donations she made to Saint Francis. The parish council ignored or laughed at Martha's obvious jealousy in a feud that began long before he got there.

When Father Melvyn first arrived at Saint Francis de Sales, a fresh-faced priest from England, the animosity between the women was already set in stone. He once asked Pastor Jameson about it, but the answer was a disinterested shrug. The accepted story was that poor Martha, who had little, was jealous of Velma, who had everything. Thereafter, he too paid little attention to the problem.

Returning to the present, he sighed. There is important parish business to attend to he consoled himself, until a twinge of something, guilt perhaps, made him uncomfortable. His cheeks flushed when that little voice in his head asked, *Aren't your parishioners the most important part of parish business?* "Ah, well," he muttered as he pushed aside his growing discomfort with the Martha-Velma feud.

He turned into the driveway. Rafael's truck was now in a proper parking spot and not planted across the entrance.
"Sorry to keep you waiting, Rafael," he said. "Here's the problem. People are complaining about the overhead branches from that tree," he said, pointing up, "and the bushy shrubs there, along the drive, scratching their cars as they pull in. Can you cut everything back, and can you do it today? Tomorrow is Ash Wednesday, and we'll have more traffic, meaning I'll have more complaints."

"Si, Si, Father. I will do it now."

"Thank you, Rafael." He looked at his watch. My, where has the time gone? Got to get ready.

At the end of the noon mass, as was his custom, and outside of most normal procedures, Father Melvyn walked back to the center of the majestic high altar and turned to face the crucifix, as if to remind everyone and anyone in church of the sacrifice made for their souls. He stood before the stone marble soaring almost to the top of the gold mosaic cupola. Carved angels flanked each side of `the crucifix bearing the body of Christ. He raised his arms then turned to the congregation to give the final blessing. "May the Lord bless you, in the name of the Father, the Son, and the Holy Ghost," he said, tracing the cross in the air. "The mass is ended. Go in peace to love and serve the Lord."

The response from the sparse congregation came back. "Thanks be to God," after which he left the altar. His eyes saw the field of pews, and he was plagued by the feeling that he was running a gauntlet as he passed through a virtual field of hate flashing across the center aisle.

Glaring at each other, the combatants were in their usual places in the same row on either side of the aisle. Not making eye contact, he swept past them aware that Martha was upright and recovered from her fall, and Velma had left her broom at home.

In the outer lobby, the narthex, at the farthest distance and directly opposite the main altar, Father Melvyn stopped to greet the few regulars, mostly retired persons, who attended midday mass. It saddened him that fifty, even twenty-five, years ago, mass was said in most parishes at seven thirty in the morning to give the faithful a chance to start their days in prayer on their way to work. Now they must tend to their own prayer needs early in the morning. His thoughts about how things had changed were interrupted by the scrappy scene approaching him.

Velma and Martha, the first ones out, raced to reach

their pastor. Elbows flew. The women crashed into each other; Velma won. Martha lost her balance but stayed upright by grabbing the ridge of the large holy water font in the center of the narthex. "I'm going to kill you and that stupid cat," Martha snarled.

Turning her back to Father Melvyn, Velma answered, "Not if I kill you first."

"Ladies, please. You are in church, and you both just received communion." Father Melvyn saw the dismay on the faces of the other parishioners who waved to him but didn't bother to stop. The Velma-Martha feud was well known. Father Melvyn stepped forward. "This is out of hand and not amusing. Threatening to kill each other in the church is a new low. I'd recommend you both go to confession."

Velma waved and apologized. "I'm sorry, Father," she said sweetly. "You're right. We aren't behaving well at all. Please forgive me?" Martha made no such apology.

"You okay?" Father Melvyn asked, watching Martha hold onto the font.

"I'm going to kill that... woman one day," Martha answered, walking off without so much as a goodbye.

After the parishioners were gone, Father Melvyn returned to the sacristy, where he removed and stored the vestments. He was more than irritated. It's time for me to put a stop to this feud, or at least order them to call a truce while on church property. He knew he needed to do something, but what? I'll talk it over with Mrs. B. She has a great sense of people and rock-solid common sense, he thought.

Originally hired as the housekeeper and cook, Mrs. B. had since become an invaluable administrative assistant. Feeling confident that together they would find a solution, his preoccupation with Martha and Velma ended when he walked through the connecting passage from the church to the rectory.

He didn't need to look at a watch. His stomach responded to the wonderful aromas coming from the kitchen. He opened the door on the rectory side of the passage and sniffed, then smiled. The fragrance of his favorite meal reached him; it was better than perfume. It was one of her signature dishes. "Eggplant parmigiana," he called out as he crossed the hall to the kitchen.

Mrs. B. smiled as if indulging a child, even though Father Melvyn wasn't much younger than she. "A simple sniff and you know what I've cooked? You're getting too good at this. Think I'll try some new recipes," she said. "Enjoy your lunch. I'll be working in the office. There are letters for you to sign. When you're finished eating, you can tell me what happened this morning between Martha and Velma."

"How did you find out?"

"I have my sources. Eat up," she quipped and walked out of the kitchen before he could ask another question.

Rafael probably told her, he thought, turning to his lunch. His mouth watered. Crossing himself, he said a quick prayer, and dug into the steaming dish. "Ah," he sighed with contentment and gratitude for the good Lord having sent this woman to Saint Francis. She'd rescued him from the clutches of the housekeeper he'd inherited and her successor.

5
The Housekeeper Saga

While he savored his meal, Father Melvyn's mind spooled back in time. He'd arrived at St. Francis de Sales in Austin via Boston to assist Father Jameson, the frail, old pastor suffering from osteoarthritis. The adjustment was challenging. Americans, he learned quickly, had a different approach than he was accustomed to in England, but Father Jameson was happy to let Father Melvyn, his new assistant, carry most of the responsibilities. Then there was Father Jameson's housekeeper, Mrs. Rangel. She was another story.

He thought about the fierce woman who, like a tiger watching over her cub, hovered over Father Jameson. She protected him from everything and everyone, including his new curate, the parish council, and his parishioners. No sense of humor, and worst of all, no cooking skills. He took another forkful of the delicious parmigiana, savoring the bite. "Ambrosia isn't the food of the gods, Mrs. B.'s eggplant parmigiana is"—at least to the Italian gods, he thought irreverently. In Mrs. Rangel's defense, he had no trouble controlling his weight when she and her successor, Mrs. Smith, cooked.

"Hmmm." He grabbed a paper napkin and scribbled a note: *See calendar—special mass in memory of Father Jameson.*

When the old pastor died unexpectedly, the bishop asked Father Melvyn to take over. A few months later Mrs. Rangel gave notice.

"I have taken the liberty of hiring a new housekeeper for you," she'd told him in her most righteous tone. At first Father Melvyn was grateful, but it didn't take long to learn that the new housekeeper was worse than Mrs. Rangel.

Mrs. Smith was bossy, critical, and uppity, and she cooked the same meals the same way as her predecessor. He once commented, "Mrs. Rangel cooked chicken this way too." He didn't speak the remainder of his thought: like rubber.

"Of course," she answered, nose high enough in the air to drown in a rainstorm. "She left me her recipes."

Father Melvyn, still a new pastor, trained himself to ignore her as long as she kept the rectory clean and neat, answered the phones, and provided some kind of food. Totally immersed in the business of Saint Francis de Sales, he didn't want to take the time to find another housekeeper. He imagined they were all the same, but the woman irritated him.

He prayed for patience to deal with her until one fateful day, when he'd returned from the midday mass extra tired because he'd been called to the hospital twice the night before.

Lying in wait, like a spider watching its prey, Mrs. Smith pounced and began her carping as soon as he walked in. "You know, Father, your room is unnecessarily sloppy. You should be more like Father Russo."

That he banged the plate down, making the dry sandwich bounce onto the table, didn't clue Mrs. Smith to stop talking. "And your office. Really, Father Kronkey," She never called him Father Melvyn. Like Mrs. Rangel, she considered it inappropriate. "Papers and files strewn all over the place. How can I keep the place clean? I piled everything in one spot." Even the memory of the encounter embarrassed him. I was not charitable, patient, or priestly, he thought, remembering his response:

"Mrs. Smith, I think it best if you don't clean our bedrooms any more. We will take care of our own personals, thank you." She huffed as if I'd blasphemed and I lost it, he remembered. "As for my office and my papers and files, KEEP YOUR HANDS OFF."

The memory of her horrified expression was vivid. She backed away, turned, and stormed out of the kitchen, spluttering in outrage. "Well, I never…"

The next day she gave notice. She said she couldn't continue working for someone "who bounded through the house like a runaway horse and laughed too much, too loud, and too long. Being a good Christian woman, however, I've placed an ad in the weekly journal. I will interview, hire, and train a new housekeeper."

Feeling like a weight had been lifted from his shoulders that day, Father Melvyn thanked her and said he'd do the interviewing and hiring.

"Well," she wheezed as she turned and propelled her ample frame through the kitchen door and into the front hallway.

Within a week they had five applicants, all meeting Mrs. Smith's uptight requirements. Having learned his lesson he didn't hire any of them. "Father Kronkey, these women were serious and of the right temperament to serve as your housekeeper and cook."

Father Melvyn felt a new flood of shame as he recalled the words he'd been about to speak that day. "Talk about being saved by the bell...literally." He still wondered what instinct or which angel pushed him to follow Mrs. Smith as she answered the doorbell.

In the doorway stood a woman with large, round, blue-rimmed glasses, rather unruly curly white hair, and an infectious smile.

"Can I help you?" Mrs. Smith asked in her usual haughty tone.

"I'm here in response to the ad in the journal," the woman said. "Can't have our pastor starving now, can we?" She chuckled and extended her hand. "I'm Samuela Buonafigliuola."

Father Melvyn set his fork down; his belly shook with laughter as he relived the scene worthy of a sitcom. He'd been standing behind Mrs. Smith. Her deep, never ending sniff almost sucked all the oxygen out of the air then she became as rigid as a statue. Something made him step forward.

"Happy to meet you, Mrs. Bon...How do you say your name?"

"B-U-O-N-A-F-I-G-L-I-U-O-L-A," the woman said slowly as if talking to a child. "Most people call me Sammi."

Exhaling in order to find her voice again, Mrs. Smith spluttered, "This is entirely unacceptable. No one will be able to pronounce that name."

"Thank you, Mrs. Smith. I'll take it from here." Turning to the newcomer with the difficult and strange name, Father Melvyn guided her to the office. "May I call you Mrs. B.?"

"That's fine, Father Kronkey."

"And I'm Father Melvyn."

Returning to his lunch, he finished his eggplant parmigiana and again thanked the good Lord. What a blessing she is. Smart, sassy and discrete, she only makes wisecracks when no one is around, and she's a great cook. He patted his belly. Maybe she's my reward for not killing the others.

It didn't take long for Father Melvyn to discover that Mrs. B. was also an excellent and much-needed administrative assistant. No one expected the population explosion in Austin, which in turn increased the number of parishioners in Saint Francis's parish, thereby increasing the amount of administrative work to be done. Mrs. B. turned out to be a whiz. What had she done for a living before? She'd told him at the interview, but he forgot.

More important, he marveled at her gift of setting people at ease, especially when they arrived for counseling. They often fidgeted, nervous about revealing secrets and problems, often looking around furtively, as if afraid someone else might hear. Mrs. B. would set them at ease and then melt away. She never hovered. Just then the subject of his reflections walked into the kitchen.

"Enjoyed your lunch, Father Melvyn?"

"You know I did. Looking for flattery, Mrs. B.?"

"Yes, but I think tonight just salad for you. More tea?" Not waiting for an answer, she placed a fresh glass of ice tea in front of him and sat down with her own. "We don't have much time; Ms. Jenkins will be here in a few minutes. Tell me what happened this morning with Martha and Velma."

Instead of giving her the details in the latest Martha Velma fracas, he expressed confusion. "I cannot fathom why, at their age, these two women have such animosity toward each other."

"Local lore says there was a problem over a man fifty-something years ago. As the story goes, Charles Maxwell and his family were newcomers to Austin. They had money from questionable sources, and they were a bit odd. Rumor says they were involved in rackets or some other disreputable business.

"Anyway, the son, Charles, was handsome. Every young girl pined for him. He started dating Martha, who was supposedly a knockout. After a few months, Martha's parents sent her out of town to break up the relationship. Then he took up with Velma. Her father was a respected doctor and sat on the city council. As Velma never lets us forget, the family had standing in the community. Velma's father, Dr. Scooterman, was not pleased when Velma eloped with Maxwell.

"About a year later, Martha came back to Austin. They say she was different, bitter, like she is today."

"She never married?" Father Melvyn asked.

"No. She didn't."

"And she hated Velma for marrying Charles?"

"So they say."

"And they've held this hatred for fifty years? Where do they find the energy for it?" Amazed and troubled, Father Melvyn's eyebrows gathered over his nose, and he held his pursed lips between his thumb and forefinger. The door buzzer interrupted his thoughts. Without a word, Mrs. B. went to answer.

"Hello, Nancy. How are you?"

"I'm great, Sammi. How about you?"

Father Melvyn heard the voices and knew Ms. Jenkins had arrived. He finished his ice tea and went to the office, listening to their amiable chatter while they waited. "Hello, Ms. Jenkins," Father Melvyn said, extending his hand.

When he walked in, Mrs. B. waved her fingers, "Ciao," she said, walked out and closed the office door.

"Before we talk school business," he began, "I have a favor to ask." Father Melvyn explained Martha Magswelle's need to have a student walk her dogs.

"Yes, we all know Ms. Magswelle. She's not shy about her dislikes…of which there are many," Ms. Jenkins made a note. "I have two nice boys who live nearby. I'll ask them to help, and I'll give them credit for community service."

"Much appreciated, Ms. Jenkins. Thank you."

Nancy Jenkins pulled out a written report and handed it to him. "As you can see from those numbers, even though it's only March, we're expecting an increase in enrollment for the next school year. Applications are coming in at a heavy rate."

Father Melvyn looked over the numbers. "We did have excellent results on the state exams last year." He looked up. "Expecting the same this year?"

"Yes, and hopefully better. We're putting more emphasis on science and math. Unfortunately, it's leaving little time for music and art. I've been discussing this with my faculty, and they have some good ideas."

"Can you share?"

"Not yet, Father. I want to get the best suggestions expanded a bit." Father Melvyn nodded. He was pleased. He and Ms. Jenkins shared similar philosophies about well-rounded educations and the balance between self-discipline, home discipline, and school discipline.

He knew from her résumé that she was a former nun. They'd discussed it at her initial interview, but since she never brought it up again, he didn't feel it was his place. He was content that they were on the same page regarding the education of young minds.

"Tomorrow is Ash Wednesday. We have the children's mass and ash distribution scheduled for eight thirty in the morning. Hopefully, that will be less disruptive to classwork than ten thirty, as we did it in years past. Father Declan will say mass in the school auditorium. Have you had much blowback about the change in time?"

"Parents will have to drop off at eight a.m., which disrupts many of their routines. There's been a lot of grumbling, but this is better." After they discussed more of the nuts and bolts of running a school, they ended their meeting by setting dates and times for the remaining school year's faculty meetings.

"The next school year starts up the third week of August, and the teachers come back August first," Ms. Jenkins reminded him. "Even with the new teachers we've hired, the expected increase in enrollment will fill each class to the max."

"You'll keep the max class size the same?"

She nodded. "On another subject, before classes begin, I have two men from a security company coming in to run safety drills with the faculty."

"What's that?" he asked.

"We live in terrible times, Father, and we must do all we can, short of carrying guns, to learn the most effective ways to protect our students in case a violent criminal, whether a nut or a terrorist, enters the building."

"Have you discussed this with the parish council?"

"No." Ms. Jenkins sat up straighter. "The fewer people who are aware of our plans, the better. The two gentlemen running the drills are doing it pro bono, so there's no budget consideration."

"I understand. If it's a council discussion, it could bogged down in arguments. I'm sure they'll find out, and when they do, you'll have my full support...on one condition.

"What's that, Father?"

"When the experts come, I want to be part of the drills."

Ms. Jenkins smiled broadly and stuck out her hand. "Deal."

***

The remainder of the day passed uneventfully.

Father Melvyn looked at the clock. "Mrs. B., it's almost five," he called out. Wherever is that woman now? he wondered. She's never still. He shouted out again. "Mrs. B., before you leave, please call Martha and ask how she's doing."

Mrs. B. appeared in the doorway. "Why are you shouting? I called her an hour ago. She's fine. Her same old crusty self and obsessed with Velma and her cat. Her exact words were 'I want that damned cat dead and Velma too.'"

Father Melvyn shook his head. "I'm going to have to do something about those two. The question is what."

"We'll talk about it," she said, pointing at the clock."Now hurry. You're late for confessions." Father Melvyn rolled his eyes and snapped on his collar. "I left you a big salad. It's in the fridge, and there's more ice tea."

"You were serious about the salad?"

Mrs. B.'s musical laughter was his answer as she walked away.

6

You Can't Choose Your Relatives

"Surprise!" he shouted when Velma opened the front door.

"Goodness, Jeffrey. Why are you here on a Tuesday?"

"I was invited to speak at a medical conference downtown. I didn't mention it last week because the original program had me presenting early in the day. I had intended to head right back to Dallas, but there was some kind of a mix-up, and I didn't speak until four this afternoon. Now it's almost six, and rush hour is terrible, so I thought I'd take my one and only aunt to dinner. How 'bout it?"

"Yes, I haven't eaten yet, and since it's just the two of us, we can have a nice chat."

"Of course, Aunt Velma. Anything you say. Where would you like to go?"

"Let's go to my favorite steak house."

"Done," he said. "Get a sweater or a jacket. It's rather cool. Still March you know."

At the restaurant they ordered wine and studied the menu. When the wine was served, they ordered their dinners. "I think I'll have the steak au poivre, medium rare," Velma told their server.

"That's a change for you, Aunt Velma. You always have their plank-grilled salmon."

"It's Fat Tuesday. Lent begins tomorrow, so I'll enjoy a nice steak. Now—" she began.

"Fat Tuesday? How did it get that name?" Jeffrey asked as if he hadn't noticed she was about to say something else. His tactic worked.

"It's derived from the French. *Mardi* is Tuesday, and *Gras* means Fat. It's significant because it's the last night before the Lenten season begins."

"Hmmm. But why Fat Tuesday? Why not Last Night before Lent?"

"You've forgotten your Catholic school lessons. Hundreds of years ago, Lent was far stricter than it is today. People had to abstain from all meats and other foods that came from animals. You know, milk, cheeses, butter, eggs, foods that required refrigeration, which they didn't have, so everything in the larder had to be eaten before Lent began. Hence, they enjoyed one last big feast-like meal the night before Ash Wednesday."

"Leave it to you to know." Jeffrey smiled at his aunt.

Their steaks arrived, and they ate in silence. Jeffrey kept his eyes on his plate. He cut and pushed the food around not eating with any enthusiasm.

Velma watched him. Bet he's going to ask for money again, she thought. "Steak OK, Jeffrey? You don't seem hungry." Jeffrey looked up at his aunt and smiled. Phony, she thought. You can't fool me.

"It's great. Probably had too many snacks at the

conference. I'll get them to wrap up whatever I don't eat. It'll be good for dinner tomorrow night."

"Not paying attention, dear? No meat tomorrow, it's Ash Wednesday. You know better."

"Right. It'll hold till Thursday." When the server returned to the table Jeffrey asked for the check and a piece of his aunt's favorite dessert to go.

With his leftovers and the cake in hand, Velma and her nephew headed back to her house. He parked in her driveway, ran around the car, and helped her out. "I should have worn a coat," she said, clutching her sweater to her chest. Jeffrey walked her into the house and headed to the kitchen.

"I brought the carrot cake in. How about a cup of hot tea?"

"That sounds lovely. Put the kettle on, and let me get changed." At the sound of Velma's voice, LaLa walked into the kitchen, hunched her back, hissed at Jeffrey then followed Velma to the bedroom.

"Can't stand that stinking cat," he muttered as he filled the kettle and set it on the stove. He took out a plate and fork for his aunt. He knew she'd never turn down carrot cake. The kettle whistled. He steeped the bags in the boiling water and added sweetness, just like his aunt liked it.

Velma returned to the kitchen. "Oh, lovely," she said. Jeffrey had the table set: fancy cake plate, matching cup and saucer, cake fork and a white linen napkin. "No carrot cake for you, dear?"

"No, thank you. I'm full."

"More for me tomorrow then. Have you spoken to Ginny lately?" she asked, not allowing him to sidestep the question as he'd done at the restaurant.

Jeffrey handed her the steaming cup of tea. "Careful, the cup is hot," was all he answered, but the look on his face told her he hadn't.

"She called me yesterday. Just to say hello." Velma peered at her nephew over the rim of her teacup. "Seems you haven't patched things up with her. Don't you think you should?"

"These things take time," Jeffrey said, standing at the stove, holding his own cup to his lips. Nothing like a hot cup of guilt, he thought, averting his eyes.

"Mmmm. This is just the way I like it," Velma said, closing her eyes and savoring her sweet tea. She sipped again and took another bite of carrot cake. "Don't take too long. She's been a good and devoted wife; think of your children. Ginny says they're very upset. The children feel they did something wrong and that's why you left."

Jeffrey sighed. His mind went to the reason he moved out. Just the thought of her made him hot. Maybe he should shock dear old Aunty Velma. Maybe she'd drop dead for him. "You're right," he said in his most soothing voice. "I'm going to have everything fixed within a few weeks."

"Even the other problem?"

"Yes. Even that." He looked at his watch. "It's getting late. I need to go. Probably won't get home till after ten." He stepped to the sink, washed and dried his cup, and put it away. "Are you done? Want me to wash your cup before I leave?"

"Just this," she said, handing him the fork and cake plate. "I'll take another cup of tea to bed with me. Get on your way, and get things back on the right track with your wife. And get some help with the other thing."

At the door, Jeffrey looked up and down the quiet street. Not a soul in sight that he could see. He kissed his aunt goodbye and assured her again. "Everything will be finished by the end of the month."

Velma closed the door. Odd way of putting it, she thought. He didn't ask for money either. Wonder what he's up to? The cup in her hand was cooling. She reheated the kettle, poured another cup, and reached for her pen and journal.

He's up to something. Ginny said he's still seeing one particular woman. He's always been a ladies' man, but this current one may be a problem. Next week I'll hire a detective to find out what's going on. Wish we could choose our relatives, but he is my brother's boy, and after all Thomas did for me, I must do what I can to save Jeffrey from himself. When I have more information, I'll give him my ultimatum, but stronger this time. While I'm at it, I'll have the detective check up on Martha. She's becoming a little too bold. Needs to be kept in her place.

A shiver ran up her spine. Velma pulled her robe tight against her chest and shook her head to stop from drowsing. Sleep was coming fast. Guess the cold night air knocked me out. She closed the journal and turned off the kitchen lights. Deep in thought about her nephew and Martha, she was unaware of eyes locked on her face, staring at her through the window. She turned off the light, blanketing the rooms in darkness.

In familiar shadows, she walked to her office and put the journal in its usual place before going to her bedroom. The grumbling in her stomach became uncomfortable. Maybe the steak au poivre was too heavy, she thought. I usually have fish and tonight I had the carrot cake too. Velma threw back the covers and crawled into bed without removing her robe. So cold, she thought and pulled the blankets up to her chin.

7

Hemmed In

From the garage, Mrs. B. dragged her overloaded shopping bags into the house. As they did every night, Sasha and Ziggy, greeted her. She spent time saying hello and petting them then filled their food bowls. Once they were settled, she got her own dinner into the oven and poured herself a glass of Chardonnay. She was tired, hungry, and out of sorts, annoyed at something, but she couldn't put her finger on the source of her discontent. Think I'll call John, she thought, not expecting her son to be home. He and his wife led very busy lives. To her surprise, he picked up on the first ring.

"Hi, Mom," he said. "I was going to call you over the weekend." Mrs. B. smiled. Sure, she thought, until something distracts you.

"How's Lisa? When did you get home?" she asked, willing herself to be upbeat.

"We got back to Dallas yesterday. We danced really well and got a standing ovation. They've invited both of us to teach in the first half of their academy's summer program."

"That's wonderful, son." John and Lisa were spending a lot of time in the Pacific Northwest. "Would you consider moving way up there?"

John chuckled. "Don't worry, Mom. It's too damp. The company is great, but the climate isn't for us. But that's not my big news."

She felt a pang of relief when John said they'd never move to Washington State. "So what is it?" Mrs. B. held her breath, hoping.

"Janice approached us this morning. It was our first day back. You remember Janice Watters, the artistic director?"

"Yes, dear. I know who Janice Watters is. I'm not a dotty old goat yet."

John laughed. "OK, Mom. Got it. Janice told us that next week we start rehearsing for the leads in her new full-length ballet, which will end the season."

"Oh, John, how exciting. Congratulations to both of you." Mrs. B. felt her face pull into a smile, even though it wasn't the news she'd hoped for. "Are you and Lisa partnered for this one?"

"Yes."

"Very smart of Janice. You two have a great chemistry on stage."

"Thanks, Mom. Will you fly up for the premier? Lisa and I want you here."

"I'll be there without a doubt, and I'll drive myself. I don't want either of you running back and forth to the airport, you'll be too busy."

"Mom. It's a three-hour drive from Austin, and we don't like you driving all that way alone."

"Thank you, love. Let's not fight about it now. If I want to bring a friend, would you be able to get two tickets?"

Mrs. B. knew the dance company had a strict policy about comps.

"No problem, Mom. Got a boyfriend?" he asked playfully.

"No, dear. No *boy*friend, but a new friend. Nancy Jenkins. This is her second year as principal of Saint Francis's school. Our paths are crossing more, and we've discovered we have a mutual love of the arts. We seem to be hitting it off. So I might want to invite her."

"Super. Just let me know as soon as you can. Gotta go. Lisa sends love. Talk to you soon. Love ya, Mom," he said and hung up.

"Love you too, son," Mrs. B. whispered to the disconnected, inanimate instrument in her hand. That is good news, she thought. They work so hard, and I'm happy for them. I sure hope they don't wait too long to have a baby, though. It's okay for John at thirty-five, but Lisa is thirty-six, and her biological clock must be ticking.

Mrs. B.'s thoughts turned to Nancy Jenkins. She surprised herself by mentioning Nancy to her son. She hadn't given it any thought, but after running into Nancy at the opera, they often talked about the arts. They were both opera fans, and Nancy expressed interest in the ballet company too. "Why not?" she asked aloud.

She hadn't told Nancy that her son and daughter-in-law were dancers, but she now felt confident she could tell Nancy without the usual explanations. She learned long ago to not discuss John's career. Most people got a peculiar look on their faces when she said her son was a ballet dancer; there isn't much general understanding of this art form, she thought.

No athletes in the world were better conditioned; the women balancing on a one-inch by half-inch pointe shoe, through leaps, turns and dance steps. The men leaping, turning, and lifting other dancers, all of them controlling their breathing, smiling, making it look easy. No football-like heaving; or resting between points. The list went on and on, which is one of the reasons she avoided the topic. Get me on my soapbox, and I can't stop myself, she thought as the aroma of roasted chicken filled the kitchen. Her dinner was ready, and she was hungry.

She carved out a hefty piece of white meat and coated it with the natural juices made by the garlic and lemon. In a separate dish, she took a generous helping of Panzanella Salad. She didn't want the chicken juice mingling with the tomato and olive oil. Another glass of chilled chardonnay completed the meal. Slowly, she savored her food, which connected her brainwaves with Father Melvyn's appreciation for her culinary skills.

She was gratified that he enjoyed her cooking and wasn't shy about complimenting her. At first she'd been surprised by his interest in how she prepared certain dishes and what spices she used. *Careful,* said the voice in her head: *pride goes before the fall,* but a modicum of pride was not terrible, given the situation she'd found at Saint Francis when she was hired. She stopped eating, threw her head back and laughed. Sasha and Ziggy, looked up. "It's still funny, at least to me," she said to her attentive cats.

On the day she arrived at Saint Francis to answer the ad for a new housekeeper/cook, within an hour Father Melvyn offered her the job in spite of poor Mrs. Smith's better judgment. The next day, as agreed, she reported to the rectory to begin working alongside Mrs. Smith for a few days. It turned out to be Mrs. Smith's last day. Mrs. B. chuckled and shook her head from side to side in disbelief at the hysterical memory.

The final straw turned out to be a teaspoon of olive oil. She suggested that they put a basil leaf and a drizzle of olive oil on the tomato in Father Melvyn's sandwich. Mrs. Smith reacted as if she'd suggested rat poison. Father Melvyn walked in at that moment, and the bomb exploded. Mrs. Smith's face was beet red. For a moment Mrs. B. was afraid the other woman would have a stroke.

"This is entirely inappropriate. You, Mrs. Buonafig-g-g-whatever. You are too rambunctious for this job, and your Eye-talian name is too difficult for parishioners to pronounce; Mrs. B. is too familiar." With a last burst of air, she spluttered, "I cannot be a party to this. I quit." Pulling off her apron, she marched out of the kitchen and flung the smock willy-nilly. It flew like a cloth rocket, landing on Father Melvyn's head.

Caught by surprise, he grappled with it and finally pulled it off his face, but it remained wrapped around his neck, leaving his hair disheveled, his glasses lopsided on his nose, and a priceless expression of shocked confusion on his face. The sound of Mrs. Smith's feet stomping to the front door, followed by a slam that rattled the doorframe, let them know she'd left the building.

Alone in her own kitchen, Mrs. B. continued to laugh, something she forced herself not to do that day. Father Melvyn looked dazed and with as much dignity as he could muster, he adjusted his glasses and pulled the apron off his neck.

"Hopefully, Mrs. B., your skills do not extend to cloth projectiles." The laughter in his eyes belied his seriousness.

I guess it's not charitable, but it was comical, she thought, and I couldn't help myself. Her thoughts turned to more bittersweet recollections.

A few months before she took the job at Saint Francis, John, her husband of forty-five years, had passed away one week after she'd received a clean bill of health from the oncologist. They'd been talking about doing some of the things on her bucket list, like a river cruise in Europe, when he keeled over. He was dead before he hit the floor.

With him gone, her life changed. After John's death, she needed something to make her feel relevant. The children were grown, making their own lives. Money wasn't a problem. They weren't rich, but they'd been careful, always keeping an eye on retirement. When she saw the ad in the weekly newsletter: "HOUSEKEEPER/COOK NEEDED. Saint Francis de Sales pastor, Father Melvyn Kronkey, needs a serious, devout person to keep house and cook," she jumped at it and answered on a lark.

Unbidden tears wet her cheeks. "You know I still miss you," she said aloud, looking toward the bedroom door. She continued talking to her beloved but deceased husband, whose ashes were in a special wood box on the dresser. "We had the usual ups and downs, but we were happy, and we fell in love with Austin as soon as we moved here. Your only complaint was we couldn't find the Italian foods that we took for granted in New York. Good thing my cousins sent whatever I asked for." She smiled. "It did get better over the years."

On the floor, side by side, Sasha and Ziggy sat at attention. Ears upright, backs strong, they looked from Mrs. B. to the bedroom door, waited, and then looked back at her. "Can you two hear his answers?" she asked. They wriggled as if to say, of course we can.

"Okay, John. I'm getting too sappy," she said, looking toward the bedroom. She forced herself out of the kitchen chair and cleaned the kitchen, after which she went to the bedroom to change.

It was a relief to remove the prosthetic bra. Looking in the mirror, she studied her medically reconfigured chest.

"Well, cancer. You can go to hell. I beat you." Turning from side to side, she admitted she needed to lose a few pounds, for health reasons, certainly not for vanity. When her cancer had been discovered, it was John who told her to have reconstruction *only* if she needed to see herself restored to her pre-cancer form. "I support your decision either way," he'd said.

She pulled a white T-shirt on and turned from the mirror. Enough of this! Spending too much time in the weeds, allowing worry about what might be lurking in her body ready to rear its ugly head was never good. "What's important is that I am energetic, curious, interested in life and what makes other people tick."

Breathing out a sigh of exasperation, she placed her hands on her hips and demanded of her reflection: "Who ever invented the notion that retirement was for lazy days of doing nothing? The fun is in doing, learning, discovering."

Walking around the house, she secured the windows and doors before activating the alarm. She ran her fingers over select pieces of furniture. This house is a bit much for me now, but I still need the space when Corinne, her husband, and their four kids visit, she thought. Their visits are less frequent because my precious grandchildren are growing up and involved in sports and the arts. That keeps them in New York most of the summer.

Corinne and her husband Mark loved Austin and hoped to make it their home after the kids went off to college. They'd bought a little house that they rented in the residential section downtown while real estate was still affordable. Mrs. B. was happy with the knowledge that even if they didn't move, they'd make a good profit when they sold it.

Returning to the kitchen, she took out her menu book to plan meals for the next two days. They'll be extra busy with ashes and mass tomorrow, she thought. I'll prepare foods that don't need to be eaten hot off the stove or out of the oven. She always took a copy of the calendar and schedules home with her in order to plan the most convenient meals. She circled the next day in red. Ash Wednesday, the first day of Lent. No meat tomorrow or on Fridays for the next six weeks. On Thursday there was a heavy schedule of funeral masses; again, she planned simple foods.

Fridays were always special. It was Father Melvyn's policy that the three priests dine together and discuss what went on during the week as well as any special events or situations. He was a great believer in being aware of his assistant's and his resident teacher's activities and concerns.

She smiled. Taking care of these guys is fun, she thought. Father Melvyn was close to her age. What a bundle of energy. He was a great boss, and she was enjoying her ever-increasing nondomestic responsibilities. He was kind and patient...most of the time, even though he didn't think so. "Guess he thinks he needs to be a saint." Main course: Flounder Oreganata. Father Melvyn loves that.

Her thoughts turned to Father Declan Ryan, a young Irish transplant. He was thirtysomething but looked eighteen. The acne he had when he came a year ago had cleared up. Austin agreed with him. He was enthusiastic but a nervous sort. Any time a girl said hello, he blushed. Mrs. B. shook her head and wrote the ingredients for bread pudding. She knew it was Father Declan's favorite dessert.

"Dear Father Joe. Can't forget you." He was a science and ethics professor at the university, and another Italian American—there were still relatively few in Austin, maybe 20,000 in a population of a million plus. Unlike Mrs. B., Father Joe had no connection to his ancestry.

When they talked about being Italian-Americans in a city so unfamiliar with their traditions and proud heritage she told him that she was an American raised from strong Italian roots. It reminded her that she owed her cousins in Italy a letter. Must write soon. It's been a while.

Her thoughts returned to Father Joe. He was endearing and funny, loved cats, and was a bit obsessive-compulsive, like herself. It amused her to watch Father Melvyn and Father Declan roll their eyes whenever Father Joe said, "Cleanliness is next to Godliness," and he said it often. Father Melvyn once challenged him on it. Father Joe answered that it was in the Bible. Father Melvyn told him it wasn't.

"OK, but the concept of washing is mentioned frequently," Father Joe answered, completely unfazed by the correction. He was the only one of the three who sometimes helped her clear away dishes and clean up the kitchen or put magazines away in the library.

As soon as she'd started working at Saint Francis, Father Melvyn told her that the priests were responsible for their own personal space. That's why obsessive-compulsive Father Joe took any opportunity, when the others were out, to run the vacuum all over the upstairs.

His favorite is puttanesca sauce with linguini. That will be the first course she decided then filled out the rest of the menu, adding a mixed salad and green beans sautéed with garlic and olive oil.

Suddenly, Sasha, the Russian blue throwback, was in her lap, purring insistently. She put away her menu book, held

Sasha with one hand, and clicked through TV programs with the other. She couldn't stand any more news of murder, mayhem, and DC corruption. "Lord, what have we become?" Disgusted, she punched the off button, went to bed, and curled up with a William Kienzle mystery.

Sasha and Ziggy joined her on the bed. They lay down, backs touching, on the side that was John's; it was now theirs. "You guys just don't like my restlessness, do you? Just as well, I hate being confined. Good night, boys."

Is that it? She asked herself. Is that the underlying feeling of annoyance that had dogged me all evening? Am I feeling hemmed in? Mrs. B. tossed, turned, kicked the covers off and then pulled them back up until she burrowed into her pillows. It was after eleven when she drifted off to sleep. Inexplicably, her final thoughts turned to Martha and Velma. Wonder what the whole story is there?

8
"...And sweet revenge grows harsh."

Shakespeare

The clock read ten-thirty. "Okay, you guys," Martha said to Barclay and Smitty. "You want to go out again before bed." The dogs sat in front of her, tails wagging, tongues hanging out; Smitty gave a low woof. Martha grabbed the leashes hanging on the key rack beside the kitchen door. She'd always walked them at night until she broke her ankle. Fearing another fall, she usually let them loose in the yard and cleaned up the mess the next morning, but not tonight. She was pleased. Tonight was different. He was here with her. Grabbing the flashlight she said, "Okay kids. Let's get this done." She moved to the kitchen door.

***

It was just after eleven when Father Declan Ryan approached the designated entrance to Saint Francis's school on Ferne Lane. He'd been at an event at the Diocesan Center, and it lasted longer than anticipated. Killing the headlamps half a block from the driveway to be sure that Father Melvyn wouldn't see his car turning into the school driveway. Father Declan was prepared to break the rules. "We can't have him running out, waving his arms and yelling," he muttered.

Father Melvyn had been known to come out and chase away anyone who thought they could use Saint Francis de Sales parking field for their personal recreations or use the back driveway as a short-cut from Ferne Lane to Cobble Drive. He threatened to put up a fence, which he hadn't done yet.

Approaching the driveway on Ferne Lane, Father Declan noticed a woman and a man with two small dogs walk past Velma's house. The streetlight illuminated them for less than a minute. That looks like Martha, he thought. Wonder who that guy is? Father Declan didn't think anything more beyond his relief that they hadn't turned to look back at the sound of his car. They didn't see me. Can't be Martha, he thought. She doesn't walk her dogs this late.

***

Velma was exhausted but couldn't sleep. It was almost midnight and her extreme drowsiness alternated with gripping stomach cramps and heartburn. TUMS hadn't helped. Every time she felt about to fall into a good sleep, her stomach contracted, and she gasped for air or LaLa jumped on the bed and poked her cold nose into Velma's cheek; then she'd jump down and run toward the front door. I'd better not let her out or I might not get her in again tonight, and I don't feel well enough to keep trying, she thought.

Dragging herself from the bed, Velma went to the cat portal and latched it shut. "LaLa," she called out, walking in and out of each room. Too late. She must have gotten out. Velma grabbed her stomach. She felt weak, her legs were wobbly, and the pain radiated up into her chest. Briefly, it crossed her mind to call 911, but she dismissed the notion. Tomorrow I'll call the cardiologist. My doctor said I should see her since my cardiogram showed some changes. I never did tell Jeffrey about those changes. Nothing to tell him yet. Don't need him counting his inheritance before I'm dead. I'll call for an appointment in the morning, she decided. "LaLa," she called out again, beads of sweat forming on her forehead. Confused and disoriented, Velma found herself outside.

Everything had a halo. She blinked. Through her double vision, she saw something the size of her cat fly out of the shadows and across the lawn. "C'mon inside, you little scamp," she called out. LaLa didn't come. Instead, Velma heard LaLa's deep belly meow. She couldn't tell where it came from. She stepped off the porch and blinked her eyes, trying to clear her vision. "You naughty cat. You'll wake the neighborhood," she said. Bile rose in her throat. I hope I'm not getting a stomach virus. Can't throw up out here. Gotta get that cat. She was getting annoyed. "LaLa, come back here, or I'll leave you out all night," she called in a hoarse whisper, as she staggered to the sidewalk and across the street, unaware that someone watched her.

Velma found herself between concrete and stone wall that formed a familiar alley. Looking around she asked, "How did I get here?" She leaned against the back wall of Saint Francis Church, trying to shake the cobwebs from her brain. Her legs buckled; she slid down the rough stone.

Inside her head, something was banging against her skull. There was a strange buzz in her ears. Something moved toward her in the alley. She looked up. A figure sheathed in black stood in front of her, or were there two? She blinked. One. Man? Woman? Again, she blinked to clear her vision.

The figure squatted down, reached up, and pulled a hood back. Velma stared into the face. She couldn't see clearly; she blinked trying to clear her vision. The face momentarily cleared, then doubled.

A pair of disembodied black orbs stared down at her. A grin showed white teeth gleaming in the dull light. Velma shivered. "Please, help me." Her voice was a croak; a strange dryness in her throat made words difficult. She reached out and grabbed at the figure in front of her.

"Remember me?" A viselike grip took hold her of wrist and yanked her hand away.

Velma's chest constricted. She was spinning. The concrete path was in front of her face, the stone wall of the church sliding away. A bitter white froth passed between her teeth and dripped down in front of a pair of black shoes on the pavement. A spasm wracked her body. She pulled her legs up to a fetal position. Her chest felt like it was being crushed. Her breath came in painful gulps; she gasped. That was the last sound Velma made in the narrow alley between the church and the rectory before she was engulfed in blackness.

***

LaLa sat behind the latched cat portal inside Velma's house. She sniffed and hissed, backed away from the front door then turned toward it again. A plaintive cry came from deep within her body and echoed through the rooms. Stress tears wet the cat's face. A noise from the kitchen reached her. Mouth slightly open, tongue protruding, LaLa panted, hair follicles pulled her fur erect, ears flat against her skull, LaLa wailed once more and then ran into Velma's office.

Pulling back the hood, the black-clad figure made a quick tour of Velma's house. I can't believe she got out of bed. Don't know when the body will be discovered. Maybe I should have tried to carry her back here but if anyone saw me carrying a body it wouldn't be good. If the police decide to search...that thought was left unfinished.

I'll start with her closets, the intruder decided. The drapes were closed tight in Velma's bedroom. Feeling it was safe, the intruder turned on the overhead light and searched the drawers with care, then the closet. "Plenty of clothes." Pushing aside dresses, there was a fireproof document box on a hidden shelf but no key. "Bet it's here."

Gripping the handle of the heavy box, the intruder checked that the closet remained neat, turned off the bedroom light and crossed the dark hall to Velma's office.

A hard ball of fur slammed into the document box, screamed and got tangled up between the intruder's feet, yowling like a creature from hell. Off balance, the heavy box slipped from the black gloved hands and hit the floor with a loud bang. Unnerved by the encounter, heart beating hard, the intruder picked it up and moved back toward the kitchen. "I'll take this and leave. I'll bet her important papers are in it. No sense pushing my luck."

Ash Wednesday
First Day of the Solemn Season of Fasting and Prayer: Lent

9
More Than Ash Wednesday Traffic

She'd intended to get to the rectory earlier than usual because the priests would be extra busy, but it was closer to nine when she turned onto Cobble Drive. Traffic was stopped. "Damn light," she muttered. Most of the bumper to bumper traffic was caused by the light just before the approach to Mopac, but Mrs. B knew that today parishioners going to get ashes were adding to the problem. Waiting to move, she tapped her fingers on the steering wheel. Finally, she thought, driving her car across the intersection of Carpenter Street and Cobble Drive then slammed her brakes.

The scene that confronted her was much more, than Ash Wednesday traffic. Ignoring the orange cones set up to keep cars away from St. Francis, she gripped the steering wheel and turned toward the driveway. Her jaw hung open. A police officer stepped forward in the street with his hands in front of him. Through the windshield she heard his command: "Stop." The parking lot was filled with police cars and EMS vehicles all askew. She peered into the lot at the shocking sight of the medical examiner's vehicle. Churchgoers were being turned away from Saint Francis on Ash Wednesday.

"Ma'am, don't you see the cones? You have to leave. There's been an accident here," the officer said when she lowered her window. Her heart skipped a beat. Her first thought was that something happened to Father Melvyn.

"Officer, I'm the pastor's assistant, Father Kronkey's assistant," she said.

The young officer spoke through a mike on his shoulder. "Woman says she's the pastor's assistant." He listened and then waved her through. "Slow down, ma'am," he said, stepping aside.

Slow! her brain commanded when all she really wanted to do was floor the accelerator and fly to the carport across from the rectory. The collection of marked and unmarked vehicles and the EMS truck with uniformed personnel swarming made her anxious; she forced herself to drive at a crawl. It felt like forever before she parked. Intending to enter the rectory, as she always did, through the kitchen door, she was again surprised by another officer.

"Sorry, ma'am, you can't go in this way," the policewoman said as she stretched yellow crime scene tape across the alley between the church and the back entrance to the rectory.

Unable to control the waver in her voice, Mrs. B. asked, "What happened here? Is it the pastor?" The lady cop shook her head no then turned away indicating she wouldn't answer any more questions.

Mrs. B. trotted around the far side of the rectory. Her thumping heart became a metronome keeping the rhythm for her legs. She saw Father Melvyn on the front porch before he saw her.

Pacing back and forth, he looked a mess, even from behind. He was in civvies, and the back of his shirt wasn't tucked into his pants. He turned. His face was ghostly white; his eyes were as wild as his hair which was almost standing on end; even his moustache looked crazy. His hands were shoved deep in his pockets, and his narrow purple prayer stole hung unevenly around his neck.

"Good God, Father Melvyn, what in hell happened here?"

The cross look he gave her was enough. "Sorry," she said, knowing he didn't like her to cuss. She climbed the steps, a bit out of breath, pushing aside the random thought that she needed to start exercising again. "Are you okay?" she asked.

"At seven, one of our ushers arrived to help with the first mass. He rang the bell in a state of high excitement. 'There's a body in the alley, Father,' he shouted. Thinking perhaps someone fell, I ran out. Sure enough, even from five feet away, I could tell the body was lifeless. Head to the side, twisted at an unnatural angle, eyes wide open. When I approached, I recognized her, ran back in to get my stole to say the prayers, and called nine-one-one before—"

"For goodness sake, who was it?" Rapid footsteps walking up and down the alley drew their attention. They moved to the small side porch to watch. There were uniformed people doing all sorts of work: taking pictures, outlining the body with chalk, looking for objects on the ground. A woman in an official looking jacket leaned over and pointed the deceased's mouth. Father Melvyn took Mrs. B.'s arm and led her back to the front of the porch.

"Who was it?" she asked again.

"It's Velma," Father Melvyn whispered. "It's Velma." They stared at each other. Not a word passed between them. The sound of scraping over cement pulled their attention back to the alley. Two men wheeled a stretcher toward a waiting ambulance. It carried the remains of Velma Scooterman-Maxwell, shrouded in a plastic body bag.

Covering her mouth with her hand, Mrs. B. whispered, "I don't believe this." Deep in her own thoughts, she didn't hear the sound of feet coming up the porch stairs.

"Sammi?" a male voice said.

She turned. "Jake?" she said, in surprise. Father Melvyn stood beside his housekeeper as a tall, trim man with iron grey hair and black rimmed glasses walked up the steps.

"Father Kronkey, this is Jake Zayas from homicide. Jake, Father Kronkey, the pastor." The two men shook hands but not before Mrs. B. caught the puzzled look from Father Melvyn.

Jake didn't waste time with unnecessary pleasantries. He took out his notepad. "Father Kronkey, is it?" The priest nodded. "Do you have any idea who the deceased is?"

"Yes. It's Velma Scooterman-Maxwell. She is...was...a parishioner."Father Melvyn watched.

The detective, who addressed Mrs. B. by her first name, scribbled in his notebook. "Any idea what she was doing in the alley? Does she live around here?"

"I don't know what she was doing in the alley. She lives across the street...over there," Father Melvyn said, pointing to Velma's house.

"Hmmm." Mrs. B. stood with her hand over her mouth and her eyebrows pulled together.

"Sammi?" Jake asked, waiting for her explanation. Mrs. B. noticed the strange look on Father Melvyn's face.

"She might have been looking for her cat, LaLa," she answered. "That cat has a bad habit of running out of the house at night. I've often suggested that she lock the cat portal after five or six, but she said she 'couldn't restrict the darling creature.'" Jake continued writing.

Father Melvyn looked bewildered. He addressed a question to the detective. "Any idea what happened?"

"Not really. On the surface the medical examiner says it looks like a heart attack, but we'll know more after an autopsy. Does she have family?"

Again it was Mrs. B. who answered. "She has a nephew in Dallas. I don't have an address or phone number, but his name is Jeffrey Scooterman; he's a doctor."

Father Melvyn chimed in: "He was here two weeks ago, Sunday. I had dinner with him and Velma after mass."

Mrs. B. felt the jolt of surprise rearrange her facial expressions at Father Melvyn's information and he looked satisfied, as if to say, *See, you aren't the only one with secrets.*

"Do you know how to contact him?" Jake Zayas asked.

Father Melvyn held his pursed lips between his thumb and forefinger. His brows almost touched between his eyes as they pulled down toward his nose. He shook his head: negative.

Jake had his detective's poker face on, but Mrs. B. noticed the telltale raised eyebrow before he shrugged. "Shouldn't be too hard to trace him," he said almost to himself and closed his notebook. "I'll be back in touch when we know what happened. I may need to speak with you again. Now I need to get a warrant to search her house. Might have to break the door lock to get in."

"I know where she keeps an extra key," Mrs. B. offered. "Want me to open up?"

"Why?" Father Melvyn blurted.

Mrs. B. understood what her boss was asking. "I'm not sure. She and I got along okay. We mostly talked about cats. Her cat, LaLa, and my Sasha are both Russian blue throwbacks. She invited me to tea one day, and unexpectedly showed me where she keeps an extra key, just in case."

It was the detective's turn to look perplexed as he watched the exchange like watching a tennis match, following the ball from one side of the court to the other.

"Since she let you know where the extra key is kept, it's all good if you let us in," Jake said. "I'll let you know when I'm ready to go." He headed down the steps, turned back, extended his hand, and said, "Father Kronkey. I'll be in touch."

Father Melvyn stood with his arms folded across his chest, his eyes as big as saucers. He finally released his pursed lips and asked, "Well, Mrs. B., you know more than I do. How *do* you know all that? And how do you know the detective?"

Mrs. B. gnawed the inside of her cheek to stop herself from laughing at her boss's poorly concealed surprise. There's a lot about me you don't know, she thought. A waving arm caught her attention. It was Jake, pointing to Velma's house. "Guess he's ready to go. After I let them in, I'll come back and tell you. Can you put up some coffee?"

Father Melvyn's eyebrows rose to his hairline. "I suppose so..." he spluttered. Mrs. B. turned away unable to contain her laughter. The housekeeper was asking the boss to put up the coffee!

***

10
Where Is LaLa?

Father Melvyn watched Mrs. B.'s face pucker as she sipped. "Oh dear, I made it too strong," he realized.

She nodded then launched into a quick synopsis of what took place at Velma's house. She didn't mention the police might come back to do a more in-depth search if the autopsy turned up anything. "They took a quick look around. Came out and said that nothing looked amiss or disturbed. Her bed was mussed as if she'd slept in it and then got up, but other than that, nothing. Neat as a pin."

"And?"

He wants to know how I know the detective, she thought. She opened her mouth to explain that she and her late husband were graduates of the Citizens Police Academy and had become friends with Detective Zayas and his wife, but she was unable to say anything as a dissonant assault of ringing broke into their conversation.

Both phones rang at the same time in alternate rhythms. B. set her cup down on the counter and answered.

"Why are the police there?" and "Is something wrong with Father Melvyn?" These were the driving questions and the first of many nonstop calls from parishioners demanding to know what had happened at the church. By the third phone call she had the script down to a science, assuring parishioners that the priests were all good, but giving no information about what had happened other than someone had died on the grounds of St. Francis. Maybe I should make a quick recording and set the message system, she thought. Somehow, between the hot phone circuits of information gatherers, one desperate call got through.

"At last. Thank God. I've been trying for fifteen minutes. Maybe you need another line," the woman sobbed. "This is Mrs. Mathers. I need to talk to Father Melvyn. It's an emergency."

Hearing the stress in her voice and her sobs, Mrs. B. didn't waste time. "I'll get him for you." She punched the hold button. "Father Melvyn, you'd better take this in the office. It's Mrs. Mathers, and she's very upset."

It didn't take but a minute for the other line to ring again with another parishioner asking why the police were at the church. After she hung up, Mrs. B. stood with her hands on her hips and murmured in the empty kitchen, "Do these people have spy drones?" She was amazed at the speed information traveled in the parish network.

When the phones finally stopped, she looked at the inanimate box on the wall and imagined it wilting from exhaustion, its plastic shell melting. She reached for her cup on the counter. It's too strong. Better pour it down the sink, she thought.

The kitchen door banged; she jumped. Father Declan Ryan walked in, ghostly pale. "Father Declan, what's wrong? Don't you feel well?"

Before the young priest answered, Father Melvyn bounded into the kitchen. "Declan, can you take the noon mass and ash distribution for me? I have to go to the hospital. Apparently Mr. Mathers had a heart attack, and his wife asked me to get over there."

"Oh...ah...sure," Father Declan answered.

Father Melvyn stopped and looked at his young assistant.

"Everything okay?" he asked.

"Yes. Bad night's sleep. Mrs. B., can I have a cup of that coffee?"

"Of course," she said then whispered, "but I'd add cream, sugar, and an ice cube."

***

For the rest of the day, Mrs. B. was on her feet, scurrying from the phone to the door, fielding questions about the police presence at the church that morning. Other than information seekers, one call was for an appointment with Father Joe, another caller wanted information on baptisms, and three asked who was hearing confessions on Saturday. While she scrambled to keep up with her daily routine, the doorbell rang several times. Each time it was a parishioner saying he or she was just passing by, which wasn't likely, given the location of the church. She wanted to scream, "Don't you have anything better to do?" but she held her tongue and tried to believe they were concerned for the well-being of Saint Francis. It didn't work.

The door buzzed again at a quarter to five. Out of patience, she pulled the door open so fast that it made a whooshing sound. Expecting another parishioner *coincidentally* passing by, she was taken aback.

"Sorry to bother you, ma'am, but I'm lost. Can you tell me how to get to William Cannon?" It was a pimply-faced youth, no more than eighteen.

She relaxed. "Not from around here?" she asked.

"No," he answered, shuffling his feet.

Relieved that it wasn't another sensation seeker, she smiled. "You're on Ferne Lane; it isn't a through street. Go to the corner and make a right on Cobble Drive then another right on Carpenter Street. It takes you to William Cannon." He thanked her and walked down the steps to his car. She followed him to the sidewalk and watched him pull away.

For the first time, she noticed the chill in the air. She shivered and wrapped her arms around her middle. Her eyes wandered to Velma's house across Ferne Lane. It looked dark, empty, dead, like its owner. Can a house be telepathic? Can it channel its owner? Gloom sucked her down like quicksand. Then it hit her. "LaLa," she blurted. "Oh dear, I have to get that cat." She headed back inside the rectory.

***

"Mrs. B.?" If he hadn't called her name, she would have known by the heavy footsteps that he'd returned from the hospital. "Mrs. B., where are you?" he called out again as she walked in the front door.

"You were gone a long time. How is Mr. Mathers?" she asked.

"He'll be okay. Good thing he hadn't left the house before he keeled over. Mrs. Mathers called nine-one-one and none too soon." He took a breath. "When I left the Mathers, I saw the Neeleys. Little Tommy fell and broke his arm. I spent some time talking with them. Everything okay here?"

"Everything is fine. The usual, augmented by a host of inquisitive neighbors from every corner of the parish. Can't believe how fast news travels." She switched subjects. "Father Melvyn, we need to get Velma's cat. Poor thing must be scared silly."

"Whoa. Slow down. You want to break into Velma's house to find her cat?"

"Not break in. I know where the extra key is, remember? I put it back in its hiding place after the detectives left." Mrs. B. watched Father Melvyn's eyebrows pull together over his nose, and he pursed his lips.

"Yes. So you said. By the way, there are a lot of things you were going to *explain* this morning after that detective fellow left, but you didn't."

"I think we've been a bit busier than usual," she answered in self-defense.

"I don't like the idea of going into Velma's house. I am not doing it, and neither should you. What if the police decide it's a crime scene?"

"If they do it will be cordoned off with crime scene tape, which it is not."

"How do you know that? Who have you been talking to? Are you gossiping with parishioners? With that police friend of yours?"

She didn't like his tone and felt a flash of heat rise to her face. Her backbone pulled her erect. Instead of putting her fists up in a fight stance, she thumped them against her hips. "I *do not* gossip."

Father Melvyn took a step back and put his hands up in a defensive gesture. "Now don't get yourself in a snit, Mrs. B." His words made it worse.

"Father Kronkey, I know something about police procedures because my late husband and I graduated from

65

the Citizens Police Academy, and I know things about people because I'm interested in what makes them tick.

I keep many confidences, and I don't share personal information...not even with you." Father Melvyn stood rooted in place with his mouth open. "Forget I said anything. Guess you don't like cats. I'll come back later and get LaLa myself." Her workday done, she turned abruptly and left without saying good night.

After she turned her car out of the driveway, a quick glance at her reflection in the rearview mirror made her ashamed. Her face was flushed with anger. He's your boss and a priest. You shouldn't have answered him that way, she thought. But gossip? How dare he? She pushed Father Melvyn's stinging accusation out of her mind and worried about the cat.

Yesterday, Martha's dogs chased LaLa into the bushes, and Martha threatened to kill her and Velma. "I'm sure Martha didn't mean it, but Velma is dead. Where is the cat?"

11

You Didn't Walk in Her Shoes

In the supermarket, along with her own shopping, Mrs. B. added what was needed for LaLa: a litter box, litter, small plastic bowls, and food. While she shopped she remembered the first time she'd met Velma's cat.

LaLa had invited herself up onto the rectory porch, ignoring Velma's calls, cooing and efforts to get the cat to obey. Mrs. B. was coming out the front door, heard Velma and saw the cat ignoring her owner. Mrs. B. reached down and picked LaLa up with practiced and confident hands; LaLa stayed in her arms without a fuss.

"Oh my, she likes you," Velma said, obviously surprised, when she caught up with her wayward feline.

Handing the cat back to Velma, Mrs. B. told her, "She looks like my Sasha, also a Russian blue throwback. I love all cats, but these have wonderful dispositions. Here. Hold her like this." Mrs. B. placed LaLa in Velma's arms and arranged Velma's well-manicured hands on the cat.

After that, she and Velma occasionally compared notes about their respective pets' characteristics and behaviors and LaLa became a routine visitor to the rectory grounds.

One day, Mrs. B. was sweeping the porch steps. LaLa was sniffing at the flowerbed and again, Velma followed her cat across the street to St. Francis. "Good morning, Mrs. B." Velma said, scooping LaLa into her arms. "Thanks so much for showing me how to hold her. It's made all the difference. Why don't you come over for tea this afternoon?"

Mrs. B. was going to decline the unexpected invitation, but Velma's eyes dared her to refuse. OK, Velma, let's see what you're all about. Mrs. B. thought, unable to resist the challenge. "Sure. After I finish work."

At five o'clock that day, despite her misgivings, Mrs. B. crossed the street to Velma's house. "Too late to turn back," she muttered. Velma is vain, and everyone who is involved in Saint Francis knows she never wastes an opportunity to flaunt her position and that of her late husband in the community and the parish. Mrs. B. smiled at the memory. She remembered that when she pressed the doorbell Velma pulled open the door before she'd taken her finger off the button.

"Glad you could come," Velma said and waved her in. "Have a seat." It was more of a command than an invitation. That was the first time she'd been in Velma's house.

I tried not to be obvious about taking inventory. Her stuff was pretty, very pretty, if you like formal furniture and so was her costume.

That afternoon Velma wore a glamorous kaftan with blue and gold threading. Her hair was well styled and her makeup applied with a degree of expertise that confirmed Mrs. B.'s belief that this woman spent a great deal of time on her looks. The conversation came back to her as though it had happened yesterday.

"Lovely kaftan." Everyone knew Velma loved compliments. Why not make her happy?

"Oh, thank you. My late husband loved this old thing. You know, he was president of the parish council, and he sat on the city council too. In his time, he was a confident of the mayor's, and he was president of the country club."

Mrs. B. smiled at the memory, remembering that Velma didn't waste a minute, reciting the litany of Scooterman-Maxwell importance before she was seated in the living room. I'm glad I was able to refrain from hinting at the rumors that the mayor, when Charles had his ear, had a reputation for sleight of hand with funds. I smiled and nodded appropriately, wondering how fast I could extricate myself from the visit.

Mrs. B. stopped reminiscing long enough to get her purchases on the counter. Waiting for the person ahead of her to check out, her mind wandered back to that one and only visit to Velma's house.

The polished silver tea service that sat on the coffee table flashed in her mind. The matching silver teapot, creamer, and sugar bowl were on a silver tray with a crystal dish holding lemon wedges.

"I made my favorite afternoon tea," Velma said, handing Mrs. B. a delicate china cup. "Sugar, lemon, cream?" she asked, waving her hand at the ingredients, an invitation for the housekeeper to take whatever she wanted.

"Just plain, thank you." Mrs. B. sipped and felt Velma's calculating, surgically lifted eyes watching, waiting. Her makeup technique enhanced the blue color of her eyes, but they held no warmth. "Delicious tea, and what a beautiful tea set," she said.

"I always say tea tastes best when served in the finest bone china. This is from the Wedgewood collection; it's the Oberon pattern." Velma was so pleased. It was another opportunity to brag, but when the phone rang everything changed.

Velma went to the kitchen to answer. It was strange hearing only one side of a conversation, but the intensity in Velma's voice was unmistakable and uncomfortable. Mrs. B. heard her clearly and was sorry she'd accepted the invitation; she tried not to listen. Fortunately, Velma didn't say much. Her last retort to whoever was on the other end confirmed that the person she was talking to didn't please her.

"No. I will not bail you out again. Get some help," she snarled and slammed the phone down. "So sorry," Velma said, returning to the living room, smoothing over her already perfect hair.

"No need to apologize. Time for me to get on my way. My babies, Ziggy and Sasha, need feeding."

"Before you go, I want someone close by to know where my emergency key is hidden." Outside on the porch, Velma pointed to the planter beside the front door. "It's taped in back, just in case...you know. I live alone, so..." Her tone was melancholy.

Velma had surprised her, and Mrs. B. surprised herself by feeling sorry for her. This unlikeable woman momentarily looked wistful. "I understand, Velma. Don't worry, I won't tell a soul." She was pitiful. "You might want to consider getting one of those emergency bracelets or necklaces. You know the kind with a button that you press in case of a fall or something? It gets help to you pretty quick."

"I was thinking of that. Jeffrey, my nephew, said I don't really need it yet." The two women waved goodbye. Mrs. B. made her way back to Saint Francis to get her car.

"Maybe one day we could introduce Sasha and LaLa," Velma shouted from the steps of her front porch. Remembering that last desperate attempt by Velma, Mrs. B. felt badly that she kept going, pretending not to hear. She didn't want to get trapped in a situation with Velma who was obviously lonely.

She had only one nephew in Dallas. What kind of a mutt was he, telling his old aunt not to get an emergency call system? Maybe it was him on the phone hitting her up for money.

Replaying that day and her reactions, Mrs. B. swallowed a large dose of Catholic guilt. She'd judged this woman harshly, but the other voice in her head, the no-nonsense voice, asked, *How does that change anything? She was cloying, deceptive, needy, always trying to rub people's noses in her perceived superiority*.

Mrs. B. pulled her thoughts into line. Get a grip. The woman is dead. You don't know what her life was. You didn't walk in her shoes. She must have had some good qualities; after all, LaLa loved her. Stop being a bitch. Thinking like this is no way to begin Lent. Go to confession, she scolded herself.

***

At home, she unpacked her bags worrying about LaLa. She must be terrified. I'll get her tonight no matter what Father Melvyn thinks, but I still need someone to take care of her until I find a permanent home. Who might be willing? "I know," she exclaimed. Sasha and Ziggy looked up from their dinner. "He'd be perfect, and he likes cats."

Like most people, she often talked out loud when no one was around. Unlike most people, she admitted it.

12
In The Crosshairs

The air was damp and misty. The trees at the curb and the dark outline of the house in the inky night created weird shadows. Neighboring houses were a distance away because Velma's house sat in the middle of a half-acre. To the right her property was bordered by a greenbelt, and the house to the left was angled away from hers on the other side of a six-foot fence. The closest light came from the church parking lot across the street, which did nothing to illuminate Velma's front door, especially in the murky night.

Mrs. B. sat in her car on Velma's driveway with the motor running and the headlights casting bright round circles against the garage door. The darkness unnerved her, and she considered leaving the headlights on until she was done in Velma's house. "And when you come out, your battery will be dead, and that will be worse," she reasoned. "Get going." She killed the headlights, turned off the engine and grabbed her purse and the carrier.

Approaching the steps to the porch she set the carrier down again. A tremor passed through her as she looked up to the barely visible front door. It's getting colder she thought and pulled her sweater closed. Her spine tingled.

Can't believe I forgot to take the flashlight. Stupid mistake. Maybe I should go home and come back tomorrow morning. Then she thought about the cat, alone in the house, without food or fresh water. "Corraggio," she hissed at herself.

Gripping the carrier, placing one foot in front of the other, she forced her feet up the three front steps. When she reached the porch she felt like she'd won a prize. Hurry up, she ordered silently. Once you get the door open you can turn a light on inside.

In the blackness she walked to the door and set the carrier down. Bending over she forced her shaky fingers to reach behind the planter. She shuddered at the thought that some insect or crawly thing might be lurking there in the dark. A creaking sound behind her raised goosebumps on her arms. Was that a floorboard? Another... closer now. She forgot the key. Her body snapped upright.

A dense black mass moved out of the deep purple shadows. She bleated, covered her mouth, and instinctively stepped back and away. She tried to turn and run. Her foot hit the carrier sending it skittering across the porch floor; it sounded like thunder in the quiet night. She propelled herself toward the steps and collided with a mass. A hand grabbed her wrist, pulling her back toward the door. The scream died in her throat.

"It's only me. I've been watching for you."

Mrs. B. put her free hand to her chest. "You scared me half to death. What are you doing here and why are you whispering?"

"I came to help. I thought you'd be here earlier." He was close enough for her to make out the depth of his eyes behind the wire-rimmed glasses. He looked contrite, or was that wishful thinking? Father Melvyn released her wrist. "I didn't think you should go in alone," he added.

She wanted to ask what changed his mind but thought better of it. Her heart banged against her breastbone so hard it hurt. She blew out her breath and said, "Let's get on with it then," relieved not to go into dead Velma's house by herself. Once more she forced her hand behind the planter, loosened the tape, gripped the key, and in one swift motion, stood up and unlocked the door. "Velma should have had timers on these lights. I don't like the house being so dark," she said. Once the door was open, she reached for the light switch.

"Don't turn it on," he commanded. "Everyone knows Velma is dead. They might call the police if they see lights." He clicked on a small penlight.

Mrs. B. looked surprised when he handed her a second one. "*I* came prepared." Is that a glint of mischief in his eyes? she wondered.

"Keep the light pointed down at the floor, so it won't be easily seen from outside."

"Hmmm." How did he know that? Once inside, she aimed her light down at the cat portal. "It's latched. The cat should be in the house, so what was Velma doing outside last night?" Father Melvyn had no answer.

"LaLa," she called in a soft voice, not wanting to further spook the cat. "LaLa," she repeated, walking around the living room where Velma had served her tea a few short weeks ago, penlight in one hand, carrier in the other. Father Melvyn walked toward the kitchen. "If you see her, don't try to grab her. Call me," she told him.

Mrs. B. made her way to the hallway on the opposite side of the living room. She opened the first door to her right. The bed was unmade. The police were right. It looked like Velma went to bed then got up again. Feeling like a voyeur, she closed the bedroom door and moved to the door on the left. It was an office. Her light caught the surface of the desk before she pointed it down. "What?" she whispered, then redirected it.

Papers were strewn all over the desk and on the floor. She aimed the beam at the file cabinet; it was open. Files were sticking up, some on the floor, some jammed back in. The room was a mess. Jake said the house was as neat as a pin. "What the hell happened here?" she asked, flipping a file on the desk with her finger, trying to read it when a sound caught her attention.

A timid *meow* reached her ears. It came from her left. "LaLa! Where are you?" More meowing, stronger. It seemed to come from under the open-shelved bookcase next to the window. Mrs. B. got down on her knees to look underneath. Her penlight illuminated LaLa pressed against the far wall, stress tears wetting her face, paws opening and closing, their contractions working the papers under her into a crumpled mess.

Mrs. B. reached out, grabbed the cat by the scuff of her neck and drew her out. Before LaLa had time to bolt or fight Mrs. B. lowered her into the carrier and closed the door. "I'm going to take care of you, LaLa, no need to worry." She reached through the cage door and scratched LaLa between her ears. She was about to stand up when she noticed the papers that came out with the cat.

She smoothed them on the floor. They looked official, but she couldn't read them. What else is under there? she wondered. Shining the penlight under the bookshelf again, a glint of shiny fabric was visible. Again, she stretched her arm under the bookcase, grabbed it, and pulled. Out came a small book; it looked like a journal.

"Mrs. B., do you have her?" Father Melvyn's voice was getting closer. Still on her knees, Mrs. B. instinctively shoved the papers and the journal into her large purse as Father Melvyn crossed the threshold of the room. His gasp made her look up. The penlight in his hand was aimed at the window. She yelped.

Eyes, black as coal peered at her. They looked iridescent in the white sclera. The pale face was suspended, floating, unattached to anything bounded by the blackness of night. Most frightening, the malice from those eyes penetrated the window and scalded her. Mrs. B. felt exposed, vulnerable, caught in the crosshairs of something evil. Time stopped. The tableau froze in place. Only the hairs on her arms moved, they stood erect, and she shuddered as the eyes disappeared.

"Don't come outside," Father Melvyn ordered and took off at a run toward the front door.

The cat's cries became strident. Mrs. B. heard LaLa twisting in the carrier. She smelled the change in the cat's body odor. Adrenaline and fear had the cat in a panic. "Me too," she muttered. Forcing herself to overcome the paralysis that gripped her legs, she pushed herself up, ran to the bathroom and found a large towel to cover LaLa's cage.

It felt like forever before Father Melvyn's tread broadcast his return.

"What was that?" she asked.

"Got away. My light startled whomever it was standing there staring at you. Didn't you see it...feel it?"

Mrs. B. shook her head. "Was it a person? It looked like a floating mask. Could it have been a prank? A ghost?"

"No ghost. Whoever it was had weight, judging by the crushed stems in the flowerbed beneath this window."

Unnerved, she picked up the carrier and her purse. "Let's get out of here," she said.

"Taking LaLa home with you?" Father Melvyn asked.

"I can't. I think it would be too difficult for her and my two cats to adjust."

"You said you had *a* cat. You have more than one?" She nodded. "What will you do with her then?"

"I spoke to Father Joe. He's willing to care for her until I can find a home. He said he couldn't take her before nine tonight. He had an evening class to teach. That's why I came so late. He's waiting for my call."

"You mean at the rectory?"

"I think he intends to keep her in the toolshed at the back of the property. I have a pan, litter, and food for him." She saw her boss's annoyed expression. "You know, Father, having LaLa is good. Helps keep creepy-crawlies and critters away, providing the critters aren't bigger than she is, of course."

Unwilling to put her hand behind the planter again, she locked the front door and pocketed the key. At her car she placed the carrier in the back seat. "Want a ride across the street? I'll text Father Joe. He'll come out to get LaLa."

***

Another trespasser searching inside Velma's house heard Father Melvyn and Mrs. B. at the front door. The unexpected sound of voices spurred the intruder to move out of Velma's office without making a sound. Slinking out the back door into the night, the third searcher thought: This is maddening. I need to get back into that office. The document box I took last night had all sorts of papers—the deed, utility bills, and a bunch of other stuff—but not Charles Maxwell's will. Who are these people and what are they doing in Velma's house?

The grounds were completely devoid of light, making it easier to watch and follow the movements of the penlights inside. When a watery illumination appeared in the office, the watcher gave no thought to the flowers in the border beneath the long window. Crushing them underfoot in order to see inside the poorly lit room, it was like viewing an old silent movie in sepia tones.

A woman with white curly hair looked around at the files that were strewn all over the desk and floor. She turned and knelt down. She was beneath the windowsill. The watcher stepped up closer to see what she was doing. A few minutes later the white haired woman pulled the cat out from under the bookcase, placed it in a carrier then reached down again and pulled out papers and a book. The watcher heard a muffled voice call out. The woman on the floor stuffed the book and papers into her large purse.

Intent on the woman's actions, the watcher failed to step back from the window and into the protection of darkness. A sudden, blinding light shone through the glass. The watcher froze. Eye contact with the woman on the floor was momentary before the watcher stepped back into darkness away from the reach of the light.

Making it to the overgrown Texas Mountain Laurel at the corner of the garage, the watcher contracted into a ball and listened to footsteps running around the property. They stopped almost directly in front of the shrub and then moved away. The watcher didn't breathe until the large bulk went back in the house. A few minutes later, a man and a woman emerged.

Remaining hidden, straining unsuccessfully to hear their muffled words, the watcher waited. The man walked across Cobble Drive, while the woman backed out of the driveway and drove across the street.

"They're going to the same place." The watcher jumped out from behind the large bush and ran across in the dark, weaving in and out of the shadows.

The car pulled up close to the building. Another man came out the back door. Leaving the car idling, the woman handed the carrier to the second man, reached back into the car and pulled out what looked like a large pan with a bag in it, and then reached into her purse and handed him what looked like a bundle of paper. A few words were exchanged, but the watcher was too far away to hear. The woman got in her car and left.

Unobserved and remaining still until the two men took everything into the house, the watcher then moved through deep shadows, returned to Velma's house, reentered through the back door, and went straight to Velma's office.

Kneeling down in front of the bookcase where the woman with white, curly hair was earlier, the watcher shone a flashlight under it. There was one piece of crumpled paper at the back. Lying flat on the floor and stretching hard to grasp the edge, the watcher brought it out and flattened it on the floor.

The words "Last Will and Testament" were legible. "Velma, you bitch. You hid it almost in plain sight." Shoving the paper in the pocket of the hooded sweater, the watcher sat on the floor to think. What just happened? I was searching the file cabinet; those people came in; the woman pulled the cat, several papers, and a book out from under the bookcase. They went across the street to the church and she gave everything to the men, including a bundle of papers from her satchel, then she left.

A master of adjustment, the watcher muttered, "I need a new plan." Minutes later, pulling the hood of the sweater tight, the watcher left Velma's house and walked several blocks to a parked car, lips moving the entire time as if in prayer: "They have the will, and I need to get it. The question is how?"

13
Who Is in Charge?

At the backdoor of the rectory, Mrs. B. handed the carrier holding LaLa to Father Joe and explained what was in the bag. Father Melvyn bristled. He was distracted and not paying attention to the conversation. Who is in charge here, he wondered. This is my parish and rectory. How am I not in control of this? He liked to think of himself as a hands-on CEO type, understanding every aspect of the company under his authority, in this case, St. Francis de Sales.

"Will you put the cat in the shed now?" Father Melvyn asked, as Mrs. B. drove away.

"I think I'll keep her in my room tonight. I don't want to be clanging and banging around in the toolshed in the dark." Father Melvyn felt Father Joe's eyes on him in the dim light from the kitchen door. "I hope you don't mind, Melvyn. I don't know how you feel about animals, but I do love cats, and Mrs. B. assured me she'll find LaLa a new home fast."

Mollified by Father Joe's apology, he decided he should be big about it. "I'm sure it's not a problem." He didn't want Joe to suspect that this woman had stepped on his authoritative toes. "Let me help you carry everything inside. What are those papers?" Father Melvyn asked, taking them along with the bag of cat food.

"Some interesting articles Mrs. B. said she had about biomedical ethics. I told her I'd like to read them." Brows furrowed, Father Melvyn couldn't understand his own discomfort with the thought that Mrs. B. had a rapport with the two priests under his authority at St. Francis and he didn't know it.

The two men went into the rectory and up the stairs to the bedrooms. "I'll take it from here, Mel. I'll close the bedroom door before I let her out of her carrier. She'll probably hide under something for a few hours, maybe a few days."

"See you in the morning," Father Melvyn said. He turned and went back downstairs. He wasn't sleepy at all. The night's adventure had his adrenaline pumping. He decided to take a cup of tea in the library. It had been an unusual day and he felt off balance. He needed to establish a feeling of security and control in his surroundings.

While the water heated on the stove, Father Melvyn made a final check of the first-floor rooms. In the front office, he clicked on the light. Neat, clean, and ready. He was satisfied.

When he took over as pastor of St. Francis, the Coyles and the Barbees, his closest friends in the parish, helped him refurnish the uncomfortable and shabby offices that held oversize desks and hard metal folding chairs, hardly a comfortable and welcoming environment. The old, cumbersome desks had since been replaced with inexpensive but sleek new ones along with more comfortable chairs.

He heard the kettle's whistle, turned off the office lights and went to the kitchen for his tea then settled in the library. You're becoming too attached to material things, he cautioned himself, but he couldn't help it. The library gave him a feeling of comfort, a feeling of home. Turning on a floor lamp he surveyed the room and smiled. It's a soothing atmosphere, even if it did happen by accident, he thought.

Fortunately, his predecessor Father Jameson had elected to keep the old bookcases flanking the fireplace. Until Father Jameson's departure, the room itself was a hodgepodge of mismatched, broken-down chairs and a couple of dim desk lamps. He looked around the library with appreciation.

The Coyles gave him a gently used brown leather couch. There were two other armchairs one of which was a recliner given to him by the Barbees when they redecorated their den; it was his favorite. An assortment of nondescript side tables and a coffee table provided plenty of places to set down coffee mugs and teacups as well as magazines and books. Several good floor lamps, perfect for reading, were added. The room was masculine yet warm and welcoming.

Father Melvyn sat in the recliner adjacent to the window. He didn't turn on a light. The chair enfolded him and the events of the day replayed, leaving him with questions. His well-ordered life caring for the needs and business of his parish and his flock was suddenly out of balance. The most disturbing actor in this unsettling drama was none other than his trusted housekeeper, cook, and clerical assistant: Mrs. Samuela Buonafigliuola.

She's been here how long? Two or three years? he wondered, not remembering exactly. I feel like I've known her all my life, yet all I know is that she's widowed and has one son in Dallas and a daughter and four grandchildren in New York. She is the most efficient assistant and a terrific cook. I never knew she had cats or that she liked animals. Then again, I didn't know that Father Joe liked cats either.

Father Melvyn was uncomfortable more by what he didn't know about Father Joe and Mrs. B. than by the easy rapport between them. He especially didn't like that she had asked Joe to take LaLa without running it past him first.

Random thoughts of Mrs. B. passed through his head. She had a quick wit and a dry, often sharp, sense of humor. He thought her to be a curious person, but maybe she was more than curious; maybe she was nosey.

A tall woman, probably slim, he thought, but who could tell under those loose layers of clothes. She was very erect, not in the least bent over, and had great energy, like me, he thought. He remembered that she was around his age and wore her white curly hair short. Her eyes were brown and the big, round, blue-framed glasses accentuated them. He didn't think she was anything special, except for her smile. It was compelling because it was real. It reached her eyes, the mirror of the soul.

The thought of Mrs. B.'s smile brought one to his face. I guess one could say Mrs. B. is still quite attractive...maybe handsome is a better word, he thought. Father Melvyn was surprised at his detailed awareness of her physical appearance. Not one to ignore beauty, he appreciated women from a distance, but he didn't think of her that way. She was his assistant and the motor that kept the place running so that he could concentrate on his work.

He sipped. The tea was cold. Still not sleepy, he went to the kitchen, reheated it then returned to his chair. His thoughts stayed on Mrs. B. and her earlier display of temper.

She'd stubbornly declared that she was going to rescue the cat in spite of his objections. *I don't know if I'm comfortable with this. Yet, I felt compelled to go to Velma's house and wait for her to show up.* He shook off his thoughts. *I'm reacting to the bizarre nature of the day, the stress of finding Velma's dead body behind the Church.*

He felt sad at the thought of having started Lent with a murder. "Ah, Velma," he said aloud. *She died alone in an alley on a chilly March night with no one to hold her hand or comfort her.* He crossed himself and said a prayer for her soul.

Finally ready for sleep, he drained the last of his tea, turned off the floor lamp and left his cup on the side table, knowing Mrs. B. would take care of it in the morning.

Friday
Two Days after Ash Wednesday

14
Resetting Boundaries

Mrs. B. arrived at St. Francis at 8:45 a.m. Father Melvyn's car was already gone. She hadn't seen him at all on Thursday. He'd left before she arrived and hadn't returned by five. We both need time to calm down and reset the boundaries of our relationship, she thought. He's the boss, and I was out of line. I shall be contrite; I will apologize. Having made her decision, she walked resolutely into the rectory to find Father Joe sitting at the table reading the newspaper.

"Good morning, Mrs. B.," Father Joe said.

"Good morning, Father Joe. Where's Father Melvyn?"

"Melvyn and Declan went to a seminar. I'm covering the noon mass." Curious, she thought. The seminar starts at ten thirty, and it's a fifteen-minute drive to the diocesan office. She kept her face neutral.

How is LaLa doing in the shed?"

"She's still upstairs in my room. Poor little thing was terrified. I think she's still hiding under the bed. I haven't seen her, but she used her litter pan and ate the food I left. I'll give it a few days before I transfer her to the shed."

Mrs. B. was surprised. "Does Father Melvyn object?"

"I'm not sure, but I think I have a little grace period before he'll tell me to get her out."

"Thank you for doing this. I promise I'll make calls this weekend and try to get her a nice home by Monday. I hope this hasn't caused any trouble between you and 'the boss,'" she whispered.

Father Joe chuckled at her cheeky statement. He gave an unconcerned shrug and walked out of the kitchen. "See you later," he called back over his shoulder.

She stood with her back against the sink, feeling unsettled. Father Melvyn is really angry. I feel as if the atmosphere in the rectory has changed. She felt awkward, even though she was alone. "What will be, will be," she uttered. "Best to get on with my work."

Moving through the day's routines, she completed her administrative tasks, left Father Melvyn a stack of letters to sign, lined up on his desk just the way he liked them then turned her attention to the Friday night dinner prep.

By five, she had the chafing dishes on the sideboard in the dining room, the ice bucket filled, and the dining table covered with a cloth. There was plenty of food in the refrigerator so that they could take care of themselves over the weekend. All that remained was to put the special meal she prepared in the chafing dishes to keep them warm until the priests were ready to eat. She was about to make her escape when the back door slammed.

Father Melvyn bounded into the kitchen with Father Declan in tow. "Well, Mrs. B., our Father Declan made a very successful speech to the conference on the difficulties of this generation entering the priesthood. We are quite proud of him. He certainly caught the bishop's attention." Father Declan stood smiling and blushing.

"Congratulations, Father Declan," she said before both priests took off up the stairs to change into civvies. "I'll be leaving now, Father Melvyn. Have a nice weekend." The sound of a bedroom doors closing was the only response. Maybe they didn't hear me she thought and left the rectory. She hadn't cleared the air with her boss.

***

As soon as she walked through the door from the garage to the kitchen, her babies, Ziggy and Sasha greeted her. As always, she fed them then changed into lounging pajamas and made her Friday night Martini. The priests in her charge weren't the only ones enjoying special dinners on Fridays.

Before leaving for work she'd washed, wrapped and placed fillet of sole in the refrigerator. The seasoned flour was on the counter in a covered dish. There were cleaned and cut red-skinned potatoes, a small onion, and one garlic clove. Everything was ready to cook. She mixed the potatoes, onion, garlic, and rosemary together on a cookie sheet, gave everything a light coating of olive oil, and popped it all into the oven. Within a few minutes, the aroma of roasting potatoes filled the kitchen. Mrs. B. sipped her drink and made a list of people she'd call tomorrow to see if they'd take LaLa.

An avid mystery fan, her usual Friday routine included reading while enjoying her dinner, but tonight she decided the real-life mystery might be more interesting. She reached for the folder with the papers and journal she'd taken from Velma's house. The papers needed sorting and more time than she wanted to put in. Instead, she picked up the journal and sat staring at it, deciding whether to open it.

Should I be reading something private and not intended for my eyes? The question bothered her. She liked to understand what motivated people, but where was the line between healthy curiosity and prying? Father Melvyn's accusation resurfaced; it stung. Was she nosey? Her honest answer was immediate. Yes! But she was not a gossip. She didn't spread rumors, try to bring others down, take shots, or denigrate, and that was a fact—and she didn't share confidences or personal information about anyone. There was an important difference between learning about people's lives and spreading tales. She put the journal down. I'll decide after dinner, she thought.

The potatoes were ready. She sautéed the fish lightly in olive oil then placed it in an oven dish, sprinkled it with white wine and capers and transferred it to the hot oven for fifteen minutes. Her own special Friday night dinner looked delicious.

15
That Damned Woman

"Keep on watching. I'll be there Monday," he said, ending the conversation.

"Good. I'll have the papers by then." The watcher was confident. It was all falling into place. Not being Catholic, the call provided information about how Catholic churches were run.

The rectory was home to the priests serving St. Francis de Sales parish. The people in Velma's house the night of her death fit the description of the pastor, Father Melvyn Kronkey and his housekeeper. Tweaking the plans based on these new facts, the watcher prepared for night and the cover of darkness.

***

Approaching St. Francis de Sales Church, the watcher killed the headlights making it more difficult for anyone to see the car, but decided against parking it on church property. What if one of the priests goes out? He might notice a strange car left there no matter where it was parked. Better park somewhere else. The watcher headed to the apartment complex down the road. It wasn't gated so parking in the visitors section wouldn't be a problem.

Anxious not to be seen or noticed, the watcher pulled the hoodie up tight and jogged back to the church, cut across the parking field and walked toward the rectory.

The crime scene tape was gone, but before settling in the alley where Velma had died, the watcher circled the building and carefully peered through the windows, staying far enough back not to be caught spying again. The windows on the church side of the rectory were dark. The center hall fixture cast enough light to make out the stationary shadows of furniture. At the back of the rectory, there were three cars in the carport. The kitchen light was on, but the windows were too high to see anything useful.

Moving to the far side of the rectory, bright light shone out of the dining room windows. The blinds were open and three men sat at the table in civilian clothes, enjoying dinner, drinks and conversation. Sounds of laughter and muffled talk filtered through the walls. Doesn't look like they're going anywhere soon the watcher thought and went back to the carport to jot down car makes and license plates. It was obvious that the woman who took the cat and the papers wasn't there, but that wasn't important as long as the papers were.

Walking back to the alley where Velma drew her last breath, the watcher made out the fading chalk outline of Velma's body. I'll wait here in the shadows until the priests turn off all the downstairs lights.

At midnight the watcher moved silently around the building checking what could be seen in each room. All was dark. "It's about time," the watcher muttered, tired of the long wait. Using the same credit card that popped Velma's kitchen door, the back door of the rectory opened easily. Maybe this is a special open a back-door-card; the amusing idea was fleeting. Pushing the door open a few inches, the watcher waited. No sounds and no alarm. There was only silence. Do these fools think because they're priests no one will break in? Feeling secure the watcher moved forward on soundless rubber-soled shoes to the front of the building and turned into the first office before clicking on a small flashlight.

There were piles of papers on the desk. Rifling through them revealed baptism certificates. Moving to the file cabinet in the corner, the top drawer gave up marriage certificates and contact information. In order to work fast the files weren't put back as they were found. Some were thrown on the floor or on the desk.

Moving across the hall to the second office, the search was repeated. The rustle of papers being searched seemed louder in the quiet night as the watcher's sensory hair cells strained to pick up any sounds outside the office. A few loose papers drifted to the floor. "Where the hell is that will?"

The sudden glare of the overhead light was accompanied by a shout: "Hey, what are you doing in here? Stop!" A voice yelled.

Swinging around hard, the watcher caught the priest on the bridge of his nose with the jagged edge of the flashlight.

"Ahhh," he screamed, grabbing his face with one hand and the intruder's jacket with the other. They struggled. The watcher fought to break free; the priest tried to hold on.

Swinging the flashlight again, the watcher felt rather than saw it connect with soft tissue. One final shove and the priest went down hard hitting his head on a chair arm. "Declan, Melvyn, help," he yelled.

No longer worried about noise, the watcher punched the priest in the face, tore away from his grip and staggered back to the kitchen, bumping against the hall table in the darkness, sending it crashing to the floor before making it to the back door. Flinging it open with a force that sounded like a gunshot when it hit the frame, the watcher escaped.

Running down the street at full speed, keeping the hood pulled tight and heaving for breath, the watcher reached the parking lot at the apartment complex. Crouched behind a car, a quick scan showed most apartment windows were dark and the grounds were deserted.

There was no sound other than the watcher's own heavy breathing. Once safely in the car and driving away, the watcher muttered, "No papers. I need to get to the damned woman. She either has them or knows where they are. Damn her to hell."

***

Father Melvyn was relieved when the police arrived. The wait felt like forever, but in reality it was only a few minutes. "Officer, help quickly please. My colleague is bleeding," he said as they entered. The officer walked into the kitchen to find three men in nightclothes. A tall, thin young redhead was standing over an older man holding a bloodied cloth at the back of his blood stained, salt-and-pepper hair.

The first officer on the scene called for another car then introduced himself. "I'm officer Tom Smith. Can I have your names please?"

"Father Melvyn Kronkey, pastor of St. Francis de Sales.

The redheaded priest identified himself: "Father Declan Ryan, associate pastor."

In a nasal voice from the pressure on his bleeding nose, the injured man answered, "Father Joe Russo. I teach at the university and I live here." The tall redhead moved to the sink to rewet the cloth with cold water for Father Joe.

The EMT came in with her bag and asked, "Who is hurt?" Officer Smith pointed. "Hey, Father Joe," the EMT said. "What have we here? Let me have a look."

"You know him?" Officer Smith asked.

"I'm a member of this parish," she answered.

"Hi Jane. How are you?" Father Joe asked.

Jane smiled. "I should be asking you that question," she answered and began her examination. "Your head wound is bleeding a lot but scalp wounds do that. You'll need a couple of sutures." She replaced the cloth at the back of his head and tilted his chin up to look at his nose. "Looks like your nose took the worst of it…you're going to have a shiner too, I think." While Jane treated Father Joe the police questioned them about the attack.

"You were all upstairs in your rooms?" The three priests nodded their assent. Officer Smith asked, "Who came downstairs and why?"

Father Joe raised his hand. "That would be me. I came down first because LaLa was mewing at my bedroom door. She seemed upset."

"LaLa?" the officer and Jane asked at the same time.

"I'm cat sitting. LaLa was pacing in front of my bedroom door and seemed agitated. I opened the door and she ran down. I followed, but I didn't call her name. I didn't want to wake Declan or Melvyn. When I got to the bottom of the stairs I heard something in the front office and thought it was LaLa. I walked in, turned on the light and saw someone pulling files out of the cabinet. Guess it wasn't smart to yell or turn on the light," Father Joe said, disparaging his actions.

"Not to worry. Most people would have had a similar reaction. What can you tell me about the intruder? Male; female; tall; short; heavy; thin?

"It all happened so fast. I don't know. Maybe as tall as me. Not heavy..." Father Joe shrugged.

"Did you see any part of the person's body?"

"No. He was wearing gloves. All black clothes"

"You think it was a man?"

"I don't know if it was a man..." he hesitated.

"Is there something else?" Officer Smith asked.

"Eyes." Everyone focused on Father Joe and waited. "The eyes were black and malicious. That's all I remember distinctly. They were chilling."

"We need to get him to the hospital. That scalp wound needs to be stitched," the EMT said.

Officer Smith turned his attention to Father Melvyn. Before he began asking questions, Father Melvyn turned to Father Declan. "Give your statement to the officer, get dressed and go to the emergency room with Joe."

Father Declan nodded and told the officer, "I was upstairs, almost asleep when I heard banging down here and Father Joe yelling for help. When I got down the stairs Father Joe was stumbling out of the office holding his head."

"You didn't see the assailant?'

"No. I didn't even try. I was concerned with Joe."

"Okay. Thanks. You can go." Father Declan went up the stairs two at a time. The police officer finished writing then turned to the pastor. "And you were upstairs too?"

"Yes, in my room. It's the first one at the head of the stairs. I was working on Sunday's homily and I didn't hear Joe or the cat. I heard a bang and Joe yell for help then Declan running past my door and down the stairs. I ran down right after him and found them both sitting on the floor in the hall. Declan was holding the back of Joe's head, trying to stop the bleeding. I ran to the phone and called 911 and the rest, as they say, is history."

Officer Smith nodded and kept writing. "Do you keep firearms here?"

Father Melvyn felt a punch of shock and shook his head vehemently: No.

Officer Smith continued. "How about money?"

"We do have some cash in the staff office across from the kitchen, but not in the front offices."

Another uniformed officer walked in while Officer Smith was writing. "Whoever it was searched both offices. There are files and papers all over the floor." The police officer examined the kitchen door. It was still open. "CSI will dust and take pictures. Probably won't find any prints."

Saturday

Three Days After Ash Wednesday

16

The Aftermath

The sun wasn't up at five a.m. Saturday morning, when Father Declan returned to the rectory, with his injured colleague. Father Joe, bruised, stitched, and bandaged plopped down into a chair. Handing him a cup of coffee, Father Melvyn asked, "How do you feel?"

"Not too bad yet. Painkillers are still working."

Father Melvyn nodded. "To be expected." Without wasting time, the pastor told his curate and his resident professor what the morning's schedule would be in the aftermath of the break-in.

"Declan, I'll take confessions this afternoon and the five o'clock mass. You'll stay in the rectory and cover the phones."

"What about me? I can answer calls," Joe offered.

"You go to bed and rest. Maybe you should call someone at the university to cover your classes on Monday. You aren't going to feel up to much for the next few days." He knew he was right when Father Joe didn't argue. "Actually, I need to cancel tonight's dinner plans with Sebastian. I'll tell him what happened. Maybe he can notify your department."

"What about tomorrow's mass schedule?" Father Declan asked. The pastor thought for a minute. "I'll ask Sebastian if he's available to take Joe's masses at eleven and five." Looking over at the wounded priest, Father Melvyn said, "You look about to fall off the chair. Go upstairs. Declan will bring you some water for your meds."

Father Joe looked around. "Mel, I hate to bother you with this, but have you seen LaLa since the incident last night?"

"No, come to think of it, I haven't."

"She's probably hiding in my room," Joe said.

Melvyn watched as his injured friend and colleague lifted himself with effort and then stood, leaning on the chair-back.

"Declan, help him get upstairs, please," the pastor whispered to his younger assistant. He watched the two make their way down the hall to the staircase, looking like two battered soldiers returning from war. What is this world coming to? he wondered, dismayed by the beating Joe had taken.

Father Melvyn waited until seven a.m. to call his close friend Father Sebastian Nunez, professor of religious studies at the university. It was he who recommended that Father Joe ask for residency at St. Francis.

"Good morning, Sebastian," Father Melvyn said as cheerfully as possible.

"This is a pretty early call, Mel. What's the problem?"

"For a peaceful parish of hardworking people, we've started Lent with a bang." Father Melvyn proceeded to explain the events of the past two days, finishing with the break-in the night before and Father Joe's injuries.

"Wow. You all have your hands full. Is Joe okay?" After Father Melvyn assured him that Joe was fine, given the beating he'd taken, Sebastian continued. "Why don't I come over and take Joe's masses tomorrow. Will that help?"

"I was about to ask. That would be a great help. Thanks. Sebastian. If you don't have any other plans, why not stay for dinner? I can only offer leftovers."

"Mrs. B.'s cooking?"

Father Melvyn smiled. "Yes." Everyone who'd ever had a meal at St. Francis looked forward to Mrs. B.'s cooking.

"It's a deal. By the way, you might want to consider installing an alarm system. It's a crazy world we live in these days."

Glad Ms. Jenkins is having those security people come soon, Father Melvyn thought hanging up the phone.

Sunday

The First Full Week of Lent

17

Potluck

On Sunday morning, Father Melvyn hit the ground running and didn't have a moment to think about murder. The phones rang incessantly and every call was from parishioners who heard about the commotion at the rectory on Friday night.

He turned to Declan. "How do these people find out so fast?" His question didn't warrant an answer. "Is there a drone spying on us?" he asked, half kidding. Noticing the time, Father Melvyn hurled himself up the stairs to get ready for the day, but first went to Father Joe's door and knocked gently. No answer. He cracked the door a bit and peeked in. Joe was sound asleep.

LaLa sat erect at the foot of the bed as if guarding the sleeping priest behind her. She cocked her head and looked up at him as if to say, Don't worry, I'm watching him. The cat's demeanor fascinated him.

Melvyn tiptoed in. Poor guy is exhausted and he's going to hurt bad for the next few days, he thought. Melvyn looked around the room. LaLa's dishes were empty. He saw the bag of food he helped bring in

Wednesday night. Trying not to let the hard pellets clank into the plastic bowl, he refilled it and then filled the water bowl. He looked up. LaLa never left her position at the foot of Joe's bed. Before leaving, Father Melvyn walked over and patted the cat on her head. LaLa accepted the gesture.

***

As was his custom, Father Melvyn stood in front of the marble altar, raised his arms, faced the congregation, and gave the final blessing then made his way to the narthex to greet his parishioners.

He exercised great patience greeting those who lined up to grill him about the goings-on at Saint Francis, as they had after the two previous masses. Their exclusive interest was Father Joe's condition and what happened. No words about the message of the readings and the gospel; no words about his homily. Oh well, he thought. At least I had a break. Sebastian said the eleven, and he will say the five this afternoon. I promised him a chilled Martini. Maybe I'll start without him. The Sunday rituals complete, his vestments returned to the Sacristy closet, Father Melvyn was happy to go back to the rectory.

He walked in to find Declan taking the initiative. Everyone knew Father Declan didn't know the difference between a hot dog and a piece of apple pie, but he was getting food out of the refrigerator under the watchful eye and instructions from Father Joe. Although obviously sore and sleepy, Joe sipped coffee and instructed the young curate about which pots and pans to use and how to preheat the oven and adjust the temperature. LaLa, who had become Father Joe's personal guard, sat next to his chair.

"Hi Melvyn," Joe said.

"Are you feeling well enough to be out of bed?" the pastor asked.

"I'm okay. As long as I don't move my mouth too much. Anyway, I can't lie in bed all day." Father Joe changed the subject. "We'll wait for Sebastian, and we'll eat in the kitchen tonight. Nothing fancy. Is that okay Mel?"

"Exactly what I was thinking."

"Mrs. B.'s potluck is better than most other people's firsts; it's bound to be good no matter where we eat it." Father Declan added.

"Since you have everything in hand here, I'm going to try picking up the mess in front," the pastor told them. He needed to organize the papers and files thrown around by the intruder during the break-in. Officer Smith told the pastor to go ahead, since the police had all the information and evidence it was possible to retrieve, which was basically nothing.

***

While Joe and Declan prepared food, Melvyn worked in the front offices stacking files and papers on the desks. Mrs. B. will get everything organized and put away, he assured himself. To Father Declan's suggestion the night before that he ask Mrs. B. to come in on Sunday, given the situation, his "no" was abrupt. "Let's leave Mrs. B. to her weekend. She'll have plenty to do on Monday," Melvyn added, not ready to ask her for extra help.

He resolved to clear the air with his housekeeper first thing Monday morning. That would be the first step in recovering the harmonious balance they'd had before all this happened. The knock at the front door broke into his thoughts.

He opened it to Sebastian's smiling face. The last Sunday mass was over. "Where's the martini you promised me?" Sebastian asked.

Monday

The First Full Week of Lent

18

It's an Insane Asylum

Determined to sort things out with Father Melvyn, Mrs. B. let herself into the kitchen. She stood rooted in place, staring at the bizarre scene before her eyes; her greeting died in her throat.

The three priests sat together at the table. Father Joe had his back to her. Father Melvyn and Father Declan were smiling as they watched LaLa, who was sitting on Father Melvyn's lap, delicately lick milk from a small saucer on the kitchen table. At the sound of the door, Father Joe turned.

"Oh my word," Mrs. B. put her hand over her mouth, shocked by the priest's black-and-blue face. "Father Joe, what on earth happened to you?" She walked over to him and turned his head from side to side, studying his facial cuts, bruises, and black eye.

"Good morning, Mrs. B." Father Melvyn boomed, startling LaLa, who jumped off his lap. "Now see what I've gone and done." LaLa returned to Father Joe's side and stared at Mrs. B.'s surprised face as if to say, No worries, I have them all in hand. She gave a soft mew and went back to Father Melvyn's lap and her milk.

Recovering from her astonishment, Mrs. B. asked, "Is anyone going to tell me what's going on?"

"Seems we had a bit of excitement over the weekend," Father Melvyn answered. "I'm surprised you haven't heard, given that news travels at the speed of light in our parish."

Mrs. B. closed the door she'd left open and stood with her hands on her hips, waiting. She felt her eyebrows pulling toward center. Father Melvyn looked amused, almost smug.

"Take a cup of coffee and sit, Mrs. B. We have a lot to tell you, but before we do, I have a question. Did you find a home for LaLa?"

Mrs. B. sighed. In spite of the picture that greeted her when she walked in, she knew Father Melvyn didn't want the cat in the rectory. Her words came in a rush. "I did make some calls, but no one has agreed to take her yet." She didn't say that she was so immersed in reading Velma's journal and Charles Maxwell's will, neither of which were any of her business that she didn't take care of the job that *was* her business: finding a home for LaLa. "I know you don't want her here, and I promise I'll have her out within a few days. Would you like me to put her in the shed this morning so she's out of the way?" While they spoke, LaLa finished her milk and jumped off Father Melvyn's lap.

"Not so fast, Mrs. B. Declan, Joe, and I decided to keep her."

"You decided what?"

"She's rather entertaining when she wants to be, you know," Father Melvyn said.

Mrs. B. turned toward the counter to get her coffee. Is

he instructing me on cats? Does he think he's telling me something I don't know? Of course she's amusing when she wants to be. She's a cat.

"Anyway," the pastor continued, "I considered what you said about cats and bugs and all that. We'll keep her." Without giving Mrs. B. a chance to ask more questions, Father Melvyn closed off further discussion by changing the subject.

"Now for today. Father Declan and I will handle all parish business. Father Joe is taking a few days off from teaching, until those stiches are out and some of those bruises fade. Wouldn't want to terrify the students, now would we, Joe?" Everyone except Mrs. B. laughed at the pastor's quip. "Let me tell you *how* Father Joe got his new look."

Father Melvyn explained about the break-in. "I can't imagine why anyone would search the files and throw papers all over the office. It's a mess, Mrs. B., and I'm sorry to say I didn't do more than pick everything up and pile it on the desks. You have a lot to organize." He cleared his throat. "There is something else I need to talk to you about. Check the appointment book; let's schedule some time." At that, Father Joe and Father Declan excused themselves. With the others gone, the kitchen was quiet.

Mrs. B. pondered the news of the break-in. In some chamber of her mind, the words *files* and *papers* triggered a sense of fear. A tendril of poisonous apprehension wrapped itself around her heart. The image of those malevolent black eyes flashed in her memory. Goosebumps rose on her arms. Someone watched her the night they rescued LaLa. Someone saw her take the papers and the journal, and someone broke in here looking for...what? Could the intruder have been looking for the papers I took? she wondered.

Her legs felt weak. Father Melvyn doesn't know I have them and he doesn't know what's in that journal. "We do need to talk," she said.

"Something wrong, Mrs. B.?" Father Melvyn was staring at her. She looked away from his penetrating brown eyes. "I think we'll have that talk now," he said and started toward the back office, waving at her to follow.

The unrelenting, brash sound of the doorbell ended all thoughts of their planned conversation. The buzzer's tone was like fingernails on a chalkboard and it tore through the rooms. Mrs. B. jumped, Father Melvyn's eyes grew big as saucers, and LaLa darted to the stairs. The person at the door held his or her finger on the button. The noise was magnified by pounding on the door and a voice yelling, "Father Melvyn. Father Melvyn." Each time his name was called at a higher pitch.

Mrs. B. flew to the front door with the pastor two steps behind. She yanked it open to a hysterical Martha Magswelle with Barklay and Smitty panting and straining at their leashes. Martha's rising hysteria increased the dogs' emotional upset. When the door opened, they barked at a fever pitch and rushed in pulling so hard that Martha let go of the leashes. The mutts flew past the priest and the housekeeper barking and yowling.

When Barklay spotted LaLa on the landing he took off after her. LaLa screamed in terror and flew up the stairs, paws barely touching the treads beneath her. Barkley tore after her with all the speed his little legs could muster; his nails scratching on the wooden steps added another level to the cacophony. Mrs. B. grabbed Smitty's leash as he dashed past her, preventing him from joining the melee.

A racket exploded upstairs. A door slammed. Father Declan yelled, "Joe, I've got the dog. Don't open your door."

Martha threw herself past Mrs. B. "Father Melvyn. I need you."

"Calm down, Martha. Why are you walking those

dogs? Didn't Ms. Jenkins send a couple of students to walk them for you?"

"Oh bother that. There's a cop ringing my doorbell. Why?" she shrieked.

"I don't know why, but why are you upset about it?" he asked. Trying to keep track of the dogs, the cat, the curate, and the housekeeper his head swiveled in each direction as far as his neck muscles allowed.

"The police are at Velma's putting up crime scene tape, and an officer is ringing my doorbell. What do they want with me?"

"My goodness, Martha. Calm down. Probably nothing more than routine questions."

Martha shook her head vehemently. "No. They want to talk to me about Velma."

"I'm afraid your imagination is running away with itself. Why on earth would they want to talk to you?"

Mrs. B. closed her eyes. There might be good reason for them to talk to Martha. Without a word, Mrs. B. handed Smitty's leash to Father Melvyn and turned toward the scuffling on the steps. Father Declan was tugging Barklay, who was panting and trying to turn back up to continue his pursuit of LaLa. Mrs. B. looped one finger in Barklay's collar, took his leash, and without a word, handed it to the pastor.

Father Declan used his arm to mop the sweat from his forehead. He and Mrs. B. made eye contact; neither laughed.

"Please, Father Melvyn, please come with me, please," Martha begged.

"Okay Martha. I'll walk you home and see what the police want." On the way out the door, Father Melvyn turned to Mrs. B. "See if Father Joe and you-know-who are okay up there."

Mrs. B. closed the door and leaned on it as if afraid they might try to come back in. She gazed at Father Declan. He looked dumbfounded.

"What just happened?" he asked.

"This isn't a rectory, it's an insane asylum," she answered. She started toward the kitchen and stopped, feeling something seriously bad was about to happen. Turning back to Father Declan she made her own contribution to the crazy drama shattering the normally controlled activities of the rectory. "Father Declan, can you cover the phones for a half hour? I forgot something at home and it's important."

"No problem," the young priest answered.

She looked hard at his face. He was pale and looked worried. Was it because of the fracas they were just involved in or was it something else? What in the world is troubling him, she wondered, then shook it off. There's no time now. I left the journal and the will on the kitchen table. I need to talk to Father Melvyn about this. She flew out the kitchen door, allowing it to slam shut.

19

Stop When You Get to the Knuckle

Father Melvyn walked out of the rectory with Martha and her dogs, leaving behind the cat, two priests, and his housekeeper. This is the stuff movies are made of, probably a slapstick comedy, he thought. Why am I doing this, Lord? Wouldn't my time be better spent in prayer, contemplation, and improving my preaching skills?

As a priest, Father Melvyn was dedicated to the concept that thought-provoking homilies were as important to his parishioners' souls as the mass itself. He was scrupulous about finding new and fresh points of view. The seasons repeated themselves, his homilies did not. He kept past sermons for reference but didn't dust them off and reuse them, and he didn't use homiletic subscription services, although there were times when he was tempted.

I'll get back to normal soon, he promised himself, as his thoughts returned to the abnormal events of the morning. Mrs. B. was strangely silent. Wonder what that's about?

Instead of cutting across the parking lot, Father Melvyn, Martha, and her dogs walked down Ferne Lane. Before turning onto the sidewalk in front of the church on Cobble Drive, they saw a police car pull away from the front of Velma's house. Her home was now cordoned off with crime scene tape. Neither said anything. Martha kept biting her thumbnail.

"Stop before you get to the knuckle," Father Melvyn said. She looked confused. "You're biting your nail so far down that you'll reach the knuckle...never mind. Just stop it before you make yourself bleed."

As Martha and Father Melvyn approached her house a police officer came down the walk. It was Officer Smith who had answered the call on Saturday night. "Good morning, Father Kronkey. How is Father Russo feeling today?"

"As well as can be expected," Father Melvyn answered. "Why are you at Ms. Magswelle's door? Everything okay?"

"Routine questions." Officer Smith looked at Martha. "Are you Mrs. Magswelle?"

"It's Ms. and yes, I'm Martha Magswelle. What do you want?"

Father Melvyn didn't say anything. Officer Smith lowered his eyes and flipped the pages of his notepad to a blank sheet; his face remained impassive.

Father Melvin wished Martha would learn some social skills. She is unpleasant and sets people on edge for no reason, he thought.

"Routine, ma'am," Officer Smith said. "Are you aware that the rectory was broken into Friday night?"

It was Martha's turn to be surprised. "No." She looked at Father Melvyn as if to ask why didn't you tell me?

Father Melvyn mouthed, "See!"

"Did you notice anything, any unusual noises outside? Did the dogs seem agitated? Did they growl or bark at anything?"

"No, nothing unusual. I can't help you. Now if you will excuse me." She snatched the leashes from Father Melvyn's hand and turned toward her front door, dragging Barklay and Smitty. She went in and slammed the door shut. Neither man said anything. They shared a knowing look.

Father Melvyn changed the subject. "There's crime scene tape around Velma Maxwell's house. Why?"

"I'm not sure but whenever crime scene tape is used, there is suspicion." Officer Smith closed his notepad, put it in his pocket, and waved. "Have a nice day, Father."

Father Melvyn stood at the curb with his arms folded. After Officer Smith pulled away, he turned, walked up to Martha's door, and pressed the doorbell hard. He would not be denied.

"What is it?" she asked through the door.

"Martha, open this door or I will shout through it, and I don't care who hears me." She pulled it open and without waiting to be invited in, Father Melvyn strode through the doorway. He had a clear sight line to the hothouse behind her kitchen, but the blossoms and greenery didn't register.

"What is it?"

"Why are you so nervous about the police being here? Is there something you need to tell me? Anything you say will be kept confidential."

"What makes you think I'm nervous about anything?" she asked, flitting around the room, jamming her hands into the pockets of her housedress.

Hardly able to believe the question, Father Melvyn's answer was almost a shout. "You come to the rectory in a panic, pound on the door, create havoc, and beg me to help you. You were rude to Officer Smith for no reason, and you're biting your thumbnail down to the nub." He grabbed her hands and turned them up. "Looks like you're biting all your nails down to the nub. What is troubling you?"

"Why was that cop here?"

"He told you. We had a break-in Friday night. It's routine to question neighbors."

"You saw the police putting crime scene tape around Velma's house," she said.

"What has that to do with you?"

Martha looked as if she'd cry. "Everyone in church heard me threaten to kill Velma last week. What if they think I had something to do with her death?"

Father Melvyn drew in a deep breath, held it, and counted to five. "Martha, everyone knows you two have been fighting all your lives. For the life of me, I can't figure out why. Although it wasn't the wisest thing to say, you said it in a moment of anger and frustration. No one believes you had anything to do with Velma's death. You need to calm down."

Once again the uncomfortable question of how he cared for his parishioners surfaced. Feeling guilty for his impatience, he softened his tone. "Martha, if there is anything you want to talk about, please come see me. I promise you the confidentiality of the confessional."

Martha nodded and opened the door for him to leave. Without another word, Father Melvyn walked out and turned back to his church, feeling as if he'd failed to help or comfort Martha Magswelle. What am I doing here? he asked himself again.

20
The Watcher

Huddled between the shed and the shrubs in the chilly morning air, the watcher waited, shifting from one hip to the other, trying not to think about the uncomfortable situation. There was no one within earshot to hear the muttering: "I hope she comes in early. I'm tired of sitting here and my butt is cold."

Using a penlight, the watcher reviewed the written comments in the notebook: the priest I wacked in the face didn't fit the description of the pastor. The watcher knew the woman who rescued the cat was the rectory housekeeper, Samuela Buonafigliuola. Who would curse their child with a name like that? Lucky break though because there's only one listed in the phone book. No wonder everyone calls her Mrs. B. The pastor, Father Melvyn was next on the list. Then there were blank spaces for others to be filled in. The watcher was detail oriented and preferred knowing everyone's identity, even if they were not involved.

The sky lightened. The surrounding grounds became more distinct. Trees and shrubs took shape in the watery light. Not willing to risk being seen, the watcher pushed farther back behind the shed and stretched.

Tires rolled over the concrete surface of the parking field. Peeking out from behind the shed, the watcher recognized the woman with white curly hair and large, round, blue-framed glasses. "It's her."

The woman got out of the white Ford, locked it, and walked in the back door of the rectory. Looking around before stepping out from behind the shed, the watcher noted the woman's car model and license plate then pulled up the hoodie.

Moving quietly, the watcher moved toward the building hoping to get a look in the windows when a disturbance burst from the front of the rectory. A woman's voice yelled, "Father Melvyn." Dogs barked furiously and other voices joined in the melee. The watcher ducked behind a shrub and waited. A few minutes later, things quieted then the pastor and a woman with two dogs circled around from Ferne Lane and onto Cobble Drive, heading toward Carpenter Street. The watcher moved to the end of the shrub-line and looked down the street.

A black-and-white was parked in front of the house they were approaching. Who is the woman with the pastor? the watcher wondered then decided: I'd better get out of here, and cut across Carpenter at a different point and jogged away from the church. Now I know the housekeeper's car and plate number. That will make it easier to spot her.

Using the laptop on the passenger seat, the watcher reviewed Mrs. B.'s address and punched it into the GPS. It shouldn't take more than fifteen minutes to get to the nosey housekeeper's street.

***

The GPS guide announced, "Your destination is on the right." The watcher canceled the guidance system and looked around. The street was a beehive of activity. Cars pulled out of garages, some with children in them, and others without. A school bus halted traffic with its STOP sign out and flashing. "Can't risk being seen. I'll get a cup of coffee and come back in an hour."

When the watcher returned the street was quiet. Looks good. I can go in. No sooner had the thought been complete than the white Ford from the church carport pulled into the driveway. The woman with white curly hair jumped out, leaving the car running and the driver's door ajar. She ran into the house and a minute later she ran back out with a file in her hands, returned to her car and drove off.

"What the hell was that about?" Taking no chances, the watcher drove around the corner, parked, and walked back to Mrs. B.'s house. Pulling on gloves and using the credit card skill that opened both Velma's and the rectory's doors, the watcher slipped into Mrs. B.'s house.

Two cats, one a delicate pearly blue-gray and another, red striped and hefty, sat upright at the sound of the door opening. The watcher was greeted by a growl and a hiss before the cats disappeared. "That's right cats make yourselves scarce if you know what's good for you."

A sense of urgency fueled the search. It was fast, but thorough. Papers were tossed first from the kitchen table and then from the desk. Charles Maxwell's will was nowhere to be found. "Damn and damn again. This woman is a real pain in the ass."

Not bothering to lock the front door, the watcher left. I'll drive back to the church and see if she's there. Fifteen minutes later, the white Ford was easily visible in the carport, the black-and-white was gone from the street, and Velma's house was cordoned with crime scene tape.

"Damn. The police know it wasn't a heart attack, and we still don't have Maxwell's will. This woman screwed everything up."

21
Dead Velma

With the will and Velma's journal stuffed in her purse, Mrs. B. got back to the rectory in record time. As she approached the driveway, she noticed activity around Velma's house. She checked her rearview mirror. No traffic behind her on Ferne Lane; she slowed her car and watched.

Jake Zayas pulled into Velma's driveway in an unmarked car. Instead of turning into the church parking lot, Mrs. B. pulled up to the curb in front of Velma's house. "Good morning, Jake. What's happening here?"

He walked over and pecked her cheek. "Good morning, Sammi. Glad I've run into you. Were your ears ringing?" he asked and chuckled. "Terri and I were talking about you last night. She's going to call you. We haven't seen you in forever. Let's get together for dinner, sooner rather than later."

"Great. I'll talk to her tonight."

In answer to her question, Jake looked around then

whispered, "It's not public knowledge yet so mum's the word, Sammi. The coroner said Velma was poisoned."

Mrs. B.'s heart skipped a beat. "You got the toxicology back fast, didn't you?"

"Yes. The M.E. had suspicions at the crime scene. He put a rush on it. We've contacted her nephew. He can't get here until tomorrow." Jake looked pensive. "Sammi, we've questioned several people in the parish. They tell me the victim had a real beef with another woman in the neighborhood, by the name of Martha. Do you know her?"

Mrs. B.'s heart clippity-clopped. "Yes. Martha Magswelle. She lives in the first house at the corner of Carpenter and Cobble, just on the other side of Saint Francis's parking lot." Mrs. B. pointed to Martha's house but didn't say anything about the ongoing feud between the two women.

"Are you aware that Martha has a greenhouse?"

Mrs. B. was puzzled. Why was he asking that? Instinct told her to be careful. "Yes. Everyone knows Martha has a greenhouse. She grows some beautiful flowers and plants. Is that important?" Jake didn't answer. Before she could ask another question, his partner came out of Velma's house.

Marv Clingman nodded to Mrs. B. "Can I see you for a moment?" he said to Jake.

Turning to Mrs. B., Jake winked and said, "Terri will call tonight. Have a good day."

She nodded and fiddled with her purse, hoping to hear what Jake's partner was telling him. The only words she picked up were "...the same... mess...and no photos..." She had a good idea of what he was telling Jake.

He raised an interesting point about the pictures, she thought. It hadn't occurred to me, but after reading his will and Velma's journal, it's not a surprise. Mrs. B. waved once more and returned to the carport. She needed to talk to Father Melvyn right away.

Inside, Father Declan was at the kitchen table, nursing a cup of coffee. "I'm back. Everything okay?" she asked.

"Yes. Only one call," he said, handing her a Post-it. "I told the woman you'd call her back with the information she wants. If there's nothing more, I need to get going."

"Thank you, Father Declan," she said to his back as he rushed out of the kitchen. Goodness, he's acting funny, she thought. He looks like he's running away. Is there a ghost chasing him? Oh, he's a priest. He doesn't believe in ghosts.

Her thoughts returned to Velma. Fear rose in her chest. Velma's death was now ruled a murder and what she'd learned from Velma's journal not only gave Martha a motive but also threw into the mix a potentially devastating scandal for Saint Francis. This worry drove all thoughts about the young priest's obvious distress out of her mind. She walked through the kitchen.

Father Melvyn was in the backoffice. The door was open. She rapped with her knuckles. "Do you have time to talk to me?"

"Yes, Mrs. B. I think we have things to discuss."

"More than you know." Without waiting to hear his concerns, she took a deep breath and launched into a confession of what she'd done the night they'd searched for LaLa. Looking down at her feet, not wanting to lose her nerve or be distracted, she rushed the words out. When she finished, there was only silence. The power of his stare forced her to look up. Her stomach dropped. She wished there was a rock she could hide under.

"Whatever possessed you?" His icy tone hit her in the face like a bucket of cold water.

Trying to be brave and reasonable, she said, "If you decide to fire me, I'll understand, but please, read the journal and the will."

"I will do no such thing. I will not pry as you have done. This is none of my business, nor is it yours. I am terribly disappointed. Mrs. B. I thought better of you. Now, you will call your detective friend, tell him that we were in the house the night Velma died and give him those papers."

Humiliated, she felt heat rush into her cheeks and tears spring to her eyes. He'd reprimanded her like a child; she fought back the emotions. With great deliberation, she took the papers and the journal from the handbag still draped over her shoulder and placed them on the desk in front of Father Melvyn.

"The information in the journal will seriously affect Saint Francis de Sales. You need to know about it before I give the journal to the police." Choking on shame, she barely got the words out. Without waiting for any further dressing down from her boss, Mrs. B. walked out of the office, relieved that she hadn't broken down and cried.

I'm glad I didn't tell him that the ME ruled Velma's death a homicide by poison. After all, Jake told me *mum's the word*. See, she rationalized, I can keep secrets. Before another thought entered her head, the phone rang, and for the rest of the day, non-stop calls kept her too busy with parish business to think much about Father Melvyn.

***

Father Declan returned from his errands a short time later and was immediately sent to the hospital to visit another parishioner.

Father Joe came down for coffee. "Do you have any aspirin Mrs. B.? I'm getting a terrible headache." Pills in hand, Father Joe told her he was going to take a nap.

Mrs. B. cleaned the kitchen and was at the sink washing dishes when she saw Father Melvyn pull out of the carport. He had an appointment at the bishop's office. Obviously, he'd left through the front door rather than walking through the kitchen on his way to the carport. "I don't want to see you either," she said in the direction of his car leaving the grounds. It was a relief that he wouldn't return for hours. I'll be gone before he gets back, she thought.

The rectory took on an unusual air of quiet by midafternoon. A gentle mewing from the hall called to her. LaLa sat in the doorway, ears perked up and held tilted as if to ask, "What's going on?"

"Here you are, LaLa. Looks like you're a femme fatale who conquered these good men with your natural feline charms," she said, looking into the cat's beautiful green eyes. "Come."

Contrary to her own directives to the priests to keep the cat's dishes on the floor, she placed a small bowl on the counter. LaLa jumped up, delicately lapped the milk, and then sat on the counter rubbing her head against Mrs. B.'s arm and watched her clean and peel vegetables.

"Let's go into the office and straighten out that mess. Maybe I should stay later and get it done in case your new owner decides to fire me tomorrow." LaLa looked at her as if she understood and followed. As soon as Mrs. B. opened the door to the front office, the cat's demeanor changed.

LaLa sniffed the air. Ears back, she lowered herself to a creeping position, belly almost on the floor. Mrs. B. watched the cat's behavior. "You've picked up on something you don't like. Hmmm, if only I spoke cat."

The cat crept around sniffing, her mouth slightly ajar and her tail puffed up. When she finished her tour of the office, she looked over her shoulder at Mrs. B., arched her back, hissed, then turned and slinked out leaving the housekeeper alone with the mess and her unsettled thoughts.

After LaLa's dramatic departure, Mrs. B.'s efficiency kicked into high gear. She proceeded to gather and sort the papers and files that had been thrown around like so much trash and were now piled on the desk. It was tedious, rote work, which left her mind free to unravel and agonize over her mistakes. Unbeknownst to her, across the street, Martha Magswelle was in her greenhouse, watering and caring for her plants; she too agonized over dead Velma.

***

No one will believe me if I tell them how their wonderful, generous Velma pelted me with insults and threats, she thought. She was a cruel witch and deserved to die. When she approached the final row of plants kept separate from the rest, Martha pushed Velma from her thoughts to focus on caring for some of her most exquisite flowers.

The leaves, stems and blooms of these had deadly powers, but they were exotic and beautiful. Oleander, foxglove, hibiscus, and nightshade had the most exquisite flowers. Martha smiled and spoke aloud to her plants. "You are a tricky bunch and I love the challenge of the diligent care you all need. You're worth it."

Martha believed that vegetation was responsive to stimuli, including the human voice, and although she knew better than to remove her protective gloves, she did make it a point to stroke and handle them. These were her one luxury.

Caring for these deadly blooms required separate equipment, especially disposable gloves. Martha wouldn't risk having non-disposable gloves. She was careful at all times. She always watered, trimmed, and fed her distinctive beauties last. Satisfied, she wrapped the trimmings in a paper bag, cleaned and stored her clippers and scissors, pulled off her work gloves, and threw them in the bag with the trimmings. Standing back, she reveled in the loveliness of their foliage.

Glancing over her shoulder, Martha saw Barklay and Smitty waiting for her at the door to the greenhouse. They were never allowed in. That was one of the reasons she'd never considered having a cat; cats are not as manageable or as obedient as dogs.

Martha thought about LaLa. I could have gotten rid of Velma's precious cat and sometimes I really did want to kill her. She could be so annoying, but it's Velma who deserved to die, and now she is dead. Good riddance.

Exiting the greenhouse, Martha didn't touch Barklay or Smitty. She returned to the kitchen and washed her hands once more for good measure then sat at the table and covered her eyes.

The thought of her last public fight with Velma at the church replayed in her head. In spite of Father Melvyn's assurances, she worried. "I should have kept my mouth shut," she whispered to Barklay and Smitty. "People heard me threaten her." The memory made Martha's stomach queasy.

22
Things Will Look Better Tomorrow

Sasha and Ziggy greeted her at the kitchen door with high pitched meows a decibel below screams. They circled her legs, pushing hard against her. With their tails puffed, backs arched, and ears flat against their heads, they were telling her there was trouble. "Goodness. What's the probl…"

Her heart dropped when she saw the mess in her kitchen. Drawers had been pulled out. Anything soft and moveable had been thrown on the floor. Thinking she couldn't feel worse after her earlier dressing down by Father Melvyn, she was shocked. "What in heaven's name happened?" she asked aloud, watching her pets trying to tell her.

Dumping her bags on the table she first scanned her home as far as her vision reached without moving. As if in a trance, placing one foot in front of the other, she walked through the rooms looking at the upheaval. Someone had invaded and violated her home, her sanctuary.

Her bedroom closet was pulled apart. Clothes were pulled off hangers; the dresser drawers were open with clothing hanging out; the money envelope with $2,450 in cash was on the floor. She picked it up and counted. All there. She looked at her jewelry box. Nothing was touched; nothing was taken. She checked her laptop. It was on the side table where she'd left it that morning.

Sasha and Ziggy walked by her side, crying and gulping, speaking their language, telling her what happened. "I know you are upset. I wish I was fluent in feline," she said to her two most trusted four-legged friends. Their cries were doleful. Still numb, she picked them up to soothe and reassure them. When they were calm, she gave them fresh food and water then picked up the phone to call the police.

She started to dial then stopped. If this was a common break-in, would the thief leave money and electronics? "No," she said aloud, answering her own question. She went back to her office and took a fresh look. The desk and file cabinet suffered the brunt of someone's search. They had been torn apart, literally. "This has something to do with Velma's murder. I know it does!"

The mounting anger began at her toes and worked its way up through her body. Her skin tingled with it, but it wasn't until she checked the front door that suspicion, fear, and anger merged. Wet beads formed at her hairline, she shivered, and her skin puckered; she was furious and afraid. The firm twist she gave the inside deadbolt snapped her fear; the rage remained. "I don't know who you are, but I know what you want," she said between clenched teeth. "The question is what am I going to do about it?"

Her nerves were strung tighter than piano wire. If I had the bastard who did this in front of me, I know I could kill. God forgive me. Feeling the need to do something violent, she settled for the physically taxing, went to the laundry room, pulled out the mop, bucket, and vacuum, prepared to do the kind of heavy cleaning that works up a gym-worthy sweat.

She pushed and pulled furniture, dusted, vacuumed, and scrubbed trying to remove any remnant of the intruder's presence, after which she restored her closet, placing blouses, skirts, dresses, and pants on hangers then rearranged the shoes that had been thrown around. What was this person looking for in my shoes? she wondered.

Housework gave her logical mind a chance to marinate in emotions, to let things bounce around, go postal, or go sentimental, allowing her to acknowledge whatever came to mind, reasonable or unreasonable. Fury was her primary emotion followed by betrayal, but by whom?

Feeling alone and vulnerable, she allowed feelings that were normally pushed aside to surface. Tears blurred her eyes. Yanking the area rug forward to reach every corner, she abruptly stopped her work, walked into the bedroom to be sure the container with her husband's ashes hadn't been disturbed and shook her fist at God while she hugged the hard vessel to her chest. "Why did you take him from me?" She sobbed for a moment and then placed the container back in its place. She went back to her housecleaning workout.

In the little space between anger at God and missing John, her grandchildren's faces appeared. As always, the very thought of them made her smile. "Lord, thank you for them. They are blessings. Please, send one to John Jr. and Lisa soon." While she prayed and labored with the ferocity of a prizefighter, the phone rang twice. She let the answering machine pick up. She didn't want to talk to anybody.

Thoughts of dead Velma, and what might be trouble for Martha if Jake's questions were any indication, pushed their way to the forefront. The more she thought about it, the more certain she became: this break-in was connected to the one at the rectory.

By the time she worked off all the adrenaline from her rampant emotions, the entire house was sparkling clean and neat once more. Her desk was once again a normal organized chaos, and the files were back in the cabinet. Once all the cleaning/exercise instruments were put away, she headed for the shower.

Exhaustion and hot water relaxed her. That's when her mixed feelings about Father Melvyn surfaced. Still upset by his harsh criticism, she scolded herself. "He hurt your pride is all. Get over it," she mumbled. "But he doesn't deserve the consideration I'm giving him," she said to Sasha and Ziggy, who were sitting on the bathroom counter supervising.

Refreshed, but tired, her mind was clearer. She looked at the clock. Not too late; she thought and returned the calls on her answering machine. The first was Nancy Jenkins.

They talked about the upcoming opera season. They shared their excitement about the next season's programming and decided to take a subscription together. She didn't want to mar the upbeat tone of the conversation by mentioning the break-in.

The second call was to Terri Zayas. They chatted about their children and grandchildren. Terri and Jake had twin granddaughters. They were adorable, and Mrs. B. always enjoyed hearing about their most recent antics. She told

Terri that she wished her daughter, Corinne lived closer and that John and Lisa would have a baby.

Throughout the conversation, Mrs. B. struggled with whether or not to tell Terri about the break-in. She decided not to, knowing that once Jake found out, she'd be forced to tell him everything and she wasn't ready. Before saying goodnight, they set a date for dinner.

At midnight, still wide awake, she felt like a caged tiger. Sasha and Ziggy sat on the kitchen table watching her. Their heads turned from side to side following her path as she pace and wrestled with her decision to give Father Melvyn time to consider the scandal that might shatter Saint Francis. Whether or not Father Melvyn read the papers, tomorrow I will call Jake and tell him, she decided. Jake will be angry with me too.

Father Melvyn was right. I shouldn't have taken those papers, and I'm not sure why I did. Maybe I'm bored, she thought. Maybe this is a sign that it's time to move on. Confused emotions flooded her. She liked to know what made others tick, and most of all, she analyzed her own feelings and actions.

A punch of nerves mixed with anticipation at the thought of what else she might do if she left Saint Francis was tempered by a twinge of sadness at the prospect; it surprised her. "Get over it. Maybe it's time for new horizons." She plopped down on her side of the bed. "Okay kids, let's get some sleep. I'm exhausted. Things will look better tomorrow."

***

"The police must have the toxicology report or Velma's house wouldn't be cordoned off with crime scene tape," he said. They argued about which substances should have been used. There was a lot at stake, and they were both distressed that the report came back so fast.

"All that matters is that they know she didn't die of natural causes and you don't have the money yet," she said, trying to soothe him. "It belongs to you. You deserve to have it. We can't screw this up."

"You don't have to remind me." He marched into the bathroom and slammed the door. When he came out, she sat beside him and rubbed his back, soothing him as one does a child.

"Soon you will have everything," she whispered. "You know Charles's will is still out there. It was never probated, or you would have been notified. We just need to find it. That will make all the difference. You'll see, things will look better tomorrow."

23
Because She *is* the Problem

It was close to eleven Monday night when Father Melvyn returned to Saint Francis. He pulled into the carport, killed the headlights and turned off the engine. Father Joe's and Father Declan's cars were parked there; he looked at them without really seeing them. The light over the kitchen door lit the walk from the carport to the rectory, and the only lights on inside were upstairs.

He'd been at the Conference of Pastors most of the day to discuss administrative concerns, including the business of running parishes in today's world, especially with the continuing fall off of priestly vocations. The pastors, under the guidance of the bishop, shared ideas about personnel, training for volunteers who work with children, budgets, and school security in the face of their vulnerability to criminal or terrorist attacks. He didn't mention Ms. Jenkins's plan to have a security seminar at Saint Francis for their faculty. He thought it best to wait until after it was done, when he'd have something concrete to report.

After the conference, the discussions continued with several friends, including Sebastian, while they enjoyed pre-dinner drinks at the annual dinner for the Dialogue Institute.

"Dialogue Institute. What a great organization. I wish I had time to be more involved with them," he murmured. We need more like it, he thought. The importance of bringing leaders of different faiths together in respect and understanding in these volatile times could not be overstated. He believed that religious extremism was driving hardline separations between faiths, and it served no one, except the extremists.

In spite of his enthusiasm for the Conference of Pastors and the Dialogue Institute's work, throughout the day thoughts about the Velma-Martha drama intruded.

Velma's death, even though an unhappy event, was a normal part of life. Rescuing LaLa, although not what he wanted to do, turned out to be a positive. His real discomfort was Mrs. B. He felt off balance, resentful. She's not who I thought she was, he reflected. Her administrative skills, added to her housekeeping and cooking have been a treasure. She's efficient and effective, smart and sassy, but discreet. No one, not even Declan and Joe, know how quick-witted she is...or do they?

He thought about how easily she went around him, speaking directly to Joe about taking care of LaLa. There's so much about her that I don't know: her friendship with the detective, her relationships with other parishioners. She's a registered member of my parish, but I've never gotten the impression that she attends mass regularly.

Father Melvyn sat in his car deep in thought. He worried that she had a tendency to gossip. She says she doesn't share confidences not even with me. Is that what's bothering me? "But she took papers and a journal that were none of her business. I can't overlook that," he said aloud. His eyes focused on the darkened rectory. He didn't know what to do about Mrs. B. "I'd better go to bed. I'll sleep on it," he muttered, unhappy that he couldn't talk it out with the one person whose insights he'd come to rely on because *she* was the problem.

Inside, he walked to the staff office and turned on the light. The journal and papers were where Mrs. B. left them that afternoon. He bundled everything together. No sense having Declan or Joe finding this stuff, he thought.

The voice in his head whispered, "You'd better read it. You've always trusted her and she said there was something that could damage Saint Francis." Irritated, he climbed the stairs and dumped everything on the bureau in his room then turned to the final prayers of the day.

Tuesday

The First Full Week of Lent

24
Not the Same

As soon as he opened his eyes the same anxiety he felt when he'd laid his head on the pillow the night before filled him. As required, Father Melvyn was disciplined about saying the Liturgy of the Hours, especially the major ones: morning and evening. He pushed everything out of his mind, determined to say the morning prayers without distraction.

Liturgy completed, he closed his well-worn prayer book; his fingers stroked the leather cover of the pre-Vatican II breviary, softened by age and wear. The memory of her was bittersweet; he missed his late mother.

The loud buzz of the doorbell startled him. The bedside clock said 8:15 a.m. What's this morning's emergency? he wondered, aware that Mrs. B. wasn't in yet.

Filled with an immense sadness because he was leaning toward firing her, he bounded down the stairs, his mind still wrapped up in the pros and cons of keeping her on and whether he would let her go immediately or give her notice. Would he give her a reference if she asked? I'll talk to her about all of it this morning, he thought. Maybe we can clear the air and firing her won't be necessary.

His thoughts were fully engaged with his housekeeper dilemma when he pulled open the door to see a man he didn't like standing there.

"May I come in, Father? Sorry to bother you this early." Jeffrey Scooterman reached out to shake Father Melvyn's hand. "I arrived in Austin early and went straight to the police station. The autopsy and the toxicology are finished and I need to tie up loose ends."

His aunt is a loose end? Father Melvyn thought, but remained silent.

"My aunt's body will be released this afternoon. I'd like to make funeral arrangements."

"Oh, ah, Dr. Scooterman. Yes, of course, please come in. I'm sorry for your loss."

"Call me Jeffrey." Father Melvyn's feelings of aversion surfaced. Something slick about him, the priest thought, leading Jeffrey Scooterman into the office. He noticed that it had been reorganized and cleaned; his sense of sadness increased.

"So was it a heart attack?" Father Melvyn asked as he walked around the desk to retrieve the calendar book.

"No, Father. They found evidence of poison, but they have no further use for her body."

Father Melvyn dropped into his desk chair. "Poison," he echoed. "I am so sorry," was all he could muster.

"The police are treating it as a homicide now. I think they have a suspect, but they didn't give me a name. They just said they're questioning parishioners, one in particular. Seems my aunt had a running feud with another parishioner who threatened to kill her and her cat."

Father Melvyn didn't react outwardly. Inwardly, his emotions clamored: his heart thumped and he felt his stomach knot into a pretzel. His breaths came in short heaves; foreboding crawled over his bones.

Glancing at Jeffrey Scooterman, he wondered, Why does he look so smug? "Here it is," Father Melvyn said, pulling the calendar out of the drawer. "When would you like the funeral mass, and where will you bury her?"

"If you can have her mass tomorrow or Thursday morning, that would be great. Then I will contact the crematorium. Far less expensive."

Father Melvyn's dislike increased; he held it in check. "Tomorrow, Wednesday, at ten a.m. okay?"

"Yes, and thank you, Father. Will you say the mass?"

He wanted to refuse but remembered how generous Velma had been to Saint Francis. "Yes, of course. Will you have a wake for her tonight?"

"At Greenwoods, from seven to ten. There's one other thing. My aunt's cat. Does anyone know where she is?"

"Yes. We have LaLa here. Do you want to take her?"

At the mention of her name, the cat made a grand entrance. She walked into the office on silent paws, head erect, tail straight up, and big green eyes wide open. She looked at Jeffrey, hissed, turned, and left.

Father Melvyn watched and bit the inside of his lip to keep from smiling. Ha! LaLa was not a Jeffrey Scooterman fan.

Frowning, Scooterman said, "No. I don't want her. Just wondered, that's all. Are you keeping her?"

"Yes, we are, if you have no objections."

"None."

The priest was relieved, happy that Velma's nephew made no pretense about wanting the cat. Odd, he thought. Scooterman didn't even ask how we got her. The two men shook hands at the front door.

"In case you need me, here's the number to the motel where I'm staying. Here's my card and my aunt's attorney's card. Don't know why you'd need the latter...just in case you can't get me."

"You're not staying at Velma's house?"

"No. The police aren't done searching yet." Father Melvyn heard the annoyance in his voice. "I don't know what they expect to find and I need to get in. You know, papers, bills, stuff that's going to need attention."

"I understand," Father Melvyn opened the front door and said a quick goodbye to Velma's nephew. Guess you can't wait to get your hands on her money, he thought, walking back into the office and pulling out the can that Mrs. B. kept in the bottom desk drawer. He wasn't sure why he felt the need to use air freshener. Scooterman didn't have an odor; Father Melvyn felt rather than smelled something foul; he sprayed anyway.

LaLa walked back into the office, wriggled her nose slightly, and stared at him as if to say, you did good. The back door slammed.

That'll be Mrs. B., he thought, walking to the kitchen. One look at her pale face with dark smudges under her eyes made him blurt, "Are you ill?" Her age is showing, he thought uncharitably.

"Bad night. I think we need to talk."

"We do. Jeffrey Scooterman just left. He made arrangements for Velma's funeral. It will be tomorrow at ten a.m. He said she was poisoned." Mrs. B. didn't answer. She didn't even raise an eyebrow.

She knew that! What else does she know? he wondered. "Let's go into the staff office and sort this out." It wasn't a request. He turned and walked out of the kitchen. Mrs. B. put up a pot of coffee and followed him.

"Father Melvyn. You were right yesterday. I shouldn't have taken those papers, and I apologize for my less-than-appropriate behavior. Nosiness leads to all sorts of trouble, and this Velma situation is getting worse." She paused.

She's waiting for me to say something, he realized. Lips pursed, leaning back in the desk chair, he gave a royal wave of his hand indicating she should continue.

"When I got home last night, my house was a mess. It was broken into. It had the same MO as the break-in here. No money or valuables were taken, but papers and files were thrown all over, as if the intruder was searching for something specific. I think the person is looking for the will and maybe even the journal."

Shocked by her words, he banged the chair into its upright position. "What? Sammi..." He corrected himself. "Mrs. B., I'm sorry. Did you call the police?"

"No. I should have. I've broken every rule, but I decided to speak with you first and then call Jake Zayas. We need to give him the papers whether or not you've read them. I think we should...I should...give him everything, even the journal. They might be pertinent to his investigation. And I think, under the circumstances, it's time for me to—" The rest of her sentence was cut off by the doorbell. "Be right back," she said and almost ran to the front door. He was gripped with a sense of relief that whatever she was about to say remained unfinished.

***

"Father Melvyn, please come out here." Something in her voice propelled him out of his chair. He emerged from the back office to see his housekeeper standing in the hall with a younger man of medium height, looking down at his feet.

His first impression was that the caller was average in every way, until the young man looked up. His eyes were arresting: coal black, rimmed by thick black lashes. Where had he seen those eyes before? They looked familiar, yet not.

"How can I help you, young man?" he asked, stepping in front of Mrs. B.

"My name is Chancey Johnson and my mother told me to come here and ask you for help."

"Who is your mother?" Father Melvyn asked.

"Martha Magswelle."

Suffering a second shock within a few minutes, Father Melvyn stood with his mouth hanging open.

Mrs. B. stepped up. "Come into the office, please," she said, gently guiding the young man to a seat. Father Melvyn pulled himself together and followed. He was blunt when he turned to face the newcomer. "I wasn't aware that Martha had a child."

"I know. My mother said you would be surprised...actually, she said you'd be shocked." Without waiting for a response, Chancey Johnson continued. "The police picked her up for questioning last night.

They kept her late. When they let her go home she called me and asked me to come to Austin. I drove here from Killeen this morning. The police came back an hour ago with a warrant to search the property then they took her back to the police station. They are questioning her about a murder. They said something about poisons. I don't know what they're talking about. She needs a lawyer. I...we...don't have much money, and I don't know any lawyers in Austin. She said you'd know what to do." The young man sniffled, as if about to cry.

Releasing his pursed lips, Father Melvyn said, "Get some tissues for him, Mrs. B." When she left the office, Father Melvyn closed the door. "Tell me what's going on."

An hour later, Father Melvyn came out of the office with Chancey. "Try not to worry. I'll make a few calls and get her a lawyer."

"Does she have to stay in jail?"

"I wish I had an answer for you. If they're charging her we may have to post bail. Let me get some legal guidance, and I'll get back to you. Where are you staying?"

"Thank you, Father. The police searched everything in the house. Made a mess too. They said I can stay there, but I can't go into the greenhouse."

***

After Chancey left, Father Melvyn went back to the kitchen. "This is shocking. Martha suspected of killing Velma? She's difficult, but I refuse to believe it. Get Tom Barbee's number for me. I'll see if he'll take Martha's case." He stopped. Mrs. B. didn't meet his eyes.

"Right away, Father," she said.

Something in her face prompted him to ask: "You knew about him?"

"Yes. It's all in the journal."

"Then why did you sound so distressed when he arrived?"

Mrs. B. looked up. Father Melvyn saw a flash of annoyance before she averted her gaze. "The eyes."

Father Melvyn scratched his head. He looked confused. "What about the eyes? I mean, they looked familiar, but I couldn't place...Oh. Those were the same eyes staring at you the night we rescued LaLa." He paused again. "Father Joe described coal-black eyes the night he was attacked."

"No. Not the same. What Father Joe and I saw felt evil, angry, dangerous. Chancey's eyes are soft, gentle."

Maybe he's a good actor. Father Melvyn pushed aside the cynical thought that popped into his mind. He paced, cupped his pursed lips with his thumb and forefinger and contemplated this new and shocking information. Mrs. B. went to the office and returned with Tom Barbee's office number.

"I'm going grocery shopping. Anything in particular you want?" He didn't answer, just waved her away, already heading to the office to call his friend.

25
Ahhh, The Housekeeper

"Hold on, Mrs. B. I'll help you with those bags," Father Declan called to her as she opened the rear door to get the groceries. He pulled his car up next to hers.

"Thank you, Father Declan. Now I don't have to make a second trip." Inside, they dumped everything on the kitchen table. "Be careful with that one," she pointed to the bag he was about to set down. "Eggs." He nodded. Mrs. B. put her hands on her hips and stared hard at the young curate. "Is something bothering you? Are you not feeling well?"

"Mrs. B., I heard that Martha is under suspicion for having something to do with Velma's death. Is that true?"

"Yes. I'm afraid it is."

"The night Velma died I thought I saw Martha and a stranger, a man I'd never seen before, across the street in front of Velma's house. They had two small dogs. Could've been Barklay and Smitty. I didn't think anything of it. I was more concerned with cutting across the school driveway and not getting caught by the boss. Then Velma was found dead between the church and the rectory. I guess I should've told the police."

"Why didn't you?"

"At first because I didn't think it was of any importance, but now..." He hesitated. Mrs. B. looked at him expectantly. "I like Martha. I don't believe she could have done this. She's been very kind to me."

Mrs. B. eyebrows popped up to her hairline, surprised to learn he had some kind of friendship with Martha. "There may be nothing to tell," she said to ease Father Declan's discomfort. "I know Ms. Jenkins arranged for a couple of boys to walk the dogs for her."

"At eleven thirty at night?"

"You have a point." She stopped putting the groceries away. "I didn't know you had any personal contact with her." Father Declan ran his fingers through his red hair. He looked distressed. "Sit. Take a cup of coffee and tell me about it," Mrs. B. said.

"Do you remember when I arrived here I had a lot of trouble with acne?"

"Yes, but your face is clear and smooth now."

He continued. "One day, after mass, there was no one in the narthex, and Martha came up to me. 'I have something natural that will help with that,' she said, pointing to my face. I was so embarrassed; I know I blushed. 'No need to be ashamed. You didn't do anything wrong. Let me help.' She was kind and gentle. That afternoon, I rang her bell. She took me back into a little greenhouse. Have you ever been in it?"

"No. I haven't," Mrs. B. was more than a little surprised at this glimpse of Martha's unexpected softer side and Father Declan's willingness to accept her offer.

"She grows beautiful orchids and flowering plants, herbs, and other things. She picked the leaves off a couple of plants and brought them in the house. She told me they were Aloe-vera and she was mixing them with chickpea flour and turmeric. She made a paste, put it in a little plastic container and told me what to do. She said after a week to use the Aloe leaves alone. Within a month, most of my acne was gone."

"I had no idea," Mrs. B. said, smiling at Father Declan. "And here I thought all the healthy food I was cooking had something to do with it."

Father Declan smiled. "I'm sure it did, but Martha was a great help. I really don't believe she killed Velma, and I don't want to say anything about seeing her. I've been struggling with this. I don't know what to do."

Mrs. B. began to pace. "Let me think, Father Declan. Let me think."

A car door slammed outside, and a minute later, Father Melvyn blew into the kitchen, allowing the door to slam shut. "I'll take a cup of that coffee, Mrs. B., and I'm going to my room. Unless there's an emergency don't disturb me for the rest of the day. Declan, you're on call."

When Father Melvyn's footsteps disappeared, they heard his bedroom door close with a bang. Mrs. B. rolled her eyes.

"Maybe he bangs doors to relieve stress," she said and returned to the subject of Martha. "There's a lot going on with Velma's death. For the moment, don't say anything. I think Father Melvyn is trying to get Martha a lawyer. Let's wait. You can tell the lawyer who represents her. Besides, I don't think she'd have taken her dogs if she was up to something nasty, especially since Barklay and Smitty would raise Cain chasing LaLa."

"That's true. Thank you, Mrs. B. I'm glad I talked to you about it. If you need me, I'll be in the library catching up on my backlog of books."

***

Putting Father Declan's concerns out of her mind, Mrs. B. focused on administrative and domestic responsibilities and the remainder of the day passed without further drama. At five, her work completed, she poked her head in the library, wished Father Declan a good evening, and left, not certain of what to do about Charles's will and Velma's journal. *I guess I'll wait until tomorrow,* she decided.

Before turning the ignition, she searched her purse for her cell phone. She had a love-hate relationship with it. *It's great for emergencies but too distracting to hear it go off while I'm driving.* She found the phone, hidden in the deepest recesses of her large purse. When she lifted it, the screen lit up with a message. It was a text from Father Melvyn: *Reading the Velma papers. I'll finish after I pay respects at Greenwoods tonight. We'll talk tomorrow.*

"Oh hell. I forgot! Tonight is Velma's wake."

***

Mrs. B. arrived at the funeral home at seven fifteen. The parking lot was crowded. She circled twice before getting a spot. When she walked in, Greenwoods was packed with everyone who was anyone in the diocese.

The bishop himself was there. He stood on the far side of the crowded room, talking with Father Melvyn and several friends, some of whom Mrs. B. recognized, including Tom and Grace Barbee. She wondered if Tom agreed to take Martha's case. Bob and Alice Coyle were talking with Father Sebastian from the university. They were deep in conversation. She was happy that none of them looked in her direction because the cloying, sweet smell of flowers in the crowded room overpowered her as soon as she walked in. I'll have a headache if I don't get out of here fast, she thought.

Head down, Mrs. B. made her way to the casket, which was half-open. Velma was laid out in a beautiful cream-colored dress, her hair coiffed as always, with a simple gold band on her ring finger and a rich-looking garnet rosary wound through her fingers, nails polished in the same garnet color. Wonder if that was deliberate? She knelt, said a prayer then stepped over to Jeffrey Scooterman to offer condolences.

"Ahhh, the housekeeper--- Father Melvyn's housekeeper." There was no mistaking the disdain.

She ignored it. "Yes, and I'm truly sorry about your aunt." He nodded, offered a brief, weak fingertip handshake, as if he couldn't bear to touch her and turned away to speak to others.

Happy to escape any further conversation with him, she ignored the snub. Father Melvyn is right. Scooterman is sleazy. She took a cloth sanitizer from her purse and cleaned her hand. How does he know I'm the housekeeper? Did Velma tell him about me? she wondered. I don't remember ever meeting him.

She made her way over to a group of women from the Saint Francis book club that were standing nearby. Careful to keep her back to Father Melvyn and his group, she joined the ladies.

"Did you know the bishop was coming?"

"No, I didn't." Changing the subject she asked, "What book are you all reading this month?" No one in the knot of women answered her. They were caught up in the awe of the church's hierarchy being present.

"Isn't it wonderful that the bishop came? Does he normally do this?" another of the women asked.

Yet another whispered conspiratorially, "You know, Velma gave a generous donation to the diocese for one of the bishop's pet projects. I'm not surprised he showed up."

The first woman cut in. "I heard His Excellency is going to lead the rosary at eight."

Mrs. B. bristled. His Excellency, indeed. She always thought the title pretentious. Are we in the Spanish court of Isabella and Ferdinand? Whatever happened to His Grace? Still, it was bad form to leave once the rosary began. People would notice. She checked her watch. "It's almost eight, and I need to get home," she said, excusing herself from the group.

"You should come back to the book club, Sammi," the first woman said.

"I will. I have the schedule." She moved toward the door speaking to a few other parishioners as she made her way out of the funeral home.

***

Outside in the cool dry air of night, she took a cleansing breath; her stomach settled. Relieved that Father Melvyn and his group hadn't noticed her, she walked to her car in the well-lit parking lot congratulating herself on escaping with minimal discomfort when she was overwhelmed, almost knocked off her feet. She grabbed on to the nearest car to steady herself and looked around for the source. There wasn't a soul in sight.

Heart pounding, the nerve endings in her back tight, she was on the verge of panic. An eerie sense of danger engulfed her. She increased her pace. Turning her head back and forth, trying to locate the threat, she hurried to her car. Her hand trembled with an irrepressible shudder as she reached for the car door handle. Yanking it open, she jumped in, locked it, and turned the ignition, ready to floor the accelerator and fly out of the parking space.

"I feel like someone walked over my grave," she said aloud, hoping the sound of her voice would dispel her sense of terror. Steering the car with one shaky hand, she used the other to turn on the radio and select a country music station. Raising the volume, she hoped the loud music would ward off the dread that menaced her.

***

At the back of the room where Velma Scooterman-Maxwell was lying in her casket, the watcher, wearing a blond wig and tinted glasses, melted into and shifted through knots of people, pretending to notice the pictures of Velma displayed around the room. Nice crowd; they couldn't have known her that well. Moving in the shadows at the edges of the room, the watcher identified players of interest, noting Father Melvyn standing with other priests and unidentified civilians.

Weaving in and out like an invisible wraith, the watcher picked up snippets of meaningless talk in the different groups standing around: some catching up on each other's lives, some gossiping about Velma. When Mrs. B. walked in, the watcher's attention locked on her like a heat-seeking missile. The watcher stayed as near to Mrs. B. as possible, trying to hear her conversations.

When Mrs. B. left the funeral home, the watcher walked to the back of the room and stared intently out the window, visualizing having the nosey housekeeper by the throat, squeezing and demanding: where is Maxwell's will?

In the parking lot the housekeeper suddenly looked disconcerted. She stopped, grabbed a car hood for balance, looked around and then ran to her car. The watcher smiled. She's spooked. What scared her? Well, Mrs. B. if I don't get Charles's will, you'll have good reason to be scared.

The watcher's thoughts turned to dead Velma and the complication that the M.E.'s ruling had created. If she'd died in her bed, like she was supposed to no one would have thought anything of it. How that bitch managed to get up and go outside is beyond me, the watcher thought and made her own way out of the funeral home.

26
Thirty Thousand Pieces of Silver

It was 2:00 a.m. Disgusted by what he'd read, Father Melvyn slammed the journal closed. Charles Maxwell was a parasite, rich as Midas and evil as Lucifer. He destroyed lives and generated hatreds that are still festering and the damage might now take Saint Francis's Church down, too. "What a cad." He stopped himself from saying the word he really wanted to use.

Dismayed, he wondered how kind old Father Jameson had allowed himself to be sucked into this terrible story. I'm sure he thought he was doing what was best, Father Melvyn reflected. Holding his pursed lips between his thumb and forefinger, Father Melvyn paced in his room. There was logic to his decision about the baby, but still...

The biggest surprise was Amy Rangel. She was Father Jameson's housekeeper when Father Melvyn arrived; she was also Martha's aunt, which he never knew. Martha never talked about her. How could Father Jameson agree to do Velma's bidding, along with Mrs. Rangel? It was cruelty. He opened the journal again and reread Velma's entry.

Amy told me about their meeting with the Magswelles last night. Amy was easy. I knew she would be. I gave her the deed to that little cottage she wanted off Guadalupe, near UT. It was Father Jameson who had me worried, but it looks like my promise of thirty grand for a new marble altar hit the spot! He told them that Martha would be ostracized, her family would be shunned by the community, she'd be a laughingstock and the child would never have a good life.

Father Melvyn closed the journal. More like thirty thousand pieces of silver, he thought bitterly. Well, that was a lot of money all those years ago. He continued to pace, thinking about Velma's journal. She seemed gleeful, almost self-congratulatory, that she had successfully bribed Amy Rangel and Father Jameson.

Mrs. B. is right. If this becomes public Saint Francis will be damaged. Another black eye for the priesthood, albeit having nothing to do with sexual harassment. He felt a strong urge to call his trusted housekeeper. "It's the middle of night. Can't do that," he scolded himself.

LaLa's meow was almost a whisper, as if she knew it was a ridiculous hour to be up and walking around. "How, LaLa, do you manage to get from room to room when the doors are closed?"

The cat looked directly at him and then at the bed.

"You're right," he said. "I'd better get some sleep. Velma's funeral mass is at ten in the morning. I'll speak to Mrs. B. after." Father Melvyn said extra prayers for Velma Scooterman-Maxwell's soul before turning out the light.

In the darkness, he made out LaLa's shadowy figure. She sniffed the air and scanned the darkened room before curling up on the rug at the foot of his bed.

Wednesday

The First Full Week of Lent

27
Another Piece of the Puzzle

Father Melvyn stood in the narthex waiting for the casket to arrive. He looked over the pews filled with parishioners. Some were merely curious, and many, in spite of their personal feelings about Velma, came to pay their respects and participate in the Catholic funeral rites. He wondered how many were there to see and be seen. There were members of the parish council and many of Austin's elites. Looking away from the congregation, he prepared his mind for prayers and the mass.

The doors at the main entrance opened, and the casket was rolled in. Velma's nephew was the sole family member in attendance. Father Melvyn was surprised that Jeffrey's wife and children hadn't come. He pushed aside all thoughts other than the Catholic ritual. "May the grace and peace of God our Father, who raised Jesus from the dead, be always with you."

The pallbearers and Scooterman responded, "And also with you." Father Melvyn sprinkled the casket with holy water. The funeral director spread the white linen pall over the casket to remind the congregation of the white garment received at Baptism. The processional music began. Father Melvyn led the casket and Jeffrey Scooterman down the center aisle. The mass for the repose of Velma's soul began.

Father Melvyn had to suppress his conflicted feelings. Now that he'd read her journal, he vacillated between pity and blame. He looked at the beautiful high altar that he so admired; it suddenly lost its luster. He felt sad at the price paid for it. "Not now," he hissed inaudibly. "Focus." Even though he understood the level of betrayal that caused Velma's bitterness, arrogance, and her insecure need to be admired, he felt she could have chosen a different path. Her schemes of revenge, some successfully carried out, gave him pause. He steeled himself. Put it out of your mind, he told himself. She's entitled to a well-said mass. God is her judge, not me.

After the gospel reading, Jeffrey Scooterman gave a tepid homily, followed by one of the women from the parish council who spoke glowingly of Velma's generosity. At the end of the mass the procession filed up the center aisle of the church. The pall was removed and Velma's remains were wheeled out to the waiting hearse.

Father Melvyn walked toward the sacristy to change out of the vestments used for the mass. Footsteps behind made him turn and to his surprise Chancey stepped out of the shadows.

"Can I speak with you, Father?"

He looked at Martha's son. The dark circles under his eyes and his pasty complexion reflected his anxiety.

"Of course Chancey. Is everything okay?"

Crestfallen, Chancey answered. "No. Mother is still being held and we don't have a lawyer. The police say she can have a public defender. Should we accept that?"

"Call Detective Zayas. He's in charge of this investigation. Tell him that your mother's lawyer will be in touch shortly. Tom Barbee has agreed to take her case. He may have already called. I must leave now, but you come to the rectory at two p.m. and we'll find out what's going on."

"Thank you, Father," Chancey said. "We're grateful for your help."

The priest patted Chancey's shoulder and turned into the sacristy. "You go home now," he said, feeling terrible for Martha's illegitimate son. Velma's journal, incomplete though it was, shed light on Martha's resentment. Does Martha know how deeply Velma was involved? he wondered.

And Velma. What an actress. She had everyone believing she was one step from sainthood. She should have thrown the bum out instead of hanging in there for the money. It turned her into a monster. Father Melvyn was not comfortable with his own uncharitable thoughts. Steeped in conflicting feelings about Martha and Velma, Father Melvyn hung the vestments in the cupboard with care. I can't wait to be finished with Velma's funeral, the luncheon, and her sordid tale, he thought.

Behind the closed door of the sacristy, he texted Mrs. B. *Please call Tom Barbee. Find out if he's contacted the police or anyone at the county jail. Chancey's coming to the rectory at two. We need to talk before he gets there. I'll be back by twelve-thirty.*

***

Blond wig and tinted glasses firmly in place, eyes glued to one person, the watcher stood alone pretending to look through prayer cards and pamphlets on the counter in the narthex. The target of the watcher's attention stood at the back of the church as the casket was rolled out. From the side, there was nothing particularly interesting about him until he turned. Recognition was immediate. The black eyes were large and startling. He's Maxwell's other child. Those eyes can't be mistaken. Another piece of the puzzle falls into place. The watcher was elated. Fate was moving things in the right direction. I'll trail him. Gotta find out his name. When he followed Father Melvyn to the side hall the watcher pretended to look for a restroom and heard the priest call him by name: "Chancey."

"Chancey who?" the watcher muttered. I'll get his plate number when he leaves. Following at a discreet distance the watcher expected him to go to one of the cars in the parking lot. Instead, he walked out, crossed Carpenter, and went into the first house. "Whoa! That's Martha Magswelle's house." This could be a real bonus.

***

Father Melvyn blew through the kitchen door like a gust of wind. "Got my text?"

"Yes," Mrs. B. answered. "Luncheon over already?"

"No. I said I had pressing business and left. Please sit down. We don't have much time."

Mrs. B. sat and pulled a note out of her pocket. "I called Tom Barbee. His secretary said he's in Dallas on business. That's why he didn't get Martha out this morning. She said that Tom spoke to Martha by phone and told her that she shouldn't answer any more questions until he gets there."

"I didn't think people in jail were allowed to receive phone calls."

"Neither did I. Tom's secretary explained. Travis County allows a person being held to make a free local call to an attorney *if* the lawyer first calls a special number and leaves the appropriate information. Then they allow the person to call back. Before we go any further, I need to apologize..."

Father Melvyn wasn't listening. He stared at the newspaper on the table. Several ads in the classified section were circled in ink. His face flushed red; he looked at his housekeeper. "What is this, Mrs. B.?"

She hesitated. "It's clear to me that you'd prefer to hire another housekeeper or secretary—or both. I'll post an ad for you in next week's journal and stay until you find someone else. It's time for me to move on."

"Well. That's abrupt," he said. "No effort to explain and set things right?"

"Over the past few days, you haven't seemed interested in talking, blowing in and out of here like the wind, avoiding me. What was I to think?"

Father Melvyn sighed. "The same thing that I think. We're both under great stress, with people's lives hanging in the balance. Let's not rush into anything else." He sounded high-handed, even to himself. "Please, Mrs. B., will you agree to suspend your departure long enough to get through this mess?

You were right," he continued. "If the information in those papers comes out it will be a big scandal for Saint Francis and tarnish Father Jameson's reputation, even though he's dead. If what Velma wrote is true, Martha will learn how her own family betrayed her, and when she finds out, who knows how she'll react." He paused and then asked again. "Can we postpone any talk of you leaving until this is over?"

"Yes, of course," she answered immediately. "Especially since I'm the reason this trouble is happening."

"Actually, after reading her journal and Maxwell's will I think it might have been heavenly guidance that made you take them." He watched her face. She wasn't mollified.

"What do you want to do now?" she asked.

"Let's start with what I don't want. I don't want you to place an ad."

28
Found and Lost

Chancey watched Velma's mass from the last row in the church. He felt nothing. After the casket and the mourners left the church, he spoke to Father Melvyn and then went back to his mother's house with a heavy heart.

Barklay and Smitty greeted him, woofing and wagging their tails. They needed attention, but his thoughts were filled with Martha's dilemma. I need to get my mother out of jail, he thought. The words played like the refrain of a song he couldn't get out of his head, taking over the rhythm of his actions as he walked the dogs, gave them food and water, cleaned the kitchen, and made his bed.

In the short time since he and Martha had found each other deep feelings took hold. Chancey didn't try to hold back his tears. I should have insisted she move to Killeen, he thought. I will when this is over. I have a good job with the bus company. She can sell this house, and we can buy something together.

Chancey remembered their first meeting. He was so nervous, afraid she'd be disappointed in him. The memory was crystal clear. He'd been overcome with emotion. When she got off the bus in Killeen he was barely able to say, "Nice to meet you."

Martha was kind and kept the conversation to general things: where he lived, his work for the bus company. He blushed again, remembering how afraid he was to admit that he was a bus mechanic. "My adopted father said I wasn't college material."

She smiled, patted his hand, and told him to be proud. "Think of the people who depend on buses running smoothly and on schedule so that they can get to their jobs," she said.

The third time they'd met, he drove to Austin and stayed at a motel even though Martha wanted him to stay at her house. It was on this visit that Martha insisted on hearing the whole story. He hadn't wanted to tell her everything. He was afraid she'd change her mind about knowing him.

"Please tell me, Chancey." Martha pleaded.

He explained that the Johnsons were good people. His adopted mother Mary was especially kind and loving. "I loved her," he told Martha. It still hurt him to dredge up the memories. "She died when I was ten. That's when my father became an alcoholic." He remembered how Martha cried while he told his story. He tried to stop. "You're getting too upset. This isn't good for you." He was afraid she wouldn't want to see him anymore.

"No. I want to know everything about your life."

Chancey condensed it as much as possible. "After Mary died, things were tough for a couple of years. Sometimes my father beat me, but I'm sure that was the alcohol. He lost his job, and the authorities showed up; I wasn't going to school. They threatened to take me away and to put me in a foster home. I thought he wouldn't care, but instead he said he'd take care of me for the sake of his wife's memory. He joined an AA group, cleaned up his act, and met another woman. She encouraged him and helped him stay clean. They got married and had a child of their own. After that they didn't pay much attention to me, but I was happy that my father had a good life, and I liked their little girl, Lisa.

"When I turned sixteen, my father told me to learn a trade. I was good with cars and motors, but after graduation I couldn't find a job. I banged around for a couple of years then enlisted in the army. By 1990 I was a sergeant and had a lot of technical abilities, but there was a shortage of medics when troops were deployed to the Middle East.

I volunteered for training and was sent to Kuwait. I thought after I got home maybe I'd be able to do something in the medical field.

One day my partner and I were trying to save a wounded soldier. The fighting had died down, and it seemed safe to move. All I remember is an explosion. Later I was told that a shoulder launched missile found us. My partner and the wounded soldier were blown to pieces. I woke up in an army hospital. My injuries weren't fatal just some shrapnel in my legs. They had to operate and that's why I have a limp, but I didn't remember anything. I still don't. When I recovered, I had a stutter, and I couldn't think clearly; I had nightmares too. They sent me back to the States where I worked as a mechanic until my discharge. That's when I got a job with the bus company in Killeen."

"Did you move back in with your father and his wife?"

"No. I got my own place. I hardly ever saw them."

"I'm so sorry," she'd said over and over, between sobs. "I should never have let them force me to give you up. I didn't want to."

Martha told Chancey about the night her aunt Amy and the pastor of Saint Francis, Father Jameson, visited her and her family. "They said life would be miserable for all of us. We'd be ostracized, rejected. They persuaded my parents that the baby would be better off in a good home, and they were in touch with a reputable agency. My aunt said I could never provide a good life for my baby, for you. I cried and begged, but I was only seventeen. They threatened to disown me if I tried to keep you."

Tears wet his face remembering her pain. That was the first time he'd hugged his mother. "I've found you now, Mom, and we'll never be separated again." From that time they visited frequently, and whenever Martha went to Killeen she stayed at his small apartment. He'd give up his bed and sleep on the couch. In Austin, she'd made up the second bedroom for him. She told him to bring some personal things for the room so that he'd always know it was his home.

Absentmindedly, he petted Barclay and Smitty, bringing himself back to the present. For the first time in his life he felt loved and important and that his existence made a difference to someone. No matter what, he was determined to find a way to help her. He wasn't going to lose her now.

Looking out the back window, he wondered if her plants needed water. The door to the greenhouse was still blocked by crime scene tape. He remembered her pride the first time she showed him her greenhouse. "Flowers and plants bring me joy," she explained.

His thoughts turned to the police investigation. His mother was accused of poisoning Velma because of the plants in her greenhouse.

From his medic training, he remembered that foxglove could be dangerous; it produced digitalis. He sighed. "C'mon, dogs, let's get you settled. I have an appointment with Father Melvyn. I found my mother and I'm not going to lose her now. We're going to get Mama back."

29
A Fragile Truce

At two o'clock, Chancey left Martha's house and walked across the street to Saint Francis de Sales. He looked up into the clear blue sky and felt warmed by the sun. Trying to extend the feeling as long as possible, instead of cutting across the parking field, he walked up Cobble Road, passed the front of the church, and turned left on Ferne Lane.

The front door opened as soon as he rang the bell and Mrs. B. greeted him. "Come in, Chancey." She smiles with her whole face, he thought. There was warmth in her eyes behind the large, round, blue-framed glasses, but he remembered his mother's warning.

Father Melvyn came down the hall. "Okay, young man. Let's get to work."

Father Melvyn, Chancey, and Mrs. B. settled into the office. "I've asked my assistant, Mrs. B., to join us. We have a lot to cover. "Tom Barbee has agreed to take your mother's case. He's in Dallas and can't get back today, but he did talk to Martha and told her not to answer any more questions until he gets there. Her hearing before the judge is tomorrow morning. Tom wants to be with her throughout. That means she'll spend the night in jail." He looked at Chancey's sad face. "Are you okay with this?"

"Can't he send someone else from his office?"Chancey asked.

"I asked that too. He said he could but felt strongly that he should be present from the beginning."

"If that's what you think is best, Father, then I'll be okay with it. Does my mother understand?"

"I'm not sure. What I am sure of is this: Tom Barbee is one of the finest and most respected attorneys in Austin— in fact, in Texas. He can be trusted to give Martha the best possible representation and defense. I'm inclined to follow his advice."

Chancey shrugged and nodded his agreement. "I want my mother home, but if this is best…"

"The other reason Tom wants to be present is he feels he'll need to make a powerful argument to get her bail lowered. It will be steep…she may be charged with murder."

Chancey's eyes welled. "I have about five grand saved…not enough?"

"Probably not, which is another reason to wait for Tom to take charge tomorrow."

Chancey blurted, "I wanted to get her out of that place today. I want her home."

"I've spoken to a friend in the police department," Mrs. B. said. "Your mother is doing fine. She's alone in a holding cell." She didn't add that Jake was convinced she was guilty, just as she hadn't told Jake or Chancey everything she and Father Melvyn knew from reading Velma's journal.

"We need to have a more complete picture of things. Tell us when and how you found Martha. We didn't know she had a child," Father Melvyn said, adding, "Did you know your biological father? Did you ever meet him or have any contact with him?"

"No. I only know his name was Charles Maxwell, and he married my mother's old friend, or supposed friend, Velma Scooterman."

"How did you find Martha?" Father Melvyn asked.

Chancey smiled. "She didn't tell anyone, but as a condition of the adoption, if her child ever wanted to know where she was, the agency was to give the information. She said that's why she never moved out of the house where she grew up, not even after her parents died. She wanted me to be able to find her.

"When I moved out of my adopted father's house, I took the photo albums Mary, my adopted mother, kept of me growing up. One day, I was looking through them again and one of my baby pictures fell out. On the back was the name of the adoption agency in Dallas and my age at the time: three days old." Chancey noticed the priest holding his pursed lips between his thumb and forefinger. The housekeeper took off her large blue-framed glasses and wiped them. No one spoke for a few minutes.

Father Melvyn cleared his throat. "There's not much we can do today. Tomorrow, Tom will go to the jail, post bail and get your mother out, and we'll meet at your house. He'll explain the next steps. How long can you stay in Austin?"

"I called the bus company in Killeen and told them it was a family emergency. I never take time off, so I have a lot of vacation days saved. No matter. I'm staying until I have my mother cleared of all this. It's nonsense."

Mrs. B. cleared her throat and looked at Father Melvyn. Chancey looked from one to the other as they made eye contact; he felt he was about to hear something unpleasant.

"One of the poisons in Velma's system was an overdose of digitalis. Apparently Martha grows foxglove in her greenhouse."

"I know that, and I know what foxglove looks like and what it can do. I was trained as a medic in the army, and we covered poisonous plants. If misused, digitalis is dangerous, but that doesn't mean she did it," Chancey said, defending his mother.

"No, it doesn't. However, a few days ago, your mother and Velma had another of their infamous public battles, and she threatened to kill Velma and her cat. I don't know if your mother told you, but she and Velma have been fighting for years...no one ever knew why. Do you?" Mrs. B. asked.

"Not really. She hardly ever talked about Velma, except to say that the woman was a vicious, nasty witch who fooled everyone. She said that people looked up to Velma that people thought she was generous and wonderful, but that in fact she used her money as a weapon to manipulate them. She said to stay away from her and not to trust—" Chancey stopped. He wasn't sure if he should finish the thought aloud.

Father Melvyn and Mrs. B. stared at him, waiting. He looked at Mrs. B. and blurted out, "Mother said to be careful of you, that you were in tight with Velma."

"In tight?" Mrs. B. thought for a moment. "No. I wouldn't say that. We only talked about cats. Why would Martha think that?"

"Apparently Velma told her that you and she were becoming friends." He paused. "You seem like a nice lady, but I don't know if I should trust you."

Father Melvyn took control of the conversation. "Mrs. B. is completely trustworthy. She has never worked against your mother's interests. Believe me you will see that in time." Father Melvyn stood up, indicating that the meeting was over. "We'll continue this tomorrow when Tom brings your mother home. For today, there are visiting hours at the jail. I'm sure you want to spend time with her."

At the front door, Chancey said, "It's strange. My mother loves animals. Why would she threaten to kill a cat?"

"Last Christmas, LaLa, that's Velma's cat, got between your mother's feet and she fell. That's how she broke her ankle. Didn't she tell you?" Father Melvyn asked.

"No. She said she tripped on the sidewalk. I wanted to take time off and come here to care for her, but she wouldn't hear of it."

"Last week," Mrs. B. continued, "she was walking Barklay and Smitty. They spotted LaLa and tried to chase after her. They pulled your mother down, making her fall again. In a fit of anger, Martha threatened to kill the cat and Velma, but it was spoken in the heat of the moment. None of us believe she did any such thing."

***

After Chancey left, Father Melvyn and Mrs. B. went back to the kitchen. She poured them freshly brewed coffee. Father Melvyn plopped down on a chair at the table and indicated that Mrs. B. should join him. "He doesn't know the whole story, and I doubt Martha knows of Velma's involvement in the plot to force her to give up her baby."

"The more we learn, the stronger Martha's motive seems, and it may point to Chancey too, especially when Jake finds out about Chancey's medic training. Once we give Jake the will he'll question Chancey. If he thinks Martha and Chancey know about Charles's bequest it will make them stronger suspects. But how could they? It doesn't add up."

"I don't see it either," Father Melvyn said. "Velma hated Martha and would never allow her in her house. In fact, throughout the journal she referred to Martha as the pretty one. 'See, Martha the pretty one doesn't always win. Charles married me, not you. '"

Mrs. B. picked up the thread. "Velma was livid when she found out Martha was pregnant; she felt that Martha tried to entrap Charles, but it didn't work. Velma saw to that. Her notes were gleeful. She was proud that she was able to bribe Martha's aunt and Father Jameson. She was vicious and determined to have Charles for herself and to be rid of his illegitimate child." Mrs. B. paused. Neither she nor Father Melvyn spoke.

"Father Declan told me he thought he saw Martha and a strange man the night of Velma's death," Mrs. B. said, changing the direction of the conversation. "She was walking her dogs across the street in front of Velma's house. He couldn't see the man's face. If it was Chancey, that's more evidence against them. One of the last entries in Velma's journal said, 'If Martha thinks she's going to embarrass me or blackmail me, she'll be sorry.' Speaking of Father Declan, I was surprised when he told me that Martha helped him with his acne problems. Did you know?"

"No. I didn't," Father Melvyn answered.

"Seems he likes Martha. He doesn't want to say anything to the police that will hurt her. I advised him to wait until Martha had representation and then to tell her lawyer. Tom will know what to do. Don't you think?"

Father Melvyn nodded. "That was probably the best way to handle it. You're right, Mrs. B., Martha will be further damaged. This information might be enough to send her to jail and the scandal for Saint Francis will be huge." He paused. "I can't believe Father Jameson took what was essentially a bribe, even though in those times it was not illogical for Martha to give up the baby."

"Logic has nothing to do with this," Mrs. B. said. "Vicious, destructive jealousy does. Martha was the one all the boys wanted to date and Velma was the plain one that no one noticed, but Velma was shrewd. The Scootermans were community leaders, movers, and shakers. Velma knew that was her selling point.

"Charles married Velma for that standing and then betrayed and humiliated her. When she found out about Martha's baby, she couldn't bear the thought of Martha raising it under her nose. Velma didn't care about Martha's or the baby's best interests. She wanted that child gone, and she bribed Father Jameson with money for a new altar." Mrs. B. went to the coffee pot to get another cup.

"Please get me another too," Father Melvyn held out his cup. She returned to the table and continued. "And that aunt of Martha's -- Amy Rangel. Didn't anyone question how Rangel could afford to buy the house she moved into?"

Father Melvyn shrugged. "All unanswered questions," he said.

"If Velma kept one journal I bet she has lots of them stashed away. Wouldn't I just love to read them." The look on Father Melvyn's face brought her back to the present situation. She changed the subject. "Let's keep in mind that there is another offspring floating around somewhere. Velma wrote that too. Out of spite Charles wouldn't tell her the name of his second illegitimate child, but she knew there was another besides Martha's son."

"God forgive me for saying it, but he was hateful, and may God forgive him. What shall we do, Mrs. B.? I would love to give Jake the information without risking Saint Francis, but I'm not sure we can. Shall we call him now?"

"Let's sleep on it, Father. He's going to be mad as hell at me. It might cost me a friendship, but it's already done."

Father Melvyn asked, "Do you think it will help if I talk to him?"

30
Let's Help Them Close This Case

She looked at him through the thick plexiglass. "What's wrong, Chancey? You look pale. Did you meet with Father Melvyn?" Martha asked her son in the prison visiting room.

"Yes. What he says makes sense, but I really wanted to get you out of here today." He went on to explain that Father Melvyn told him the same thing Tom told her on the phone.

Martha held her emotions in check. She forced a smile. "Don't worry. Tom Barbee will be here tomorrow, and I'll be home. You need to get a good night's rest. I'll be fine. It's only a few more hours."

"I know. Father Melvyn said it's to your advantage to wait for Tom." Martha placed her hand on the glass, and Chancey did the same from his side. "I love you, Mom," he whispered.

Martha's eyes filled with tears. "Love you too, son. See you tomorrow." After Chancey left Martha returned to her cell and knelt beside her cot. She held the pillow in front of her face to muffle the sound of her tearful prayers.

"Please, God," she prayed, "get me out of this mess. I promise I will be a better person and make up for everything wrong I've done." She comforted herself with dreams of the future, a future she wasn't sure she'd have. "When this is over I want Chancey to move to Austin. What little I have in this life belongs to him. I want to make up for all those lost years. I'll shout from the rooftops that Chancey is my son, and I don't care who doesn't like it. Thank you, Lord, for bringing him back to me."

"Everything okay in there?" The guard's voice interrupted her prayers.

"Yes."

"Time to eat. Come out into the common area." Martha obeyed without another word. She sat at one of the tables with two other inmates and looked at the sandwich. Bologna and cheese, an apple and a bottle of water. Just like the last meal. Better than nothing, she thought. Tomorrow I'll be home with Chancey, and I'll cook us a nice dinner. That thought made her happy. She wiped her tears away, sniffled, and bit into her unappetizing sandwich.

"Hey, Momma," the woman to her left said. "Stop your crying. Don't let these guards see you break down."

"Thanks. I'm trying."

"Good. Did you say you don't want that apple?" Martha looked up. A stab of fear made her shiver. The inmate speaking to her had snakelike eyes and a smile that revealed broken and yellowed teeth.

"Would you like to have it?" The inmate put out her hand. Martha placed the apple in her palm and then forced the remains of the sandwich down her dry throat, sipping her water. When the lunch period was over, she returned to her cell. I can't wait to get out of here, she thought.

Relieved to be alone, she napped, woke, and napped again. The constant light in the cell, along with the scratchy blanket, hard mattress, and flat pillow, didn't help. Her mind was empty, and her emotions were full. Her heart ached; tears ran down her cheeks. She wanted to go home. She wanted her son.

***

After the luncheon for his aunt, Jeffrey Scooterman returned to the motel. "Glad that's over. We ate while Velma burned, he quipped. Everyone was grateful and gracious at the luncheon," he said. He hung up his jacket and kicked off his shoes, lay on the bed, and propped himself up on the pillows. "I'm sure the bishop and the parish council members are hoping for at least one final contribution." He chuckled, "and they can wait until hell freezes over."

He glanced over at the person seated at the desk, writing furiously. "I need to get into my aunt's house to get her bank accounts. The funeral director said I'll need a death certificate for the bank. Since her death is being investigated as a homicide, the certificate will state the cause as "pending," but the bank won't care about that.

"Unfortunately, getting the death certificate might take a couple of weeks. The funeral director was sympathetic and said he'll see what he can do..." Realizing the person at the desk wasn't paying attention, he asked, "What the hell are you doing? You didn't hear a word I said."

"I found the other one."

"The other one what?" Silence. He was about to ask again then bolted upright on the bed. "Are you kidding?"

"No. I'm not. He was right under our noses."

"What do you mean? Are you talking about Martha Magswelle's kid? She gave him up for adoption. How did you find him?"

"I'll tell you later. Let me finish this."

172

Jeffrey returned to his own thoughts. "After the service, Detective Zayas approached me. He wants me to talk to me tomorrow. Said he has a few more questions. Do you think it's anything?"

"I think we need to help them close this case, sooner rather than later, before you end up under suspicion."

"Why would I end up under suspicion?" What are you thinking?" he asked.

"Hello? You stand to inherit everything. If the police find out you were here in Austin the night she died you'll be a prime suspect, but if the police learn that Martha had an illegitimate kid with Charles that would give her strong motives too: revenge and money. If we throw more suspicion on Martha and involve her son Chancey, now that we've found him, the police will close the case without involving anyone else.

"We don't want them to find out that Charles's last will and testament is out there and was never executed. If they learn you would have been excluded from the estate, the spotlight will be on you."

"I doubt they could know. My aunt spent her miserable life keeping up appearances and hiding Charles's peccadillos."

Jeffrey's companion threw the pen down in disgust and shot a series of rapid-fire questions at him. "Are you sure Chancey and his mother didn't find out about Charles's bequest? Do you know for sure whether Charles contacted them?

"No. I'm not sure about anything," Jeffrey said.

"How did Velma get her hands on Charles's will in the first place.?"

"My father was very close to his sister. He was outraged by Charles's behavior. When Charles died, Aunt Velma told my dad that Charles's attorney, Lucas Browne, called her in to discuss the terms of the will before he put it in probate. He said he was giving her time to put her affairs in order because other than the checking and savings accounts, which amounted to maybe a hundred grand, Charles's estate, including half of Velma's house, amounted to four million, give or take, and was left to his illegitimate children.

"Browne knew about Martha's son, but he didn't have a last name, and he didn't have the name of the other kid because Charles died suddenly before giving Lucas the information. Lucas told my aunt that to uphold Charles's wishes, he was going to hire a P.I. Lucas was old and frail, and happily he dropped dead a couple of days later."

"Like Charles died suddenly?"

"Coincidence, I suppose," Jeffrey continued, ignoring the implication of the remark. "Being a lawyer and circulating in the legal networks here, my father learned that Lucas's widow wanted to sell his practice. Not knowing how much information Mrs. Browne had, Dad used an intermediary and bought it. That's how he got hold of Charles's will.

"Dad told me that Charles was a real bastard. He laughed at Velma and decided that the Maxwell millions were to be split between his two illegitimate children. My father told her to burn it, but the bitch didn't. As far as the world was concerned, Charles died intestate."

"And she paid all the taxes and penalties to get the money and the house into her own name?"

"Worth it, don't you think?" He laughed and threw himself back on the bed. "Dear Aunt Velma thought she was going to use it against me."

Jeffrey's companion was pensive. "No one else knows what we know, but if there's any suspicion, this could get tied up in court for years."

"I don't need to be reminded," Jeffrey snapped. "The money in the accounts will get me out of my immediate trouble, and we can wait a few months for the rest."

"That would be true if Velma died in her bed, but she didn't. Now there's a murder investigation and there's no statute of limitations on murder. We need the case closed, fast."

"Fast," he parroted. "Sure, but what can we do?"

"Hmmm. Let's see. Chancey was adopted, but now he's here. When I realized who he was, I followed him and watched him go into his *mommy's* house. Didn't the police tell you about the feud between Martha and Velma?"

"Yes and I talked about it with the priest when I made the funeral arrangements. I told him that the police said they were looking into a long running feud between my aunt and another parishioner, but—"

"I think we need to help the police tie up the loose ends. Who has a motive to kill Velma? Besides you, that is."

"Not funny," he snapped.

"Your aunt and Martha were archenemies. Why? Because of Martha's son by Charles? We don't know if Charles told Martha anything about leaving money to Chancey. Let's close this case. We need to establish a different motive for Velma's murder and we need to do it now."

Jeffrey watched his companion go back to writing. He didn't argue or ask more questions. He knew better.

Thursday

The First Full Week of Lent

31
The Note

The dogs' snarling and woofing woke him. He opened his eyes; it was still night. The bedside clock read 4:00 a.m. The dogs became more insistent. "What's all the fuss?" he asked, getting out of bed. He yawned, and walked into the kitchen. Still half-asleep, he ran his hand up the wall to find the light switch when something hard was pressed into his side.

"Hands over your head," a raspy voice ordered.

"What is this?" He tried to turn and was shoved hard against the wall. "Take what you want. I don't have any money."

"Shut those dogs up, or I'll shoot them," a raspy voice ordered. "Put them out in the yard."

He reached for the leashes on the rack next to the kitchen door. "No need to hurt them. I'll get them out. Quiet. Go outside, boys," he said to the dogs, dragging them to the door. He tried to step out. The leashes were pulled from his hand, and a foot kicked the dogs out; they whimpered. "Hey, don't kick them," he yelled and tried to turn toward his assailant when splotches of red and black exploded in front of his eyes. A rush of air blew out of his lungs from the blow to the back of his head. He fell to the floor. The last things he saw were two black-clad figures.

***

The assailants looked down at his motionless body and then at the tire iron. "Wipe it clean," the shorter one ordered, "and put it in the garage." Pulling a container and a cloth out of a pocket, the shorter of the two wiped away fingerprints, leaned down, wrapped the unconscious man's fingers around the container, and handed it off. "Put this in the pantry on a shelf. Hold it by the nozzle, and don't smear the prints."

The taller one nodded. "I can hear the dogs outside. Should we let them in?"

No. They're loose, and we won't be able to grab them so easily. They'll bark and howl even more, and we don't want the neighbors awakened too soon. Let's do this."

Together, they dragged the unconscious man across the floor and placed him next to the stove face up so that the injury would appear to have happened when he passed out and fell. The taller of the two checked for blood at the back door and wiped the floor with bleach soaked paper towels for good measure. "Hurry up. We need to be sure someone finds him before the house explodes. Move his car. Block St Francis's driveway."

"Why would he leave his car blocking the driveway?"

"He's distraught; he's about to commit suicide and obviously not thinking straight. Maybe they'll think he wanted to be stopped. Just do it."

When everything was set the shorter one turned on the stove top, blew out the flames, and then ran to the bedrooms. Bypassing the master and pulling the door closed, the assailant went to the second bedroom. There, on the corner of the dresser, was a wallet with his driver's license. "Last name Johnson. That won't be hard to remember."

"Let's get out of here," the taller one said, looking at the crumpled note again. The other pulled it away, crossed out and changed a few words, leaving it on the table.

"What are you doing?"

"Making it look like he struggled with what to say." They made one last check that all windows and doors to other rooms were tightly shut to speed the concentration of gas in the kitchen.

"Let's go. It's getting stinky. How about the oven jets?"

"Too much. Can't have the house blow up. It would get rid of Chancey, but it wouldn't close the Velma investigation." Looking around, satisfied they'd done everything right, they left.

***

Martha awoke with a start. Where am I? she wondered. This isn't my bed. She looked around, disoriented. Is this still the dream? The dim, yellowish cell light brought the truth crashing back. She sat up on her bed, hands folded in her lap. The nightmare was still vivid. She wanted to lean her head against the wall but was afraid to in case of roaches. The images from the dream remained sharp.

Velma had her hands around Chancey's throat. She squeezed, laughing like a maniac. "He's a loser like you, and you'll never enjoy him. I won't let you," she spat the words. Her laughter rang out. Then LaLa appeared. The cat screamed and wriggled under Velma's shoe, blood spurting from the wound caused by Velma's heel on the cat's neck.

Chancey cried out, "Mom. Help me." She tried to move, to pull Velma off her son, but her feet were glued to the floor. She woke up shuddering. Martha shut her eyes again and tried to push the images away. She felt the residue of pain in her legs from the adrenaline that released as she tried to force her frozen legs to move during the nightmare. I wish I could call him to be sure he's okay, she thought. The abdominal pressure made her realize that she had to pee.

There was no one in the observation in the window in the cell door, no guard looking in. She padded over to the exposed toilet and took care of business without being spied on then made her way back to the cot. Martha lay down, not wanting a guard to check her cell and find her sitting up. Morning light couldn't come fast enough.

Turning her back to the door, she prayed: "Please, God, don't punish my son for my sins." Burying her face in the unforgiving pillow, Martha wept.

32
A Terrible Accident

It was barely daylight when Mrs. B. rushed into the rectory, disheveled and still in shock from Father Melvyn's call. "What is it, Father? What couldn't you tell me on the phone and why is the entrance on Cobble Drive blocked?" She shouted her questions before getting all the way through the door. One look at his face, and she knew it was something really bad. He was pale and tousled; he looked like he'd just gotten out of bed.

"Rafael woke me. He was passing St. Francis and saw a car blocking the driveway on Cobble Road. When I went out, I recognized Chancey's car. I ran over and banged on the door. No answer. The dogs are outside in the yard, barking like crazy. Something is very wrong." He paused for a moment. "You wouldn't know where *she* keeps an emergency key, would you?"

Rafael stuck his head in the door without knocking. "Padre, the police are here."

Father Melvyn took off at a run across the parking field toward Carpenter Street, with Rafael and Mrs. B. on his heels. They trotted across the street as fast as the morning traffic allowed.

The officer was banging on Martha's front door, ringing the bell, and calling out, "Hello, hello. Police. Can anyone hear me?"

Father Melvyn rushed up the walk. "I'm worried. I tried the front door too. Chancey didn't answer."

"You know the owner?"

"Yes. Her son is in the house." By now the dogs were barking full out.

"I'll need to get animal control. I don't want to shoot them, but we can't risk being bitten if we have to go in from the yard."

"Let me do this," Father Melvyn said to the officer. He turned to Mrs. B. "Martha will be home this morning. I can't let her come in here and find her beloved dogs shot dead."

Stepping through the gate, he approached the dogs. "Barklay, Smitty, shush." The dogs had a positive reaction to him. He pet the two whimpering, shaking animals, took their leashes, and pulled them to the far side of the yard. He motioned for the police officer and Mrs. B. to walk through the gate while he held and soothed the dogs. They look desperate, he thought as they stared helplessly at him.

The officer walked around and tried the back door. It was unlocked. She walked in and then turned right around and walked out. "Get away from the house, ma'am." She pushed Mrs. B. back and spoke into her mike: "We need emergency services and an ambulance. We have a gas leak here. Going in through the back door. It's unlocked, and someone is on the floor."

Within minutes sirens made their way up the street drawing a crowd on the sidewalk, in spite of the early hour.

Several police cars and emergency services arrived, followed by EMS. The first officer was inside opening every window and door she could reach. From the doorway, Mrs. B. heard her say, "Turned off the stove top. Can't find a pulse."

"Mrs. B.," Father Melvyn called to her. "Help me tie them to the fence so that the police and EMS can move freely." A short time later, they watched five emergency personnel carry Chancey's body out. One held his head, with the others on each leg and arm; they placed him on a stretcher. An EMT put a stethoscope to his chest.

"Alive...barely," she said. "Let's go. We need to get him to the hospital ASAP."

Father Melvyn ran over. "May I ride with him?" He didn't wait for an answer. Mrs. B. watched as he pulled the narrow purple stole from his pocket and jump into the ambulance. Before the door closed, he kissed the stole and draped it over his neck, prepared to pray over Chancey on the way to the hospital.

***

The ambulance pulled away, siren blaring. The police continued to do their work while the gas company examined the property inside and out. Not sure of what to do, Mrs. B. stayed at the fence with the dogs.

The original officer on the scene walked over and questioned her about who she was, who the priest was, and the name and relationship of the victim to the owner. She answered as best she could. Another car pulled up. It was Tom Barbee with Martha, who barely allowed the car to stop before she jumped out and ran to Mrs. B.

"What's happened? Where's Chancey? Where's my son?" Not waiting for an answer, Martha ran toward the house, but the police wouldn't let her go in. "Where is my son?" she screamed again. The officers held her back.

"Calm down, ma'am. Are you the owner?"

"Yes. Where is my son?" Her voice rose to a screech.

"He's on his way to the hospital. We'll talk to you in a minute" the officer said and walked back toward the house.

"Martha, come here," Mrs. B. called to her. "I'll tell you. Help me calm Barklay and Smitty." The dogs, still tied to the fence, were barking furiously again, their voices hoarse and dry. Tom walked over and took Martha's arm, leading her to Mrs. B.

"What happened here? Why didn't Chancey show up at the jail this morning?" Tom asked.

"It looks like a terrible accident," Mrs. B. said, nervous about Martha's reaction. "Chancey is in that ambulance. There was a gas leak during the night." Martha was bent over, trying to calm her dogs. Her head snapped up.

"Gas leak? That can't be. I'm careful. I have the heating unit and the gas lines checked every year." Martha began to untie the dogs.

"Don't loosen them yet, ma'am," the policewoman called to her.

Watching Martha, Mrs. B. whispered to Tom. "Father Melvyn went in the ambulance with Chancey. Maybe we'd better take Martha to the rectory. I don't think she should stay here."

Tom agreed. He walked over and talked to Martha. She nodded. "Officers, I'm Ms. Magswelle's attorney. We're going to take the dogs out of the yard. When you're finished here, you can find Ms. Magswelle at the Saint Francis rectory, across the street." He didn't wait for consent or agreement.

Tom and Mrs. B. were on either side of Martha, who was being tugged by Barklay and Smitty, as if they wanted to escape the scene in Martha's yard. Together, they crossed Carpenter and were about to turn into the church parking field when Jake Zayas pulled up. Without so much as a hello, he called out the window, "Where are you going, Ms. Magswelle?"

Tom stepped in front of a distraught Martha. "There's been a terrible accident, and we're going to wait in the rectory. Is that okay detective...and why are you here? This is a gas leak."

"Stay at the rectory until I get there," Jake answered tersely.

"I don't want you talking to my client if I'm not there."

Jake nodded, his face showing nothing, but his eyes were on Martha.

I don't like this, Mrs. B. thought, but she knew better than to ask him anything. He pulled away from the curb and drove the few feet to Martha's house.

"What is going on? I want my son." Martha burst into tears.

"Let's get inside," Tom said, stroking her shoulders.

Mrs. B. whispered to Tom, "Wait at the front door. I need to lock Father Melvyn's cat in his room."

"Father Melvyn has a cat?" Tom asked.

"Long story," she answered and trotted ahead of Martha and Tom. She wanted to avoid the fracas that happened the last time Barklay and Smitty got loose in the rectory. Don't need that commotion again, she thought.

33
I Just Wanted to Kill the Cat

Tom and Martha settled in the front office of the rectory. While he tried to explain what happened, Mrs. B. took Barklay and Smitty to the kitchen and gave them water.

The dogs drank greedily, parched from incessant barking. She found some scraps of meat in the refrigerator and fed them. "You poor guys. You were beside yourselves." The dogs, understanding they were safe now, sat down flat on the kitchen carpet, laid their heads on their front paws, and sighed. Mrs. B. smiled. "You wouldn't be so calm if I hadn't locked LaLa in Father Melvyn's room. She's going to be pissed when I let her out and she smells your scent in her kitchen."

Barklay and Smitty began to whimper. The sound of sobs reached her ears. "OK, boys, I'll go check." She made her way to the front office. Tom was holding Martha around the shoulders while she cried.

"This is all my fault. If he hadn't come here this wouldn't have happened to him. I want to go to the hospital now. I want to see my son."

"It's not your fault, Martha. Do not keep saying that. It's not good for you and you don't want anyone else to hear it. They will misinterpret your meaning," Tom said in a firm voice. Martha tried to pull away from her attorney, but he held her fast, his eyes pleading with Mrs. B. to help.

"I'll get you some tea. You need to calm down, Martha. Father Melvyn is with Chancey," she added, hoping to comfort the woman. Tom got Martha into one of the chairs and handed her the box of tissues from the desk. "We must wait for Detective Zayas. Then I'll take you to the hospital. Mrs. B., can you call Father Melvyn and get an update?"

***

It felt like hours before Jake Zayas showed up. Martha was calmer after having spoken to Father Melvyn twice. Mrs. B. opened the door before Jake rang. He walked into the office where Martha and Tom waited.

"Please step out and close the door, Sammi," he ordered. Without preamble, the detective showed Martha the note found on the kitchen table. "Your son confessed to killing Velma." Martha read the note:

I did not mean to kill Velma. I just wanted to kill her cat. That damned cat made you fall, and ~~she~~ Velma didn' t care. She was a mean, vindictive, horrible woman, but it was an accident. I was looking for the cat' s dish when I heard her come in. I panicked, threw the poisoned water in the tea kettle on the stove and got out the back door. I didn' t think about what might happen. I' m so sorry.

"This isn't possible," Martha cried. "My son doesn't write that way. I want to go to the hospital…NOW," she shouted. "I want to see my son."

"It's block printed, Mrs. Magswelle, so it's difficult to say who wrote it."

"I keep telling you it's Ms., not Mrs.," Martha yelled back at him. "My son didn't know anything about that stupid cat making me fall. I never told him."

Jake realized he was getting nowhere on this line. He changed direction. "Does your son live here with you? No one seems to know about him. Did you mix the poison cocktail from the plants in your greenhouse and the antifreeze we found in your pantry?"

"I don't know what you're talking about. I don't have any antifreeze," Martha shouted. "I'm telling you, he didn't write that. And I want to go to the hospital—now."

Tom Barbee spoke up. "Detective Zayas, Ms. Magswelle is obviously distraught and with good reason. Now, unless you intend to charge her with something else, she is out on bail and I assure you she isn't leaving Austin. We can continue this after she sees Chancey."

Jake ignored the lawyer's statement. "'I just wanted to kill the cat'? You don't seriously think I believe this, do you?" he said, moving into Martha's space, putting his face close to hers. "Maybe you and your son colluded to kill Velma, and then he got scared. He wanted out and tried to cover for you." Jake's tone was cold. Martha stepped back.

Tom stepped in front of her. "At this time we have nothing more to say and you are bordering on harassment. I'm taking Ms. Magswelle to the hospital." Tom Barbee took hold of Martha's arm and led her to the front door.

Perched on the corner of the desk, Jake Zayas watched them leave. The antifreeze container would be checked for prints. He was sure either or both of their prints would be found on it, but something wasn't making sense. Tucking the plastic bag holding the suicide note into his pocket he walked out of the office and turned to the front door.

"Jake." Mrs. B. placed a hand on his arm. "Can you come back later this afternoon? Father Melvyn and I need to speak to you. It's really important."

"Sammi, if it's about this case, you know I can't discuss it." "Please, come back. It's critically important and Father Melvyn needs to be here."

Jake sighed in exasperation. "Okay Sammi, I'll be back at four-thirty. This better be good."

***

Deep in her own thoughts, Mrs. B. closed the door behind her friend. Once he finds out about the will and Chancey's birthright, he might be more convinced of Martha's and Chancey's guilt, but then he'll know that there is another offspring with the same motive: money. My impression of Chancey doesn't fit with that note. Something's not right.

34
Is He Catholic?

"He's going to survive," Father Melvyn announced entering the kitchen from the back door.

"Thank God," Mrs. B. answered. "Sit. Let me get you something to eat. I made fresh coffee...I think we both need it." Mrs. B. served Father Melvyn the salad she prepared and a fresh cup of coffee. He ate, and she updated him on what had taken place at Saint Francis while he was gone.

"There were no emergencies. Father Declan covered the noon mass, and Father Joe said he'll be back early to take tonight's evening service. There are two funerals booked, one tomorrow and another for Saturday morning. Both Father Declan and Father Joe said they'll cover." She waited until he finished the salad before asking, "Were you there when Martha came?"

"Yes. I've never felt sorrier for that woman." Father Melvyn ran his fingers through his gray-shot reddish hair, took off his wire-rimmed glasses, and wiped them clean with a napkin.

"Did she say anything about a suicide note?"

"No. Tom told me while she wept piteously over Chancey."

"Detective Zayas is coming back at four thirty. What do you want to do about the journal?"

Father Melvyn thought for a moment. "After studying the will left by Charles Maxwell and the journal, which is a random collection of Velma's bitter feelings and an incomplete time line of what she *says* she did, I don't see anything in the journal that would add to Detective Zayas's case—or impede it if he doesn't know."

"And?"

"I think we give your friend Detective Zayas the will. I'm sure he'll be annoyed that we went into Velma's house and even more upset that you took papers out with the cat and didn't tell him." He paused for a moment and then made the case for not giving the investigating detective the journal.

"I suppose if he had the journal, it would fill in a lot of background information, but the will speaks to that. And I don't think exposing Father Jameson's very bad judgment contributes anything constructive to the investigation. After all, Charles Maxwell's bequests make his lack of regard for Velma very clear. The will states in detail that his two children by other women are to inherit his estate and not Velma." Mrs. B. didn't comment.

He continued. "Jake will wonder how Velma came into possession of the will. Those answers are in the journal. We'll be forcing the police to work harder to uncover motives and connections, but we can tell Jake that Velma's brother, Thomas is Jeffrey Scooterman's father and was Velma's lawyer. He can question Scooterman. I suppose if things get too out of hand, we can always give the detective the journal at a later date. - Yes? "

"Yes." Mrs. B. thought for a moment. "You don't think that Martha has the right to know about her aunt's betrayal?"

"To what end?" Father Melvyn's eyebrows arched down over his nose. "Are you advocating revenge?"

"No, of course not. I know it won't change anything, but I suspect once this is over and she and Chancey have recovered from the nightmare, Martha will let everyone know, including her aunt, that her son found her and they are reunited. Velma's notes say the aunt was paid off to help push Martha into giving her baby up for adoption. Amy Rangel might not have a good reaction and Martha won't understand."

"That's a family matter to be resolved internally. It's none of our business." Mrs. B.'s expression made Father Melvyn squirm. She wants me to do something to head off a confrontation, he thought. He stressed again, "if necessary, we will give Detective Zayas the journal later. Is Jake Zayas Catholic?" he asked.

"Yes, but not a churchgoer."

"No matter. Perhaps I can swear him to secrecy about Father Jameson."

Mrs. B.'s eyebrows lifted. "You can try, but you don't know Jake Zayas." The front doorbell buzzed. Mrs. B. glanced at her watch. She walked into the hall toward the front door. "Speak of the devil. Hopefully, we'll never have to reveal the journal," she murmured.

***

Mrs. B. led Jake to the office. Father Melvyn walked in behind them. The two men shook hands. "Sammi said there was vital information you want me to have, but no matter what you tell me, I cannot discuss this case with you."

Father Melvyn bristled at the detective's high-handed manner. "Mrs. B., why don't you explain to Detective Zayas what happened and what we found?" She and the detective both looked surprised that Father Melvyn was asking her to lead the explanation.

"Jake, we— I did something that perhaps wasn't right. I didn't intend to interfere, but at the time, we all believed Velma died of a heart attack, and—"

"Sammi, what are you trying to tell me?"

As simply as she could, Mrs. B. explained what happened the night Velma died. "I was only thinking about rescuing LaLa, Velma's cat. If you recall, I returned the key to its hiding place after you and your partner left. Later that night I went into her house and found the cat hiding under the bookcase. When I pulled her out, she was sitting on crumpled papers that slid out with her."

Father Melvyn reached across the desk and gave the detective the papers. They watched Jake examine the condition of the will. It had been smoothed out, but evidence of LaLa's treatment was clearly visible, with little pinholes from her nails as well as deep creases where she'd gotten the pages scrunched under her body.

Father Melvyn took over the explanation. "Apparently this is Charles Maxwell's will. He makes it clear that the majority of his estate is left to his two illegitimate children, one by Martha Magswelle, given up for adoption, and another, a girl. It's all in there." He didn't add that Mrs. B. also took Velma's journal, which gave a great deal of background information on everyone involved in the drama, as well as instructions from Velma's brother to "burn it," which she didn't do.

The detective pulled out a pair of reading glasses and looked through the pages. "Obviously, you both read this." His tone chilled the air.

"Yes. We did. I'm sorry, Jake. It was wrong of me to take the papers and not tell you immediately, but it was not my intent—"

"Lack of intent and ignorance are not acceptable excuses under the law. You should know that, Sammi." Turning to Father Melvyn, he asked, "And you padre? When Sammi came to you and told you what she'd done, why didn't you tell her to bring this to me immediately?" Jake waved the papers at Father Melvyn.

Icicle for icicle, Father Melvyn's tone matched Jake's. "She did not come to me after the fact. I was with her in the house." The priest and the detective stared at each other; neither blinked. The temperature in the room dropped significantly. "What you need to know, d*etective,* is that there are others with strong motives to kill Velma. There is another illegitimate child, for one, and if her nephew, Jeffrey Scooterman, knew about the bequest, that might also be a motive." Father Melvyn didn't give the detective a chance to answer. "You should also know that when Mrs. B. pulled the cat out from under the bookcase, I walked into the office and my penlight lit up the window. Someone was staring in, watching her."

Mrs. B. cleared her throat, breaking the eye-lock they had on each other.

Jake turned to her. "Did you see who it was?" he asked.

"No. I can only tell you the person had the most arresting black eyes." She paused. "Jake, my house was broken into Monday night. Nothing was taken or destroyed, but drawers were pulled out, and files and papers were strewn all over, like they were in the rectory break-in last week." Zayas took out his notepad and pen and made notes.

"Did you call it in? Did you make a report?"

"No. I knew once I did that I'd have to talk about the will. I think someone is searching for those papers. And Jake, when you came out of Velma's house last week, after her body was found, I overheard your partner comment that the house was as neat as a pin. It wasn't later that night when we went to rescue LaLa."

Jake stopped writing. He looked from Mrs. B. to Father Melvyn and threw up his hands. "Don't you have enough to do running this parish, Padre? And Sammi. I'm shocked. You know I could charge both of you." He looked from one to the other. "Well?" he asked.

Neither responded. Jake Zayas stood up. "I'll decide what to do about you later. For now I have a murder to solve." With that he left slamming the front door behind him.

35
Cry Later

Father Melvyn looked at Mrs. B.'s downcast face. She was flushed and there were tears on her cheeks. He had a moment of sympathy, but pushed it back. "Fine mess we've gotten ourselves into, yes?"

"Not we. Me. It was all my doing. I'm sorry, Father Melvyn."

"I'm sure you are, but we're in it now." Holding up one finger, he lectured. "Number one, we have information that cannot be ignored because two lives are at stake. Number two," he added a second finger, "even though we have more information than your detective friend, what we know doesn't get Martha and Chancey out of trouble, and number three," another finger went up, "we agree that for all her cantankerousness, we don't believe that Martha or her son killed Velma." He waited for a response. There was only silence. Trying humor, he added, "Mrs. B., wishing someone dead doesn't get them killed, does it? Or do you believe in voodoo?" She remained silent with her head lowered. "We have work to do. Cry later."

Her head snapped up at his cold tone. Pinpoints of anger flashed from her eyes. He was relieved. Good show, old girl, he thought. Softening his tone, he said, "Shall we get on with it?"

Mrs. B. swiped the wetness from her cheeks. In her most businesslike tone, she said, "We forgot to tell Jake that Father Declan may have seen Martha and a man walking her dogs outside of Velma's house the night she died."

Father Melvyn chuckled. "We're in trouble already; what's a little more? If we can show your detective friend that Chancey and Martha couldn't have done it, it won't matter, but we will tell Tom. He needs to know that." He stood up. "Charles Maxwell's other offspring noted in the will, what's her name?"

"Laurette Deene."

"Can we do a computer search? We know from Velma's entries that the "other one" lived in Dallas. Maybe she's still there."

The back door slammed. From the corner of his eye, Father Melvyn caught Mrs. B.'s wince. "Get Hannigan in here next week to fix that door," he said, controlling his urge to smile.

"About time," she muttered under her breath, heading for the staff office.

Father Melvyn went to the kitchen. "Joe," he said, "glad you're back. I know you're taking the mass later, but may I impose on you to cover the phones? There's some urgent work for me to do with Mrs. B. I believe she left a lovely cold dinner in the fridge for us. Help yourself."

"Sure, Melvyn." Before Father Melvyn left the kitchen, a muffled and distant meow reached them.

"Where's LaLa?" Father Melvyn asked. Footsteps ran down the hall and up the stairs. A minute later, LaLa who'd been forgotten in Father Melvyn's room, walked into the kitchen in her most regal and offended posture. She sniffed, snorted, and bristled as if to say, How could you allow me to be locked away in my own house?

Mrs. B. followed the cat into the kitchen. "Sorry, LaLa," she said, bent over and scratched the cat between her ears. "I locked her in your room, Father Melvyn. We brought Martha and her dogs back here this morning after Chancey was found unconscious. I forgot to let her out after I took Barklay and Smitty back to Martha's house." Mrs. B. left the two men in the kitchen with the cat and returned to the office.

LaLa crept around the kitchen. She caught the dogs' scent and meowed loudly, walking from one priest to the other, growling and hissing. She rubbed against Father Melvyn's leg then sat and stared him full in the eye as if to warn him: You allowed those canines in my house? And she locked me up? Make it up to me, or there will be consequences.

"Maybe we should feed you," Father Joe said.

Father Melvyn picked up the cat and stroked her head, while Father Joe went to the pantry. "My oh my, you lovely creature. What a fine kettle of fish your last owner got us into. If only you could talk."

Glancing over his shoulder to be sure Mrs. B. wasn't where she could see them he placed LaLa on the counter, in spite of instructions to keep her dishes on the floor. He and Father Joe smiled conspiratorially.

"Melvyn, let's give her an early treat," Father Joe whispered.

Once LaLa was placated and content, Father Melvyn strode into the back office. "Find anything?"

"There are seven Laurette Deenes. All but one live in other states. Our subject is a nurse in Dallas. Can't get the home number and address without paying a fee." In a flash, Father Melvyn's hand was in front of Mrs. B.'s face with his credit card sticking out between two fingers.

The old printer chugged and droned and spit out the paper with Laurette Deene's contact information. While they waited, every cliché he knew ran through his mind: in for a penny, in for a pound; jump in with both feet. For no reason, random thoughts of his boss, the bishop, came to mind. I wonder how he'll react if he gets wind of me being involved in a police investigation?

He studied Mrs. B., who was reading the information as it came off the printer. What makes people tick? Isn't that what fascinates her? What drives humans to commit monstrous acts against one another? Questions for the ages.

Pulling his focus back to Velma's murder, a thrill of anticipation traveled along his nerve endings. The prospect of proving Martha's innocence and finding out who killed Velma, if not a happy thought, was unexpectedly energizing.

36
Someone Really Wanted Her Dead

Jake walked to his desk and dumped his notebook and Charles Maxwell's will on it. His partner's desk abutted his. Marv Clingman looked up with a question in his eyes. "We've got new information," Jake said. "We like Chancey and Martha, but there are other possibilities we need to examine and eliminate."

"Okay. What new information, and where did you get it?"

"Where? Long story. Read this then let's rework what we've got," Jake answered, thrusting the will at Clingman. "I think we need to redo the trail of evidence. This is a little more complicated than we originally thought."

While Marv read the will, Jake's anger at Sammi and the priest resurfaced. He was surprised at Sammi. Now he had two amateurs involved. His annoyance caused him to take out his frustration on the eraser as he wiped the evidence board with vigorous strokes.

Starting over, he placed Velma in the middle in a circle with arrows connecting her name with others then he made a new list of what they knew.

Lab report—poison: <u>antifreeze/digitalis</u>
- ✓ Antifreeze found in Martha's garage, foxglove in her greenhouse.
- ✓ The overdose of Digitalis triggered a fatal heart attack, especially combined with the antifreeze.
- ✓ Why antifreeze? Possibly because it's super sweet and would cover any bitterness from the digitalis.
- ✓ Foxglove—*Digitalis purpurea*—is a common biennial garden plant; contains digitalis and other chemicals that affect the heart. Poisonous; may be fatal, even in small doses. Found in Magswelle's greenhouse. Quick acting—but not quick enough. Velma wandered out and died between the church and the rectory of Saint Francis de Sales.
- ✓ Martha Magswelle grows poisonous plants in her greenhouse.

Velma's home—initial search
- ✓ House neat. No sign of a break-in.
- ✓ Crime scene established after coroner's report; house was a mess. Search found residue in teakettle on stove.
- ✓ Smelled sweet; lab results supported coroner's findings: poison cocktail.

Today—new information
- ✓ Priest and Sammi said they went to rescue the cat the night after Velma's death. Velma's office ransacked.
- ✓ Breakin at Sammi's. Connected to break-in at rectory? Nothing taken. Someone searched for papers. She didn't make police report. Why? Again, nothing taken. Papers and files searched.
- ✓ Intruders—known: Father Melvyn Kronkey and Mrs. B. after Velma's death. No apparent motive. Described

someone watching from outside. Arresting black eyes staring in.

✓ Possible intruders: Martha Magswelle, Chancey (Maxwell) Johnson—Martha's illegitimate son. Chancey's eyes fit Mrs. B.'s description of the person watching her; fit description Father Joe Russo gave of the intruder at the rectory.

Main Suspects, Whereabouts, and Motives

✓ Martha Magswelle: at home/out on bail. Revenge and money; running feud with victim, reason unknown.

✓ Chancey (Maxwell) Johnson: in hospital. Possible suicide attempt. Motive: Money

Other Possible Suspects

✓ Laurette (Maxwell) Deene: money; whereabouts unknown.

✓ Jeffrey Scooterman, MD. Why use a crude method? Where was he the night Velma died? When was last time he saw her? Motive: Money

Background—incidentals

✓ Charles Maxwell: Date of death? Cause of death? Find death certificate.

✓ Suicide note left by Chancey confesses to killing Velma over the cat. Thin at best. Money is a better motive. Did he and Martha know about Charles's money and will?

Staring at the board, Jake folded his arms across his chest. "Digitalis and anti-freeze. Someone really wanted her dead," he muttered.

"Sure looks that way," Marv said, walking up behind him. "This doesn't mean Martha didn't do it, but you're right—it does complicate matters. By the way," he added, handing a paper to Jake, "seems Chancey served as a medic in the Middle East years ago. He'd have knowledge of how the body responds to digitalis. He was wounded and developed PTSD. After that he was sent back to the States, where he finished his tour as a mechanic; his prints are on the antifreeze container found in Martha's pantry."

Jake took the paper and made notes on the evidence board. "Mother and son look real good for this, and I'm not buying the cat thing."

"I agree," Marv said. "We still need more information on Velma's nephew and the other one: Deene. Scooterman is a doctor, Velma's only living relative, and has access to drugs. If he knew about Charles's will, he'd have a strong motive to kill Velma. And why was Charles's will never probated? We need answers to that before we clear him."

"Laurette Deene is Charles Maxwell's illegitimate daughter. Don't know anything about her. Marv. Let's find her and see if she's a player in this, and let's talk to Velma's current lawyer."

Jake picked up his cell phone and dialed. While he waited for an answer, he said to Clingman, "I'm trying the busybody padre and Mrs. B. I'd rather not ask Scooterman the attorney's name. " Clingman leaned against his desk and waited. "Hello, Sammi. It's Jake. Do you or the padre know Velma's lawyer's name?"

Clingman heard the voice on the other end say, "Give me a minute."

"Thanks, Sammi," Jake said a moment later and ended the call. "Okay Marv. It's Zoe Snelling."

Clingman sat at his computer and did a fast search. "Got her address and phone number.""Get a subpoena for Velma Maxwell's will."

"Will do," Marv answered as he stepped up close to the board and looked at the new notes Jake had made. "What's this?" he asked, pointing to the note about Father

Kronkey and Mrs. B. going into the house the night after Velma's death.

Jake Zayas answered. "The pastor of Saint Francis and his housekeeper decided to rescue Velma's cat. Apparently Sammi, that's Mrs. B., found the cat hidden under a bookcase. When she pulled the cat out the papers came with her. Instead of telling me immediately, they held on to the will and read it. We now have a couple of amateur sleuths who are going to get in the way; I feel it."

"We can throw a good scare into them for interfering in a murder investigation," Marv offered.

"Maybe, but not now. We have to solve this thing first. Get that warrant, Okay?"

"You got it," Marv said. "then I'll check the databases for anything on Laurette Deene."

37
Lent:

A Time for Spiritual Growth and Renewal, but First…

Mrs. B. dragged her groceries into the house. Sasha and Ziggy waited at the garage door, meowing as if to say, Where were you? It's late; we're hungry.

"I know. Let's get you fed," she said, knowing there was no sense trying to do anything else with them circling between her feet. Once they were happy, she checked her phone messages.

"Hi, Mom," Corinne said. "Just checking in. Haven't heard from you in days. No news is good news, yes?" Mrs. B. smiled. Typical Corinne message.

John's message followed. "Hi, Mom. Lisa and I thought we'd come down for Easter. Call me. Let's make plans." She dialed her son immediately. The message machine picked up.

"Got your message. I'd love to have you and Lisa

here for Easter. I'll prepare a traditional dinner, pizza rustica, too. Love to both of you. We'll talk over the weekend."

After she ate her own dinner and cleaned up, Mrs. B. made notes in her menu book for the second Friday of Lent and for the weekend. "Here we are almost at the end of the first week of Lent, and I've done nothing," she said aloud.

Lent was always a special time for her, a very personal time. She didn't shout from the rooftops or burden others with her thoughts. She didn't consider herself a madly devout person, but Lenten observations were an important part of her life, a time she looked forward to each year.

Even before her cancer surgery and successful treatment, Lent was a time for realigning perspectives, resetting what was important, and continuing spiritual growth.

She thought about the intent and meaning of Lent when Catholics are called to renew their faith through fasting, prayer, contemplation and by giving money and/or providing service to those in need.

"This was a terrible beginning," she muttered. The drama around Velma's death and the possibility that two innocent people might pay the price for a crime they didn't commit was worrisome.

Didn't Jesus say to help your fellow man in times of great need? she asked herself. "Hopefully, the Velma drama will be over soon and I can concentrate more on spirituality, but first..."

Satisfied that she had the shopping list sorted according to the foods she wanted to cook for her three charges at Saint Francis de Sales, she sat at the computer and finished the research on Laurette Deene. She and Father Melvyn ran out of time earlier in the day because the nuts and bolts of running the parish and seeing to the needs of parishioners occupied the remainder of the afternoon. She already had Laurette Deene's home address and phone number, and a little more focused searching brought her to the woman's professional information.

Laurette Deene worked at FamilyCare Best LLC. When she looked it up, she found three locations but no staff listings. Too often the Internet allowed too much information on others to be easily accessible. This website required searchers to leave contact information first. I'm not doing that, she thought. Looking at the information she already had, she wondered if she should take a chance and call it. She lifted the phone but then set it down again. These days everyone had caller ID. She'll be able to trace it back to me, Mrs. B. thought. Where can I make a phone call? Are there any public phones left in this world?

Thirty minutes later, to her complete surprise, Mrs. B. had a list of Austin's public pay phones but no idea if they were still there or in working order. She sent Father Melvyn a text:

I found sketchy work information on Deene. I was going to call her home number, but I don't want to call from my phone because of caller id. I found a list of public pay phones in the area. Tomorrow I'll go to the one on Guadalupe, at the food co-op, and try it.

Father Melvyn answered immediately: *Don't do anything without me. I'm not needed here, as you arranged for Father Declan to take the funeral mass. Pick me up at seven.*

Feeling worn out by the day's events, Mrs. B. did her nightly check of the windows and doors. She went to her office bookcase and reached for a well-worn volume and then walked to the bedroom and called her cats; they were already sitting upright on her bed waiting for her.

Thoughts about St. Francis and the murder drama brought an underlying sadness to the surface, but she was too tired to think about it. Shutting it out of her mind, she decided to take one positive step.

She opened her favorite Lenten reading, *The Life of Christ* by Bishop Fulton J. Sheen. After five pages, exhaustion and a dreamless sleep claimed her.

Friday

The First Full Week of Lent

38
No Time for Murder

The air was cold. Father Melvyn paced along the curb on Cobble Drive. A wind gust blew his hair back and ruffled his moustache. He pulled his cardigan closed and buttoned it against the damp morning air.

He sniffed. Smells like rain and it feels like rain, he thought. The forecast predicted a twenty-percent chance, but it's Central Texas. Probably won't.

Cars began turning into the driveway. He approached them on the drivers' side and bent over. Staring at the drivers, he wagged his finger and mouthed *"Gotcha!"* The kids in the passenger seats scrunched down, embarrassed. Some of the men looked annoyed, but most, especially the women, had the good grace to look sheepish. "Obviously not expecting to see me so early," he said, pleased with himself.

They were breaking the rule: no entry to the school from Cobble Drive. It was for their children's own safety. The kids arriving early for sports practice now had to cross the active driveway and cars coming in from Ferne Lane. Parents in a hurry trying to avoid the jam-up of cars risked their children's safety. "Why can't they obey the rules?" he wondered aloud. "I must make a note for Ms. Jenkins." We need to send another reminder to parents who put their convenience before their children's safety. Maybe Rafael could figure out a hedge to block the open space.

He checked his watch. Where is she? He walked back and forth on the sidewalk, steeped in reflection. His morning prayers rekindled a deeper sense of trusting all things to God, and he was prepared to do that, but also, as Saint Augustine said, "...work as if the matter was entirely in your own hands."

Of course, my ever so efficient and unpredictable Mrs. B. is the wild card, he thought. Another breeze made his neck feel unusually cold. He wasn't wearing his clergy collar. Ever conscious of appearances, he'd opted not to wear it. It draws attention, and I'll be in a car with a woman, a very feisty and unpredictable woman. "Whatever possessed you to take those papers?" he said aloud as if she was standing beside him.

Once the words were out, as if by magic, she pulled to the curb. It's uncanny he thought and jumped into the passenger seat.

"Fresh coffee," she said, pointing to the cup holder before pulling away from the curb. Glancing sideways at him she asked, "Your lips were moving when I pulled up. Talking to someone?"

"Yes. Asking our better angels to guide us and keep us out of trouble today. By the way, when we get back, please call Rafael. I want him to plant hedges to stop these parents from driving through the parking field as a shortcut to the school. It's dangerous for the children." She nodded. They drove in silence to their first pay phone destination.

The parking lot at the food co-op, where the pay phone was located, was fairly empty. Father Melvyn stayed in the car and sipped his coffee. Mrs. B. got went to the phone booth, lifted the receiver, and gave him a thumbs-up. He imagined he could hear the coins clanging as she inserted a dollar's worth of quarters and dialed. He didn't imagine the sound as the phone slammed back into its holder. She's not happy, he thought as she jogged back to the car.

"Disconnected," she said, jumping back into the driver's seat. "I have a cell number listed for her, but even if she answers, it won't tell us where she is."

"You have the name of the medical practice where she works. Maybe you could call there and see if she's working today."

"I only have the central number. I don't know if they give information about personnel in each office, but we can try." Her wristwatch read 8:20 a.m. "I hope it's not too early." Mrs. B. looked over at Father Melvyn. "Would you like to do this one?"

"No."

She laughed. "Didn't think so. How many quarters do you have?" He handed her four more. She walked back to the phone booth, and Father Melvyn peered at her face as she dialed, talked, and hung up. He couldn't tell anything by her expression. She stood in the booth for a moment before returning to the car. When she sat in the driver's seat, her eyebrows were pulled together; she looked pensive.

"Uh-oh. What did you find out?"

"It was a central receptionist. I asked at which location Laurette Deene worked and if she was there. The receptionist said she only takes care of appointments, but in this case, since the person I was asking for was listed as out on leave and they are referring all her calls to a different nurse, she didn't see any problem telling me that Deene isn't in."

"Out on leave," Father Melvyn echoed. "That could mean anything. No real help."

Mrs. B. looked sly. "No, but Deene is here in Austin." She saw the question in Father Melvyn's eyes. She waited.

"And how do you know that?" he finally asked.

"I lied. I took a chance and told the receptionist that I'm Laurette's cousin from New York, here on business. I heard about the family problem and hoped to travel with her. I said I didn't have her cell number on me and then I held my breath, waiting for her to question my identity or to say she didn't know whether a family matter was the reason for Laurette's leave or where she went. Instead, she seemed happy to talk."

"'Oh, too bad,' she said. ' Laurette left for Austin a few days ago,' but she couldn't give me Laurette's cell number. I told her it wasn't a problem." Mrs. B. looked away and mumbled, "Guess I'll have to go to confession tomorrow." She sat stone still, staring at the papers on her lap with the information on Laurette Deene.

***

Immersed in his own thoughts, Father Melvyn didn't answer her snarky remark about confession. A horn honked. The parking area was filling up. "Let's get out of here," she said. Holding his pursed lips between his thumb and forefinger, Father Melvyn was silent while they drove back to St. Francis. What are we missing? The feeling that they weren't seeing everything was bothering him. There are gaps in what we know, he thought.

When he looked up, he realized they were close to Saint Francis. "Go around to Ferne Lane. Let's see if Scooterman's car is at Velma's house. The police removed the crime scene tape."

"Do you think Scooterman will move in?"

"I don't know, but I did get a call from Zoe Snelling, Velma's lawyer. She wants Scooterman and me to meet with her on Tuesday to go over certain aspects of the will before probate."

"Why you?"

"Because Saint Francis de Sales is mentioned in the will."

Mrs. B.'s drove around to Ferne Lane and made a right. When Velma's property came into view they saw the driveway was empty. Scooterman's car wasn't there. Wanting to get back to the rectory faster, she decided to break the rule about driveway usage even with the boss in the car. She turned into the church property from Ferne Lane, cutting across to the carport behind the rectory.

"Ahem." His eyebrows were almost in his hairline. "It's clear to me that it's a must for Rafael to plant some hedges to block the drive so this doesn't continue."

She smiled. "Since you mentioned it before, I thought I'd take advantage of the shortcut while I still could." She parked in the carport and turned off the engine. "Why don't you call Jeffrey Scooterman. Tell him Velma's lawyer contacted you. He doesn't know how much we already know. Maybe he'll relax and talk to you."

"Good idea. He told me where he was staying."

While Mrs. B. put up fresh coffee, Father Melvyn called the Starlight Motel. "Dr. Jeffrey Scooterman's room please." He listened for a moment then said: "No message. Thanks."

"What happened?"

"Nothing. He's not answering, and I didn't leave a message."

"Maybe he is moving to Velma's, but he's not there yet," she said. "Do you have his cell number? "

Father Melvyn rummaged through his wallet and

pulled out Dr. Scooterman's card. The printed cell number was scratched out; there was a handwritten number on the back. He dialed, and the automated voice gave generic instructions to leave a message.

"Hello, Jeffrey. Father Melvyn here. I received a call from your aunt's attorney. She wants me to join you on Tuesday to discuss the will and probate. Why don't you come to dinner Sunday night and we can talk about it?"

As soon as he hung up, the phone rang. "Father Melvyn here," he said. "I see. I'll be there as fast as possible." Turning to Mrs. B. he said, "Mr. Mather took an unexpected turn for the worse. I'm going to the hospital." Absently, he tucked Jeffrey Scooterman's card between the phone and the wall before trotting out of the kitchen to get his collar, stole, and kit for anointing the sick.

The phone rang again. Mrs. B. answered. "Saint Francis Rectory," Her distraction ended abruptly. "No, Father Melvyn isn't here. Yes, Father Declan is. I'll get him." Mrs. B. ran to the library. Not there. His car was in the carport, so he must be upstairs. "Father Declan?" she called out from the foot of the stairs.

"Yes, Mrs. B.?"

"Emergency. You need to go to Breckenridge. Mrs. Mallory's daughter said her mom is on the brink, and she requested you."

"Tell them I'm on my way," he yelled down. Mrs. B. relayed the message and hung up.

After Father Declan left for the hospital, the phone took center stage for the remainder of the day. Between answering calls she cleaned, cooked, and took care of administrative tasks. There was no time for murder, but it wasn't far from her consciousness.

Mrs. B. opened the refrigerator and took out the container of red sauce she'd prepared earlier in the week and then took out the eggplant. She'd planned baked rigatoni with a Sicilian twist and a side salad. With practiced hands, she poured the red sauce into a large pot. While it simmered, she set another large pot of water to boil, cut the eggplant into chunks and gave them a quick fry in hot olive oil. Draining them briefly on paper towels, she then prepared the ricotta with eggs, fresh parsley, mozzarella and a pinch of sugar. When the water reached a rolling boil, she added salt and the rigatoni pasta.

When the macaroni was cooked to just pliable, she drained and transferred them to a baking dish, added the ricotta mixture and red sauce, covered the top with grated Parmesan cheese, and baked it for twenty minutes to set the eggs. While the pasta baked in the oven, she made a big salad for the priests, covered it, and put it in the fridge. She took the main course out of the oven, covered it, and left it on the stove with heating instructions: "Remember to put the eggplant on the plate <u>before</u> the pasta."

In the dining room, she arranged the sideboard and set the table. "Here's hoping tonight's dinner doesn't end like last week's," she said, thinking about the break-in that left Father Joe's face a kaleidoscope of colors.

The feeling of warm fur rubbing against her leg made her look down. LaLa sat on the floor beside her. "OK. I'll feed you too. Don't try that innocent look on me. Like I don't know they spoil you and give you all sorts of treats," she said to the cat.

If cats smiled, LaLa did, before turning toward the kitchen.

***

Jake Zayas and Marv Clingman parked. "Couldn't she meet any earlier?" Clingman asked.

"No. She was in court all day. At least she agreed to come back on a Friday afternoon. On the face of it, this shouldn't take long. A few questions, a copy of Velma's will, and we can be on our way. As for Laurette Deene, working backward, her information stops at high school in Dallas. There's no record of her birth or any other information before that—and no driver's license."

"We'll need to dig deeper," Marv said as they entered Zoe Snelling's law office.

Saturday

The First Full Week of Lent

39
This Isn't Opera

Saturday proved to be a normal day. It was filled with the usual work of a parish priest, for which Father Melvyn was grateful. One wedding, confessions, now called reconciliation and the five o'clock mass. He felt in balance again.

Dinner the night before with Declan and Joe also felt good. They focused on religious and scholarly topics instead of crime. While the three men dined and talked the new addition to the household, LaLa, sat in the doorway watching and listening.

"If she could talk, I bet she'd give Mrs. B. a full report first thing Monday morning," Father Joe said to everyone's amusement. For a few hours, at least, Father Melvyn was able to forget about Velma's murder, until Jeffrey Scooterman called and accepted the invitation to Sunday dinner at the rectory. What to do about food?

Father Melvyn called Mrs. B.'s home number several times Saturday evening. He didn't leave a message. Where could she be? He wondered if he should try her cell or if he was being a nuisance, but didn't allow the thought to stop him. After three rings her cell phone went to voice messaging. Heaving a big sigh, he waited for the beep and spoke. "Mrs. B., Father Melvyn here. I wanted to tell you that Scooterman called back. He's coming to dinner tomorrow night. May I trouble you to come in and make something special? Maybe if I wine and dine him nicely I can get him to give us more information."

After leaving the message he busied himself tweaking his homily for Sunday's masses. When he was satisfied, he fussed and mussed with laundry and minor tasks. Both Declan and Joe were out for the evening, and there was nothing interesting on TV. He hit the power button in disgust. All gratuitous violence; no mystery, no suspense, just blood, guts, and gore. Feeling peeved at the TV and Mrs. B. because she hadn't called back, he turned to LaLa.

"Well, cat. Looks like it's you and me tonight." LaLa exhibited her feline comprehension and answered with a meow. He smiled. Maybe she did understand. To think he never considered having a cat for a pet until LaLa. "Let's you and I break the rules," he whispered conspiratorially.

Thudding down the steps with LaLa behind him, he went to the pantry and took out a can of food that was reserved as a special treat. "I won't tell if you don't," he said. In a flash she was on the counter eating greedily while he stroked her silky blue-gray coat. At least the cat is responsive, he thought, still peevish because he hadn't heard from Mrs. B. After LaLa licked her dish clean, he turned off the lights and went back up to his room. He was at the top of the stairs when he heard the cat's paws. She followed him up, which he found comforting.

Preparing to say evening prayers, he lifted his breviary, closed his eyes and focused on breathing until he relaxed.

When he was ready, he opened the prayer book, paced the length of the room and began the evening's readings. His lips moved as he recited the prayers in a whisper. After completing the obligatory litanies, Father Melvyn crossed himself, set the breviary down and took up his rosary. He knelt, and offered it for the special intentions of his congregation.

Prayers complete he turned on the TV again and found a mindless comedy. He tossed, turned and thrashed, unable to relax and feel comfortable. It was after eleven when his cell phone bonged informing him of an incoming message. He reached for it and squinted at the screen. The letters appeared blurred. Giving up, he put on his glasses. *Sorry I couldn't answer sooner the opera just let out. Il Trovatore, a tale of revenge and murder. fitting, isn't it? Yes, I'll come in early tomorrow to make a nice dinner.*

"Harrumph," he muttered, "Does she think that's funny? This isn't opera this is real life and a real murder." Still irritated, he gave a one word answer: *Thanks*. Finally able to relax, he drowsed.

***

"Chancey Johnson's room, please," he said to the hospital switchboard operator.

"I'm sorry, sir, but we cannot connect to that room."

"Then I'd like to send flowers; can you tell me the room number?" The operator came back on the line and gave him the information; he thanked her and hung up.

"Got it. Now what are we going to do?"

"We need to get this right. You've screwed up enough."

40
The Constitution of a Horse

"I screwed up?" he yelled. "You promised to watch out for me. You were going to be my eyes and ears. You were going to be the one in the shadows seeing and hearing everything so we could make a foolproof plan. You were supposed to be *the watcher*. You didn't do such a good job. You haven't been able to get Maxwell's will and if you'd listened to me and used the SUX," he shouted. "she would have died in her bed."

"Yes, you told me. Shortsighted as usual. I was protecting you. If I had used the Succinylcholine someone might have noticed a needle mark on her body. You *doctor,* would have been the first suspect. Who knew the old bat had the constitution of a horse. She should never have been able to get up. I watched her. She drank two cups."

"Well, it's done, and so is our plan to get Chancey's confession in and him out of the way. I told you to light the oven too," he said.

"Yeah. You told me a lot of things. Now I'm telling you we can't let him recover."

"There's no telling if he'll regain consciousness, and even if he does his memory will be fuzzy. I don't think he'll remember what happened. In any case, he didn't see our faces."

"Do you *really* want to take that chance?" Jeffrey's partner paced the room, thinking. The stupid ass wants to depend on Chancey not recovering or remembering. I'd love to slap him. He's so deep in debt to the mob that they're going to kill him and I need to keep him healthy awhile longer. His gambling served its purpose. He had no choice but to get rid of the old bitch, but these screw-ups are getting old.

Forcing a reasonable tone, the watcher said, "We can't go anywhere right now. You can't touch the monies until you get a death certificate, and we must get Charles's will and whatever else that woman pulled out from under the bookcase, besides the damned cat...and there's no alternative—we have to do something about Chancey."

Jeffrey's face was dejected. He's pathetic, the watcher thought with disgust. I'll take care of him soon enough. "What we can't do is sit around hoping that it will work out in our favor." Pretending not to know, the watcher asked, "Where is your medical bag?"

"It's in the closet."

"Get it."

Jeffrey pulled the bag out of the closet only to have it snatched from his hands. The watcher rummaged through it, pulled out a vial, read the label, smiled, and said one word—"Good"—then sat down at the desk and made a list.

"You love making lists, don't you?" Jeffrey said.

"It's called organization." Jeffrey's partner stopped writing and looked up. "Did you follow up on the death certificate?"

"I called the funeral director again. I can get it Monday and we can move the money from her accounts," he said, holding up his hands to stop another lecture. "We'll do it your way. We'll stay in Austin and make the withdrawals over a couple of weeks."

"Fine. Monday we transfer the money. Tonight, we tie up loose ends." Consulting the list the watcher began checking off items.

"Did you open three accounts in three different banks, like I told you to?"

"Yes. I have all the paperwork here with the account numbers," Jeffrey answered.

"With the death certificate the transfers won't take more than a day. We need to be careful making withdrawals. Even spreading those over a couple of weeks might not be enough for the IRS not to notice, but by the time they piece it all together, we'll be gone. What about the probate?

"I meet with Velma's lawyer on Tuesday. She wants the pastor of Saint Francis there because Velma left something to the church. She said she'd go over everything with us."

Jeffrey paced. "I need to get the money from the savings and checking accounts and get back to Dallas ASAP. Once I've paid off my debt to Snake we can head to the Caribbean."

"Snake doesn't know where you are, does he? Please tell me you didn't mention where you were going."

"No. I didn't."

The watcher brought the conversation back to the lawyer. "Did she tell you who *else* is mentioned in Velma's will?"

"No."

"And you didn't think to ask?"

Jeffrey ignored the question. Fixated on his fear of Snake, he returned to the subject of his gambling debt.

"Maybe I should withdraw all of it, not worry about the IRS, go back to Dallas, and pay off Snake."

"Don't be stupid. If you get tagged, you'll have the IRS up your butt before Snake gets to you."

"The IRS is better than Snake."

"I don't think so. They will tie you and the estate up in knots forever. I think I'd better come with you on Monday to make sure you don't do anything stupid."

"You don't trust me?"

"I know better."

Jeffrey shrugged off the answer and changed the subject. "The police are finished with her house."

"Maybe you should move in there."

"It gives me the creeps."

This conversation is going nowhere. Looking at the list, the watcher said "Let's go."

"Where are we going?" Jeffrey asked, looking puzzled.

"First stop: Target. They're open until midnight. This is what we're going to do."

Sunday
First Day of the Second Full Week of Lent

41
"Doing the same thing over and over, the same way and expecting a different result...
A. Einstein

At 2 a.m., under the cover of darkness, two people dressed like all other medical personnel strode purposefully from the visitors' parking lot to the emergency room. They had what looked like hospital badges clipped to their V-neck scrubs and stethoscopes dangling from their front pockets. Any duty nurses or doctors within earshot would hear medical speak about a case. What no one could see was the syringe and small vial hidden in one of their uniforms.

Rather than use the elevators, they found the exit signs for the stairwells. When they exited on the second floor it was quiet. "Pay attention. This is the riskiest time," he whispered.

They glanced furtively at the room numbers and walked with feigned assurance in the direction of numbers going up. "Lucky break for us," he said, as they rounded a corner. "It's out of the nurses' station's sight line."

The door to his room was open and a nurse stood over the patient checking the IV line. Without missing a step, they passed the room and scooted down another stairwell, waited fifteen minutes, and returned the same way. All was quiet.

The steady hum and beep of machines was the only sound. A quick glance revealed a man with a shock of dark hair lying motionless in the bed. They sidled in, closed the door and checked the patient's wristband. His name and his patient number were clearly visible.

Jeffrey filled the syringe and thrust the needle into the IV port. Voices approached the door. "Doctors want another look at his blood gasses." Jeffrey yanked the syringe out of the port, grabbed his partner and ducked into the dark bathroom. Leaving the door cracked, they watched the technician enter the room, look at the sleeping patient's credentials, walk to the other side of the bed and draw blood. The process was over in a couple of minutes. As soon as the technician left they returned to the Chancey's bedside and the IV port.

"Oh shit." The watcher hissed. There was a puddle on the floor.

Jeffrey looked at the syringe he was about to reinsert. The plunger was all the way down the barrel. Realizing he made another mistake, his voice wobbled: "I must have kept the plunger depressed when I yanked the needle out."

"How much did you inject?"

"I think about half."

The watcher grabbed tissues from the side table and wiped the puddle off the floor. "You can't do anything right, can you? I have to do everything. Let's get out of here before we get caught." They elected to use the same route making their way out of the hospital through the emergency room.

In the car neither spoke. Once inside their hotel room the watcher turned on Jeffrey. "You're losing it. We need to get this finished before you come apart. I don't intend to end up in jail because of you."

"Don't look at me that way." Jeffrey turned away from the eyes boring through him like lasers. He feared what was behind those eyes.

"I'm going to take a shower. I need to think," the watcher said, stripping off the hospital scrubs.

***

Hot water steamed the bathroom. Jeffrey's partner stood under the shower spray waiting for the heat to unknot twisted back muscles and muttered: "I need to think this through without him crowding me. He's a baby, a spoiled baby and needs constant reassurances. " The sound of running water muffled the words inside the mini echo chamber of the shower stall.

"I've worked too hard to get this far, and he isn't going to ruin everything." Leaning back against the warm tiles, hot water flowed together with hot memories and rage.

Charles Maxwell was a bastard. True. I didn't know him, but I knew about him and I've analyzed him like a bug under a microscope. More like a parasite.

Then there's Velma, surrounded by sudden, fortuitous deaths. I wonder who she helped along. Charles? Charles's lawyer? Then again, maybe the Magswelle woman did Charles in. If someone killed him he deserved it. Bet no one ever thought to do an autopsy on him because Velma had everyone fooled. No matter.

"I think it was Einstein who said insanity is doing the same thing over the same way and expecting a different result. This fool is going to end up dead, and I could end up in jail. How do I get the money and get out of this mess?"

42
I Feel It in My Bones

At nine thirty on Sunday morning, Jake Zayas rang the rectory's doorbell. To his surprise, Mrs. B. answered. "Sammi, good morning. Do you work on Sundays too?"

"No. I'm here by special request." Jake looked puzzled. "Scooterman is having dinner with Father Melvyn tonight and my boss asked me to prepare it for them. He's over at the church. Come in." Leading him to the kitchen, she asked if he'd like a cup of coffee.

The detective didn't like the sound of it. It wasn't a good idea for the priest and Scooterman to spend time together. The padre and Mrs. B. were already too involved, and he still hadn't decided what to do about their behavior. "Why?" he asked.

"Why what?"

"Why is Scooterman having dinner here tonight?"

"Velma Maxwell's lawyer called Father Melvyn and asked him to meet with them on Tuesday. Apparently Saint Francis is included in the will."

"No mention of Charles Maxwell's will?"

Mrs. B. shrugged to indicate she didn't know. "Coffee?" she asked again.

"Thank you." He took the cup she handed him. It was black, just as he liked it. "I read Charles's will. Although it could muddy everything for years, it's not my problem. I have a murder to solve. Velma was poisoned, and Martha and her son still look good for it."

"I'm not a detective, Jake, and Martha Magswelle is a very difficult, thorny old-woman, but she didn't do it. I feel it in my bones."

"Feel it in your bones," he muttered. "That will look great in a police report. Maybe you should hire out as a clairvoyant."

Gritting her teeth and ignoring the remark, she asked. "Have you located the Deene woman?" Before he answered her the phone rang.

The caller's voice was loud enough to make Mrs. B. hold the phone away from her ear. "I need Father Melvyn now. He must come to the hospital. Something's happened." Garbled words were followed by uncontrollable sobs.

"Martha, take a deep breath. I can't understand you. Father is at the church. What happened?"

"It's Chancey. He's still in a coma. They called me at six thirty this morning. I've been in the hospital since. His vital signs changed, setting off machines at the nurse's station. They checked his blood and found some kind of drug was given to him...maybe by mistake. My son might die," Martha wailed.

"Please give me the phone." It wasn't a request. "Ms. Magswelle, this is Detective Zayas. Tell me what happened." He listened. "I want you to stay with your son. I'll be right there." He hung up the phone. "Sammi, I'm going to the hospital. Please tell the padre to call me. I have other questions for him about the Velma-Martha feud," Jake said and headed for the front door.

"What about the Velma-Martha feud?"

"No time to explain now. Tell the padre to call me."

"Martha asked for Father Melvyn. I'll send him to the hospital."

Jake didn't answer. I can't say he shouldn't come since Martha asked for him. I just wish Sammi and the priest would stay the hell out of this now and let me do my job, he thought, walking doggedly out of the rectory.

***

Father Melvyn walked into the hall from the passage between the church and the rectory in time to hear the front door close. "Who left?"

"That was Jake Zayas. He has more questions for you, but while we were talking, Martha called. She's at the hospital, and she's hysterical. She wants you to go. Chancey is still in a coma, and she said something muddled about them finding a drug in his system that he was not supposed to receive. They think it was administered in error.

"Do you believe that?" he asked.

"It's certainly possible," she began reasonably. "Medical people are human and…" The look on Father Melvyn's face stopped her. "No. Do you?"

"I certainly do not. I'm heading over there now."

"Shall I wait until you get back in case you're detained?"

"That would be helpful."

43
Naughty Cat

Monday morning, Mrs. B. arrived earlier than usual. Father Melvyn was sitting at the kitchen table drinking coffee. Their eyes met. He looks tired, she thought. "Thanks for the update on Chancey," she said. "Anything new?"

"No. He's still in a coma but breathing okay. Jake Zayas was at the hospital waiting for me. He asked questions again about the Martha-Velma feud. I had nothing new to add even though there's much to be said, given what Velma wrote in her journal."

"How was dinner with Scooterman last night? Learn anything?"

"No. This guy is slippery. He put on his humble face and said he was glad that his aunt made a bequest to the church, but I don't believe him. Just a front, if you ask me." Mrs. B. nodded. "You know," he continued, "LaLa did it again. What is that cat thinking?"

"What did she do?"

"When Scooterman arrived she came to the bottom of the stairs, hissed at him then turned and ran back up. I asked again if he wanted to take her. As expected, he said no, we are welcome to keep her. He's not into cats and she certainly isn't "in to him," Father Melvyn said making quote marks in the air. "The only other thing I learned is that he's not staying at Velma's. 'Too creepy,' he said."

Mrs. B. took a cup of coffee and sat down. She looked around the kitchen. There was a lot of cleaning to be done.

"I have a bad feeling about this meeting with Zoe Snelling tomorrow," Father Melvyn said.

"Maybe we should reconsider giving Jake the journal." Her suggestion was barely audible.

"What?" he asked then realized what she said. "Why? Has something else happened?"

"No, but this thing with Chancey. It might be an attempt on his life—" Before she finished her sentence, the phone rang. It was Martha. Mrs. B. handed the phone to Father Melvyn.

"I see. Yes. Okay. As soon as I can." He hung up.

"Chancey is out of the coma. She wants me to go to the hospital."

"That's good news."

"Yes. I'll go later this afternoon." With that, Father Melvyn walked out of the kitchen to begin the day's work of running the parish.

* * *

After he left, Mrs. B. began the cleanup. At least he soaked the roast pan, she thought. First, she cleaned the dining room, vacuumed, and put everything back in order. When she returned to the kitchen to tackle the sink, the phone rang. She wiped her wet hands and grabbed the receiver; it was a wrong number.

Placing the phone back in its cradle, her hand swiped the card tucked between the phone base and the wall. It fell to the floor. She picked it up and returned it to its niche. A cell number was scratched out, with a handwritten one on the back. It looked familiar, but the running water called her back to her cleanup.

She continued her domestic chores. The physical tasks to get things back in order kept her hands engaged for the remainder of the day, leaving her mind to wander elsewhere.

She was happy to hear that Chancey woke up and was recovering, but she had a nagging feeling that something terrible was about to happen. Guess I'm extra tired, she thought while repurposing the leftovers into a light dinner for the three priests.

At the sound of footsteps coming down the hall she looked up to see Father Declan followed by LaLa. The cat seemed to divide her time equally between the three men and was involved in all their comings and goings. LaLa announced their arrival with a meow.

Mrs. B. looked at the wall clock. "Oh my," she exclaimed. "Where did the time go today?" Watching Father Declan sit down and pull off his clerical collar, she added. "How are you?" she asked.

"I haven't had a chance to talk to you alone," he answered. "I did talk with Tom Barbee and told him I thought I saw Martha and a man walking her dogs in front of Velma's house the night of the murder.

"He said it didn't mean anything. Even if it was Martha walking in front of the victim's house it isn't indicative of guilt, especially since whomever it was seemed to be walking dogs, but he was glad I told him. He asked me who else knew. I told him you and Father Melvyn. His exact words were, 'I'm glad you told me and I'll question Martha about it. If there's any reason to tell the police, we will.' He asked me to keep the conversation confidential. Guess I shouldn't have told you, but since you advised me to say nothing until I spoke with him, I felt I owed it to you. Somehow, it still doesn't feel right. Am I being too much of a Boy Scout?"

"Well, I think what he said makes perfect sense. You admitted you weren't sure it was Martha. Tom is the lawyer, so I guess we take his advice. It's his job to provide Martha with the best defense possible. He has no legal obligation to help the police build a case against her, and he's bound by certain rules of confidentiality," she answered.

The back door banged. I must get Hannigan here to fix that, she thought. In walked Father Joe. "You look much better," she said.

"Yes. I decided the students wouldn't die of fright, so I've gone back to my classes. I was going stir-crazy staying home." He looked around. "Where is Father Melvyn?"

"He went to the hospital. Chancey is out of his coma and Martha wanted Father to visit."

"That's good news," Father Joe said.

"Yes, it is. I've left you a light supper. It's in the fridge. It's been a long day, and I want to get home." The two priests wished her a good evening, excused themselves, and went upstairs, leaving LaLa in the kitchen, patiently waiting for Mrs. B. to feed her. The phone rang again.

A gravelly, unfamiliar voice asked, "Who's hearing confessions today?"

"There's no reconciliation until Thursday. If it's an emergency I can get one of the priests to meet you now."

"No emergency," the voice said and hung up. Returning the phone to the cradle, Mrs. B.'s hand again brushed the card protruding from the base; it floated down.

LaLa leaped across the floor and jumped up to bat it. She began playing, tossing the business card up and pushing it on the floor between her paws in typical cat fashion.

"What have you got there?" Mrs. B. asked, reaching down for it. LaLa flicked it away with her paw. Sitting still, eyes wide open and shining, LaLa wriggled and waiting to pounce. As soon as Mrs. B. reached for the card, the cat lunged, flicked it across the kitchen, ran over, picked it up in her teeth, and dropped in at Mrs. B.'s feet. "You are being a naughty cat," Mrs. B. said, and scratched LaLa's chin . The cat, now tired of the game, turned and walked away. Mrs. B. picked up the card and placed it in her apron pocket without thinking.

"C'mon. Let's get you fed before I go home."

***

"The nosey housekeeper is still at the rectory. I have time to go through her house once more to see if Charles's will is there. Maybe I'll wait for her to get home and put a gun to her head. Where the hell are you?"

The watcher ended the call. I'd better slow down and not rush into anything. There have been too many mistakes already. I need to get back in control. Jeffrey's a fool, but I still need him. It's more important than ever to find Charles's will.

44
The Situation is Fluid

Jake sighed. He and Marv Clingman stood staring at the evidence board. "The picture is changing as we speak," he said. "Was the weak suicide note a setup? Then the mix-up with the medicine in the hospital. This is starting to smell. The bequests in Maxwell's will, establishes strong motives for others."

"Yes," Marv answered. The way he used his illegitimate kids to wound Velma complicates everything."

"Chancey is in the hospital, so he's not going anywhere, but the other, the daughter. Where is she?" Jake asked.

"We found her working at a medical practice in Dallas. I searched it and got a central receptionist for the office. Deene is a nurse. They said she took a leave of absence. Some family thing here in Austin, *and* the talky receptionist mentioned that a cousin from New York also called asking about her."

Jake scratched his head. "That's good luck for us, but I thought the personnel in doctors' offices were taught not to give out information."

"More than that," Clingman said, with a lopsided smile. "She wrote down the number from which the cousin called and gave it to me." He handed Jake a slip of paper with the phone number.

Jake's look said, "You're kidding, right?"

Clingman laughed. "She won't have that job for long."

"Let's see." Jake dialed the number. There was no answer. He was about to hang up when a male voice answered. It sounded youngish, like a teen. "Hello. I'm looking for Laurette. Is she there?" Jake said.

"Hey, man, if she is, she'd be in the parking lot. Only one or two cars here. Want me to yell for her?"

"What parking lot? Where?"

"This is the phone on Guadalupe, outside the food store."

"No. Don't bother. By the way, how old are you?"

"I'm twelve. My father is inside buying food."

"Maybe you shouldn't go answering calls on public phones, young man."

"Screw off," the boy said and hung up.

Jake Zayas looked at the phone. "That kid needs some old-fashioned discipline. Anyway, the call was made from here in Austin. If there is a *cousin* from New York, which I doubt, then she's here too. Looks like we have the other Maxwell offspring roaming around with someone else looking for her." Jake had his suspicions of the identity of the *cousin*. This is not going to end well, he thought, making notes on the evidence board.

"We need to take a good look at Scooterman," Jake said. "Does he know about Charles Maxwell's will? Think about it. Coming so close to getting all that money and then possibly losing it?"

Marv gave a derisive laugh. "That's not all he has to worry about. Wish I could be a fly on the wall when Scooterman hears the terms of Velma's will. She left everything to him, but it's in a trust to be paid out in monthly increments. Velma also left a nice bequest to Saint Francis and another to one of the bishop's charities but also in payouts, not one lump sum.

"Most interesting, Velma's will says that Jeffrey must get back with his wife and end his extramarital affairs permanently. He must also prove he's getting help with his gambling addiction. If his wife should notify the executor that Jeffrey is having another affair or is gambling again, the payments stop." Marv laughed again. "Wonder how Scooterman will take this. Darling Aunt Velma maintains control from the grave."

"Let's find Jeffrey Scooterman and have a talk." Jake said. "According to the lawyer, the bank accounts weren't included in the will. They go directly to him. Let's find out about his gambling and women problems. Once he gets his hands on the bank accounts, he'll take off. He doesn't need to be here while the will is probated."

"I'm with ya," Marv answered. The two detectives left the station. From the car, Jake called Zoe Snelling. He explained that the situation was fluid and he reminded her not to tell Scooterman they had a copy of Velma's will.

"Should I go ahead with the probate?"

"Yes," Jake said. "If there's any reason to stop it, we'll be in touch."

Marv said, "What do the major players in this little drama know about Charles's will and about each other? Is Laurette involved? She and Chancey are both threats to

Jeffrey's claim. Could Dr. Scooterman be gunning for Chancey and Deene?"

Jake dialed the Starlight Motel. The desk clerk rang Scooterman's room. No answer. Jake didn't leave a message. He tried Scooterman's cell phone. No answer. He was about to leave a message when Clingman interrupted him.

"Check your incoming." Jake disconnected his call, punched his phone screen and stared at the information. A Dallas snitch said that Snake Williams is looking for a doctor supplying drugs to him. Apparently this guy is deep in debt.

"Could be someone else," Jake said.

"Coincidence again? " Marv asked.

Jake didn't answer. He shrugged, but his face said he wasn't really buying it.

"I think we'd better find the good doctor, fast," Marv said.

Jake called the cell phone again. "Dr. Scooterman, important new information has just come to our attention, and we'd like to speak to you. Please call as soon as you hear this."

"I hate to say this, Jake, but maybe we should try the padre and the housekeeper. Think they'd know where he is?"

Jake blew out an expletive. He dialed the rectory and put it on speaker. "Saint Francis Rectory, Father Declan speaking. How may I help you?" Jake identified himself and asked for Father Kronkey. The young assistant told him the pastor was not available. Jake told him there was no message; then he called his wife.

"Terri, do you have Sammi's cell phone number handy? I need to ask her a couple of questions." He knew Terri wouldn't ask why. Jake called Sammi's cell. No answer.

Another expletive. "These two have been under my feet since Velma's death. Now that I want them, they're nowhere to be found. Let's go over to the motel. Maybe Scooterman is there but not answering."

At the Starlight Motel, they showed their badges to the desk clerk. He assured them that Dr. Scooterman left several hours earlier and hadn't returned.

Jake took a chance. "Is Dr. Scooterman staying here alone?"

"No. There's a woman with him. He signed in with his name and 'guest.'"

"Can you describe her?"

The desk clerk thought a moment. "Pretty, but not exceptional. Forty, maybe fifty. Medium height, about five-five. Black hair, fair complexion. Slim. That's about it." The detectives thanked him and turned to leave. "Just one thing," the clerk added.

"Yes?" Marv asked.

"She has the most startling eyes I've ever seen."

"In what way?" Jake asked.

The desk clerk looked troubled. "I'm not quite sure how to describe them."

"Black by any chance?" Marv asked.

"Maybe. They are dark. Intense, disconcerting, maybe even scary are the words I'd use."

Jake and Marv looked at each other, thanked the desk clerk, and told him not to mention their visit to Dr. Scooterman. They didn't speak on the way back to the station.

"This is getting weird," Marv said. "We've met Chancey Johnson and agree that he has arresting eyes, pardon the pun, and he doesn't look like his mother. Martha's eyes are light.

"That was also the description given by Sammi and Father Melvyn about the person staring in Velma's window the night they rescued the cat, and by the other priest Father Russo, when he described the intruder who broke into the rectory. None of them could say if it was a man or a woman. Are we connecting the dots by connecting eyes?" Jack asked.

"Who haven't we seen or have a picture of?" Marv asked.

"We don't have pictures of either Deene or Charles Maxwell. There were no pictures of him around Velma's house." Jake continued. "Charles Maxwell was well-connected in Austin. There must be a newspaper picture of him somewhere. Let's find one, and let's get a copy of Laurette Deene's license. That will have her picture," Jake said.

"I've already combed the Texas databases. There is no Laurette Deene," Marv told him.

"We need to expand the search. I'm going to call my wife and tell her not to wait up for me. I feel like if we don't get answers tonight, someone else might get killed. Let's drive past Velma's and see if the good doctor is there. We can go across to Saint Francis and speak to the pastor too before we go back to central."

***

While they waited for someone to answer the door at Saint Francis, the detectives looked across Ferne Lane. They could see Velma's house clearly from the front porch, even in the fading daylight. The rectory door opened. It wasn't Father Kronkey.

"I need to speak with the pastor," Jake said, holding up his badge as explanation.

"Father Melvyn is at the hospital. Can I help?"

"You are?"

"I'm Father Declan Ryan."

"We're investigating Velma Maxwell's murder. You wouldn't know if there was anyone parked in Velma's driveway today, would you?" Jake asked, pointing across the street.

"In fact, there was a car parked there for a couple of hours." The priest folded his arms across his chest and looked across Ferne Lane.

"What kind of car?" Marv Clingman asked.

"I don't know. A sedan, dark, probably black. It left maybe half-an-hour ago."

"Did you see the driver? Was it a man or a woman?"

"No. I didn't see anyone. I just noticed a car parked there."

"Thank you," Jake said. "When Father Kronkey gets back, or if you hear from him, tell him to call me. It's very important." Jake handed Father Declan a card.

The detectives left the rectory, picked up sandwiches and returned to the station. It was going to be a late night.

45
Monster

"I don't care what you told the nosey priest. You have every right to be in that house. We're going over there. One more thorough search. We need that will."

"What if it's not there?"

"It probably isn't, but we need to be sure. If it's not there then that damned nosey housekeeper has it or knows where it is. What right did she have going into your aunt's house?"

"At dinner last night, Father Melvyn told me they went to rescue the cat. He asked me again if I wanted to take her. Of course I don't, but I thought it best to show some concern, even if I do hate that creature. It would have been better had Martha killed it like she threatened."

"Well, she didn't. You're set to inherit everything, but if Charles's will comes to light all is lost. We don't know if Charles communicated with Chancey. If he survives and it turns out he knows about it, things could be tied up in court for years. We've got to get it. The housekeeper is the key." Jeffrey's face became ashen. "Don't worry. I won't ask you to do anything. I'll take care of it. We wouldn't be in this predicament if you'd kept your nerve and hadn't messed up the Diazapam," she spat the words and marched into the bathroom.

Jeffrey jumped at the sound of the door banging shut. He sat on in the one chair in the room and asked himself how he ever got involved with this woman, but he knew how. The memories were vivid.

***

They'd met at the racetrack. It was great. He'd win some and lose some, but she never criticized. She was fun to be with and loved to play the horses, even though she didn't have much money.

Fun at the track became even more fun in the sack and the sex was over the top. He called her his Foxy Lady. Just the memory of that first night made him hot. He'd even asked if she was ever a working girl. She'd laughed.

A few weeks after the red-hot sex started he mentioned that his nurse gave notice. She jumped on it. "I'm a registered nurse. We'll keep it strictly professional. I'll send you my résumé. Hire me if you think I'd be best for the job. If not, no hard feelings."

The thought of having her nearby throughout the day was intoxicating and he hired her. That was the first time he'd allowed any of his women access to his life, and he learned within a few months the magnitude of this mistake.

She was competent and a good nurse, medically speaking. She was also bossy, letting the rest of the staff know she had an inside track with him; they disliked her. He thought about firing her but knew he couldn't.

It was too late. He should have listened to his aunt; her words rang in his head.

"You are a doctor, a man of stature and respect. You must comport yourself appropriately, which he didn't, and you must have the *right* spouse;" on that he agreed.

He knew from day one that he'd married for position and connections. Ginny was exactly the right spouse... to the outside world. He liked her, and she did have good qualities. Ginny was an asset to his position but just okay in bed. They'd produced children after which he felt entitled to something more exciting.

He smiled remembering his many women. He loved variety and he sampled everything. The affairs were short-lived. He had no interest in leaving Ginny and he didn't think she ever knew of his extracurricular activities, until this one.

Nights in bed with his Foxy Lady couldn't be matched. He took more chances and spent more nights out. At one point he was ready to leave his wife for this one.

Ginny found out about the affair and called Velma.

When Jeffrey told his aunt that his private life was none of her business, she dropped the bomb on him.

"You know Charles left a will. Maybe your father told you that he left everything to his two illegitimate brats, and you'll be cut out if it's ever revealed. Your father told me to burn it, but I didn't."

"Why?" he asked her.

Velma smiled at his shock. It wasn't a pleasant smile, more like a snake pulling its lips back, exposing its fangs.

"Because you never know when something like this can be useful." She then told him that if he didn't stop the affairs, fire the "current whore, return to his wife, and stop gambling," she was going to let the world know about Charles's betrayal and allow his children to inherit.

Forced to choose between the life he'd built and keeping his sex queen, he was on the verge of breaking off the affair. I should have kept my mouth shut and found a way to end it, he recalled, but she already had her fangs in my practice. Instead, he made his second major mistake: he told her about his aunt's threat. Everything changed.

She laughed. "That old witch will never let the world know what Charles did and be humiliated after all these years of covering it up. You're like a puppet dancing on her strings. Get rid of her."

"What do you mean, 'get rid of her'? What do you know about my aunt?" That's when she sprung her trap.

Steam billowing out of the bathroom when the door opened pulled him back to the present. Nude, she walked across the room; he sat in the chair and watched her. The muscles in her taut body undulated like ocean waves as she moved around the bedroom. His body responded. He was still a captive of her curvaceous physique and the promise of her sex skills, but as he stared at the back of her head he became aware of something else. She's a monster. He almost said the words out loud. I've got to get her out of my life, even if I never have that kind of sex again, he resolved.

Fully dressed, she demanded "Why are you sitting there? Turn off that TV. Let's go."

46
The Dead Can't Hurt You

Jeffrey used the key to his aunt's front door. Once inside she took charge of the search. "Go through her bedroom, every inch of it. Drawers, closets, under her pillows, under her mattress. Check the bathroom too. I'm going to rip the office apart."

Two hours later, empty-handed, Jeffrey went to the office. She had pulled the drapes closed and turned on the overhead light. Papers and books were strewn all over the floor. She was sitting in the middle of a stack of journals.

"Seems your aunt loved to write. "Listen to this," she said and opened a journal. "'You've humiliated me for the last time. Sleep well, my darling. You look like an angel, so peaceful, but under that thick black hair there are horns. Are you sleeping well, my darling Charles, or have you descended to the lowest rung in hell? No matter. One day I'll meet you there, but not yet.'

"Nice lady, your aunt and very organized. These journal dates are marked in chronological order up to last year, and the last entry in this one says it's continued in January. Guess what, Jeffrey, that would be the latest journal, and I can't find it." Stacking them, she ordered, "Get a shopping bag. We're taking them. Can't read them all now, but there's too much information to leave behind for anyone else to find."

Three hours after going in, they left Velma's fastidious house a mess and came out with her journals, except for the last one, but not Charles's will. "You know, you can stay here," she said again.

"I told you, I don't want to."

"Oh hell, Jeffrey. You're losing it. The dead can't hurt you—" she finished the sentence in her head, but I can.

When they arrived at the motel, she let him out of the car. "I'm going for a ride. I need to think."

***

Allowing her mind to shut down, she drove in and out of unfamiliar streets without seeing. Unaware of dusk turning to night, she drove up William Cannon, past Mopac, took a right on Brodie, a right on Convict Hill, and then wound her way in and out of another community she didn't recognize.

Pulling alongside a school on a quiet street, she turned off the engine and headlights, leaned her head back, and closed her eyes. Maybe I should cut my losses, leave Texas, and start over somewhere else, she thought. I've done it before. She smiled, knowing full well how resourceful she was. Hell, her driver's license wasn't even in her own name.

She'd learned a lot of lessons the hard way and knew

how to keep several identities current and separate. She'd started young, to her mother's great distress. Poor Mom, she thought.

At fourteen, I was already a handful: smoking, drinking, and screwing with that dago, Danny. God, he was gorgeous, she remembered. One night she and Danny broke into a small liquor store. When the owner refused to open the register they beat him bloody. Somehow the old man reached the silent alarm button under the counter and the police were there in no time. After that unfortunate brush with the law, she ended up in a juvenile detention facility for a year. What a trip that was. The memories were sharp as if it all happened yesterday.

Spoiled-brat Jeffrey wonders where I learned the things I know about sex. Ha! Guess he never read anything about rape and sex in juvenile detention centers.

On her first day home, her mother showed her a picture of a gorgeous man with arresting black eyes. "He is your father," she said. That's the day Laurette learned the truth.

Her mother worked as an emergency room nurse in a Virginia hospital. She met him when he came in for a case of food poisoning. He said he was in Virginia on business. He returned to Virginia often and he wined and dined her. She fell in love. The affair lasted for almost a year until she got pregnant. That's when he told her that he was married. He offered to pay for an abortion, but she refused. Then her charming father said he'd give her financial support but could never leave his wife. "My momma was a proud woman," Laurette whispered, although alone in her car.

Her mother told him to get lost, moved out of the

apartment and got another job in a different hospital, so he couldn't find her. Obviously, he didn't try too hard, Laurette thought, cynically.

"I told you he was dead because I thought I could raise you without him," her mother told her. "That was a mistake. Maybe I should have kept him involved; maybe it would have been better for you. "When you ended up in trouble, I realized I couldn't handle you alone."

"What's his name?" Laurette asked, interrupting her mother's story.

"His name *was* Charles Maxwell. When I tried to contact him I hit a brick wall: his wife, Velma. He died of a heart attack a few months later." Laurette remembered how her mother cried telling the story. "If it was a mistake, I'm sorry. Now you must get a grip on your life, my darling. I won't be around forever."

Laurette continued with her timeline of events. We moved from Virginia and Mom got her Texas nurse's license. To make a fresh start she legally changed my name from Smillen to Deene, and I did change my ways, at least on the surface. No harm in having a good profession to cover everything else, she thought. My high school grades were good, and I got into nursing school without any trouble. Mom was proud of me.

It still made Laurette sad to remember that her mother had a tough life and a tough death. At least she had the consolation of knowing I got my shit together. I did love her. Laurette felt the pain of loss.

After she died, Laurette was cleaning out her mother's things and found a letter from her father, Charles Maxwell. Apparently, he did find her. The letter said that Laurette, along with an unnamed half-brother, would inherit his estate. Her mother never showed it to her, but she didn't destroy it either.

Laurette thought about Velma, who also didn't destroy Charles's will. "What's with these women? What kind of power did Charles Maxwell have over them?"

After finding the letter, Laurette looked Velma up and tried to talk to her. I showed her the letter, but she threw me out. The memory evoked shame and fury.

Laurette remembered how Velma spoke to her the one and only time they'd met. I tried to be nice, to understand her position, but she was a nasty, vindictive bitch. She called my mother a whore and said I'd probably turn out like that too. This from a woman who'd sold her self-respect. "A whore of another stripe," Laurette mumbled, as she sat in the dark car reminiscing.

"You should have been nicer to me, Velma. It would have been better for you and your nephew." A smile spread across her face. After her one degrading meeting with Velma, she'd done her research and found Velma's nephew.

Jeffrey is a good doctor, but he doesn't have the nerve for life on the edge, she thought. "The fool should have been one of those uptight, law-abiding, bible-beating citizens. He could have joined the hypocrites' club. Noses in the air, self-congratulatory elitists: church on Sunday, mistresses on Monday and Wednesday, golf on Friday and Saturday. He would have had a good life if he hadn't gotten involved with gambling and horses...and me."

Laurette giggled, remembering how she found Jeffrey Scooterman and worked him. I followed him to the track, made conversation, and finally seduced him. She smiled again, satisfied with her achievements. Maybe I should leave nursing and become a PI, she mused. If Snake and his mob kill him he'll die happy after what we did in bed, but not yet. The old rage engulfed her.

You got yours, Velma, she thought. Your nephew is next.

"Cut my losses and go? No way. I'm not going anywhere. I've worked too hard and I don't intend to lose that money, even if it means dragging deadweight Jeffrey along." Decision made, she started the car and drove back to the motel.

***

Alone in the hotel room, Jeffrey was relieved that Laurette hadn't come in with him. He sat on the bed and held his head. This wasn't going the way they'd planned. They'd completed the money transfers and he intended to start withdrawing cash after his meeting with Snelling. He remembered what Laurette said: "Don't withdraw more than nine thousand dollars each time, not from the same bank and not on the same day."

He no longer cared what she said. He needed to get that cash and get back to Dallas. He'd worry about the IRS later. If Snake found him and he didn't have the money, he knew he'd be dead. Jeffrey hadn't told Snake where he was going, but he did tell him that he'd be out of town and Snake had his ways. Jeffrey ran his fingers through his hair.

His aunt was right. He should have broken off this affair months ago. The memory of the night he told Laurette about his aunt's ultimatum haunted him.

"What do I know about your aunt?" she'd snarled. "*I am Charles Maxwell's daughter*," she said. "I contacted your aunt after my mother died. I tried to be reasonable. I even showing her the letter Charles sent to my mother, which she kept hidden from me. Your aunt wasn't having any of it."

"You never told me...You hid this from me."

"Why tell you? We were having fun, right? We still are." Laurette changed the subject that night by pulling him down on the bed.

To drive the point home, a few days later she showed him Charles's letter explaining that he was splitting his estate between her and an unnamed half-brother. After that, she never brought up the subject again.

Over the following months his gambling got heavier, his losses greater and the sex hotter. She had him spinning. He forgot about everything other than nights with his sex queen. When it became obvious that his gambling had him in deep, it was Laurette who devised the plan to gain time.

"Prescription drugs are the in thing," she'd said. "Tell Snake you can supply him; buy some time."

I should have refused, but she really scared me, he psychologically excused himself.

"You're in trouble, my dear, and your trouble's name is Snake. He leads the Red Aces. Do you know how they kill people? It ain't pretty or fast. There's only one way out."

Jeffrey squirmed, remembering his last meeting with Snake on a deserted road a few weeks earlier. He still owed the money, but Snake was happy to keep him on the hook for the drugs and his demands were getting bigger every month.

"You can pay off the gambling debt, but do you really think he'll let you off the hook?" Laurette said. "Why do you think he gave you a month to come up with the money? Now you are a major drug supplier," she said. "Don't be stupid. The only answer is to keep Snake appeased. We knock off your aunt you get the money from the accounts to pay him. Once the estate is settled, we disappear. Why do you think I helped you? I can end up in jail too, or worse—dead." Her words played over in his mind, like a CD stuck on one track.

She's out of control. Killing my old bitch of an aunt who tried to control my life was one thing, then Chancey, but who else will be on her hit list? Like a lightning bolt, it struck him. *Maybe me*. That realization was like a punch in the stomach; he ran to the bathroom and threw up.

I need to find that letter, he thought desperately. Hoping she'd brought it with her, Jeffrey decided to search her stuff before she came back. Knowing she was a neat freak, he was careful to replace everything as he found it.

If Charles's will turns up Chancey will be entitled to a share of everything. If we find it and destroyed it like Velma should have done years ago, the letter is Laurette's insurance that I will split everything with her. If I get hold of the letter Laurette will have no power over me after we destroy Charles's will. If I can't find it I guess I could challenge the authenticity of it, but it would take time, something I don't have, as well as a lot of money. His mind returned to Snake.

There was the problem of supplying Snake with drugs. I neeed to pay Snake and disappear. Who would Laurette complain to, the police? It was her idea to volunteer the drugs to Snake. She was as guilty as he was. She couldn't complain to Snake. She'd end up dead.

He wondered again how he allowed himself to fall under her spell. She's driving me to do things I never thought I was capable of. It's those eyes, he thought.

Laurette's resemblance to her father was uncanny, except for the malevolence sitting behind her pupils. I should have made the connection long ago.

Jeffrey remembered his uncle Charles, whose black eyes were startling, but always seemed to be laughing, like he knew a secret. "Yeah. He knew lots of secrets," Jeffrey muttered while he searched.

He knew it wasn't just her eyes that still made his heart race. Sex with her was like nothing he'd ever experienced. *Maybe I should go to a sex clinic,* he thought as he continued to hunt for the letter.

He opened drawers and ran his hands over lingerie and pajamas, feeling and listening for the crinkle of paper. Nothing. Before he tackled the desk, he went to the door and peered through the peephole lens that expanded the visual field into the hallway. No one. He didn't know when she'd be back. "Hurry," he whispered as if the spoken word could make him move faster.

His hands flipped through random notes and lists of things to do. "Anal-retentive, aren't you?" he mumbled. The page header read: Players.

- Mrs. B.—nosey housekeeper
- Priests—don't know their names: dumb and dumber
- Pastor Kronkey—naive
- Martha—chump
- Chancey—half-brother, not the brightest bulb in the box
- JS—my ticket

Jeffrey went through every drawer. The letter wasn't there. "I don't know what to do." Tears rolled down his face. *Buck up,* his internal voice ordered. *She can't come in here and find you crying.* "There's got to be a way," he repeated, heading to the shower.

***

Calmer and more determined, Laurette walked into the hotel room expecting Jeffrey to be asleep. Instead, he sat on the bed, channel surfing. "Still up? I thought you'd be sleeping by now. Having fun? Found any good porn?"

"Don't be cute." She noted the gruffness in his tone. "Any ideas?" he asked.

"I'm thinking."

"You don't have much time to think, Laurette. I meet with the lawyer tomorrow morning. After that I want to make the withdrawals and get back to Dallas." Laurette was staring at her cell phone. "Did you hear me?"

"Yes. I heard you. Here's a new wrinkle," she said. "Jean, the central receptionist just thought to send me a text. It says a woman called *the other day* asking if I was working. The caller said she was a relative from New York. She told the woman that I was in Austin for a family emergency. Jean has the IQ of a gnat and she talks too much. Fire her when we get back to Dallas."

"Why is that a problem?" Jeffrey asked.

"The problem is I don't have any cousins, and I don't know anyone in New York."

"Maybe it was a mistake."

Laurette rolled her eyes. "Maybe it's a coincidence," he added.

"Don't try my patience. You know I don't believe in coincidence."

"It does happen." She didn't answer. Her look was fierce. Jeffrey felt weak, exposed. He withered under her glare. No matter what he said, it would be wrong. He shrugged and remained silent.

The expression on her face made Jeffrey's skin crawl as if a poisonous insect was creeping up his arm. He didn't want to know what she was thinking. If it wasn't for the money I owe Snake, I'd skip out right now, he thought. He sat like a statue and watched Laurette take the gun out of the room safe, check the safety and shove it in her sweater pocket. Without another word, she left the room.

47
Working Together

Filled with a new resolve, but without a set plan, Laurette left the motel. A woman called asking for me? Who? Martha? No. She doesn't have the smarts or the nerve. Jeffrey said the detectives on his aunt's case were men. She parked across from Mrs. B.'s house feeling certain that it was the housekeeper who called the office looking for her.

Tapping her fingers on the steering wheel, Laurette fought to control the white-hot anger she felt toward this meddlesome woman who screwed up her plans. I should go in there, hold the gun to her head, and force her to tell me where the will is, she thought.

Killing her headlights, she realized she was parked under a street lamp. Laurette backed the car down the street until she was out of the light. She got out and pressed the door shut without making a sound. First checking that the gun was secure in her pocket she zipped her sweater and pulled the hood up to cover as much of her face as possible without obstructing her vision.

Moving in shadows, she crossed to Mrs. B.'s house, walked across the front grass, slid through the side gate, and walked around to the yard, which sloped down. At the foot of the steps leading to the deck she stopped and looked around. No signs of life. Not even a little wild rabbit hopping across the garden. The only partial light came from a fixture beside the back door. Her rubber-soled shoes were silent on the steps, but on the deck her foot hit a chair leg. It scraped. In the silence of night, it sounded like a rumble of thunder.

Flattening herself against the natural stone of the house adjacent to the door, she waited with her hand on the revolver, ready to act fast. Standing motionless she heard only one sound: her own shallow breathing. She listened; she watched. Nothing moved outside and no lights went on inside.

***

Her eyes snapped open. A rumble penetrated her sleep. Was that thunder? She lay still and listened to the usual creaks and groans of the house: the air kicked on and flowed through the vents, a crack of ice as cubes fell into the ice bin in the freezer. I should disconnect that damned thing, she thought. Her heart raced. She suddenly felt hot under the sheet. Sasha and Ziggy sat upright.

In the darkness, her hearing intensified; there was no sound. Reason said an animal probably wandered onto the deck. She turned over, sat up and put her feet on the floor. She listened. Nothing. She sat with one hand over her heart, as if to hold the blood pumping muscle in place. The wood floor under her feet was cool. Barefoot, she tiptoed to the window across from her bed.

The light outside the kitchen door wasn't bright, but it allowed her to see across the yard. Without touching the blinds she narrowed her eyes and peered through the slats. Nothing. Don't turn on any lights, her internal voice said. The bedroom remained shrouded in darkness. The red light on the panel told her the alarm was activated and secure. Moving back to the bed she grabbed the throw on the tufted foot bench, wrapped it around her shivering arms, and walked out of the bedroom.

The fixture outside the house sent shafts of mellow light through the front door glass, helping her walk from room to room without colliding with furniture. She placed her feet with care. She didn't need a "pee break" on top of everything else. That's what friends called their broken pinky toes, suffered by going to the bathroom in the middle of the night, in the dark.

***

Instinct kicked in. This isn't a good idea, Laurette realized. She descended the steps, slinked along the wall of the house beneath the windows, and crept back to her car, relieved that she'd changed her mind. Even if she told me where to find it I couldn't kill her until I got hold of it. That would be more complicated. I'd better get back to the motel. I feel as if a noose is tightening around my neck. I don't like it. I'm smarter than this.

Think, she ordered herself. On the short drive back, another idea formulated in her head.

***

On silent feet, Mrs. B. moved to the front of the house. Lifting one slat a fraction of an inch she squinted to look outside. The dark form of a car with its headlights out pulled away from the opposite curb. All she could tell was that it was a sedan. The cold shiver gave way to a flush, making her face hot. She was angry. "This ends tomorrow," she said aloud. She stood there for a moment. "No sense going back to bed. I'll never sleep."

For the second time, she checked that the doors and windows were secure in spite of the red light on the alarm panel telling her all was well. Her jittery nerves annoyed her. Walking back into the bedroom, she peered out the window once more. There was nothing to see. She turned on the bedroom light and looked at the urn with John's ashes. "This isn't me," she said, picking it up. She sat on the edge of the bed and hugged her husband's ashes to her. She imagined him standing beside her. She squeezed her eyes shut and felt him there.

"It's okay, Sammi. You're safe. Calm down."

She saw his face, his bright eyes filled with love...and a hint of amusement. His smile brought tears to her eyes. She didn't want to move.

A soft murmur to her left and a cold nose against her cheek made her open her eyes. Ziggy and Sasha sat beside her giving comfort in their feline ways. She reached over and scratched her two companions' heads. "Okay." Placing the urn back on the bureau, she went to the kitchen, followed by her cats. "Too early for food, you guys. Let's see what we can turn up." The business card she'd left on the table earlier was in the same place.

She'd found it in the pocket of her apron when she come home from work. Good thing it's still chilly out and I had on my long sweater, she thought. I must have looked like an idiot in the supermarket. At home, she ran her hands over both pockets of the apron, looking for stray tissues that make a mess in the dryer. Instead, she found Jeffrey Scooterman's card with a handwritten number.

Picking it up again, she turned it back and forth, noting the printed number crossed out on the front of the card and a handwritten one on the back. When she'd texted Father Melvyn earlier to let him know she'd inadvertently taken it, she asked about the number. He answered that it was the one Scooterman told him to use.

He signed off with question: *Tomorrow we meet with the lawyer. What should we do about Velma's journal and Charles's will?* She didn't have an answer for him then, and she didn't have one now.

She was wired. Her nerves were raw from the sound that had disturbed her sleep and the car she saw pulling away with its lights out. Her heart was still pounding. Over a cup of tea, she sat and looked at the scattered papers spread over the kitchen table. "I'm missing something." She decided to start again with the medical practices.

FamilyCare Best LLC, where Laurette Deene worked had three locations in the Dallas area. *Maybe, if I access the individual offices I'd get some personnel information.* The central operator's words echoed—*Laurette Deene took a leave of absence*—but she hadn't mentioned in which office Deene worked. Mrs. B. realized she forgot to mention that to Jake. He probably knew already, but she resolved to call him in the morning.

"Let's take these separately," she whispered as if someone was there to hear her. "FamilyCare Best LLC, Frisco, Texas." The web page came up for that location, giving the address, direct phone number, and a list of doctors. Nothing helpful. Her thoughts wandered to friends who'd lived there for years before moving to the Carolinas. *I must pay them a visit soon,* she thought. *It's been too long.*

Next, she googled the Dallas location. The doctors' names were listed alphabetically. This office separated the staff by individual teams working for each doctor. Scanning the information without reading closely, her fingers moved faster on the keyboard than her brain registered what was on the screen. She clicked off just as she reached the last name on the list. "What?" she pulled up the Dallas location again. The last doctor on the list was Jeffrey Scooterman, with direct phone numbers to his staff.

The team included administrative assistant Andrea Crane, physician's assistant Jane Wells and nurse Laurette Deene. Mrs. B. covered her mouth. "Oh my God!" She rose from her chair and paced back and forth under the watchful eyes of Ziggy and Sasha as new questions bubbled to the surface.

Did Jeffrey Scooterman know who Laurette was? He couldn't possibly. Did Velma know? Velma's last entry mentioned hiring a detective to get information on Jeffrey's affair. Did she write down the name of the woman? Father Melvyn had the journal. "Damn it." She tried to remember. Her brain refused to retrieve the information. The oven clock read 2:20 a.m. "Can't call him now. Okay. Let's be logical and thorough." She boiled more water, took another cup of tea then forced herself to sit and read Scooterman's bio.

He was listed as a doctor of internal medicine, along with his years in practice and the schools he'd attended. She noticed he had published several articles on eldercare but nothing over the last couple of years. His professional rating was good. The only complaint was that he was slow getting back to patients.

Knowing an automated service would answer, and not expecting to learn anything useful, she dialed Jeffrey's number at the Dallas office anyway. The disembodied mechanical voice spoke.

"You have reached Dr. Jeffrey Scooterman's line at FamilyCare Best of Dallas. If this is a medical emergency, hang up and call nine-one-one. If you need to speak to the answering service, please press one now. To leave a message for Jane, press two; for Amy, press three; and for Laurette, press four. All others please leave a message at the tone or call back during regular business hours." As expected, there was nothing extraordinary there. She hung up.

Does Scooterman know who Laurette is? A worse thought took her breath away. It was like a gut punch. Are they in this together? No! He wouldn't.

Unable to be still, she resumed pacing, holding her head with both hands as if it might crack apart if she let go.

According to Charles's will, Laurette was to split the Maxwell estate with Chancey. Jake knew that and thought it made Martha and Chancey stronger suspects. Did he believe the suicide note supposedly left by Chancey? Did he think the dose of medication given to Chancey in the hospital was an accident?

If Deene and Scooterman were in this together, they'd have at least as strong a motive as Martha and her son, and they'd have a lot more medical knowledge. Maybe Chancey's attempted suicide really was attempted murder.

Velma wrote in her journal that Jeffrey was having another affair, but Mrs. B. couldn't remember if Velma had made any mention of a specific woman. She only wrote that she was about to hire a P.I. to spy on him. Jeffrey was deep in debt for gambling, and Velma had threatened to reveal Charles's will, which would cost Jeffrey his inheritance.

Her eyes went to her own notes on Laurette Deene. She looked at the cell phone number. She picked up the business card Scooterman had given Father Melvyn with the handwritten number on it. "It's Deene's number," she exclaimed. "He's using her phone. Why?"

Her heart sank. "Oh my God. They *are* in this together. They killed Velma and tried to kill Chancey. One of them is the intruder who broke into the rectory and my house. It must be Deene. Jeffrey Scooterman has beady little blue eyes. They could never be mistaken for black, startling and creepy.

She made notes: Jeffrey is using Laurette's cell phone. Why? Deene works for Scooterman; they are in it together. We need to give Jake the journal. Ask him not to reveal Father Jameson's involvement with Velma's sordid scheme. She looked at the time again and added a note: Call Jake and Father Melvyn at seven thirty. Tell Jake to meet me and Father Melvyn at the rectory.

She reached for two aspirin to ward off the headache gripping the base of her skull. Sleep would not be possible now, but she'd take the aspirin, which was the strongest medication she allowed herself. *No sense doping the senses* was her motto.

Returning to her bed she allowed the pills to ease the headache. Tossing and turning, wishing it was daylight, she felt certain she was on the right track. The puzzle pieces were falling into place in a logical pattern.

A random thought popped up. She intended to give the journal to Jake, who would be mad as hell. She wondered if she'd be able to repair her friendship with Jake and Terri? She hoped she could. With that, she drifted into a light sleep.

Tuesday

The Second Full Week of Lent

48
Time's Up

Laurette woke up at five. A soft snore told her that Jeffrey was sound asleep beside her. She looked down at him and smiled. Did all men sleep like babies, no matter the pressure and danger, or was it just him?

She showered, dressed, and made a cup of watery coffee from the individual coffee maker that most motels provided for their guests. My, isn't this place upscale? They even supply mugs instead of awful Styrofoam cups. Tastes like piss water, but it will have to do, she thought, sipping from the mug.

She checked the messages on her cell phone. That was a real inspiration, making him think he'd forgotten his phone in Dallas. She'd hidden it, forcing him to use hers so she could monitor who he was talking to and who knew he was in Austin.

Jeffrey did exactly what she expected. He texted

several people and said that he'd forgotten his cell phone at home and gave them her number. Keeping his charged when he wasn't looking, it was time to give it back to him.

Laurette looked through his messages. Four from his wife. A couple from his golf buddies. The one she hoped not to see arrived as a text at 3:00 a.m. "What a dummy," she hissed at the screen. *Where are you, my man? Time's up. My money's due on Friday. Don't make me come find you. I need more Ox.*

She knew he was never going to let Jeffrey off the hook for drugs. She answered. *OK. money and OX on Friday.* Whatever possessed him to contact Snake?

It would take time for the will to be probated. She had to work out a way to keep Snake from killing Jeffrey, but she couldn't worry about that now. Right now the most important thing is to be sure Charles's will doesn't turn up. Once I get my share, I'm out of this, she thought. Making herself a second cup of coffee she sat at the desk. Jeffrey was still asleep.

She wrote a note: *Here's your cell phone. Found it at the bottom of your medical bag. Charged it for you.* Aware of how flakey Jeffrey could be, she added: *Keep it on when you leave for the lawyer's office. I'll let you know if there are any problems.*

She closed her eyes. Not usually one to indulge in daydreaming she allowed herself to visualize a new start with a lot of money. She planned to keep it offshore; no sense bringing it into the socialist countries in Europe— she'd never get it out again. Where do I want to go? she mused.

According to what she read, Brazil was number one on the corruption list in Latin America, but she preferred Argentina; there was lots of corruption there. It was an exciting thought. Laurette envisioned herself living the high life in Buenos Aires, the home of Eva Peron, whom she admired. There was a woman who knew how to climb.

I'm going to do it differently, she thought. On my own, not on the coattails of some man. Love 'em and leave 'em, that's my motto. No man will do to me what daddy dearest did to my mother. He got her pregnant, broke her heart and left her to fend for herself. I don't buy that BS that Velma wouldn't let him leave. The money was his. He could do what he wanted. Well, no matter. He's dead, and I took care of Velma. Laurette smiled. Her wristwatch said five thirty. Time to go.

***

Fully awake again by five, Mrs. B. was exhausted from the night. She kept her eyes closed as the havoc wrought by Scooterman and Deene played over again in her head. She was determined to put an end to the danger enveloping all of them. The rectory and her home had been broken into; Father Joe hurt; Martha in jail, accused of murder; Chancey almost killed, not to mention the fact that Velma was poisoned, and she was being stalked.

Turning over, she looked at Sasha and Ziggy. They sat as still as sphinxes, eyes wide open, waiting patiently on their side of the bed; both sets of eyes focused intently on her face. She smiled at her feline babies. That was their cue to move. They nuzzled her cheek and meowed. Mrs. B. reached over and scratched their heads. "I love you too," she said, sitting up and massaging her temples. "Come on, let's get you fed. Mama's got a big day today. Time's up. This needs to end."

Before going to the kitchen she cleaned and refilled their litter boxes. "All ready," she said and left them in the bathroom. In the kitchen she went about her morning routine: coffee pot brewing, cat dishes washed and refilled with water and hard food. Pouring herself a cup of much-needed caffeine she organized all the papers and notes with her list on top and stuffed them into her satchel. After she showered and dressed, she looked around the house once more, making certain everything was in order then lifted the phone to make her first call.

Terri answered. "Sammi, what's wrong? You never call this early."

Of course Terri knows it's me, she thought. They have caller ID. "I'm sorry to disturb you, Terri, but I need to speak to Jake. It's urgent."

"What's up, Sammi?" He was on the extension.

Her words came out in a rush. "Deene is here in Austin. She's involved in this. I'm on my way to the rectory. Meet me there." She hung up before Jake could press her for more information.

Before going to the garage, she texted Father Melvyn in caps for emphasis: *I'M ON MY WAY AND SO IS JAKE. DEENE IS HERE AND SHE'S WORKING WITH SCOOTERMAN. BE THERE IN FIFTEEN IF TRAFFIC ISN'T BAD.* As always, she set her cell phone to mute, threw it in her handbag, jumped in her car, flung her scarf over the handbag on the passenger seat, and backed out of the garage.

Driving familiar streets allowed her mind to wander until her reverie was interrupted by traffic. Cars idled but didn't move. Sitting bumper-to-bumper on the street leading to the highway, her thoughts about the case retreated. It was only three miles to Saint Francis, but it could take an hour. At Mopac, she could see the backup approaching the ramp. "Shit," she muttered.

When the light turned green, she maneuvered her car into the right lane and made a right turn in the opposite direction of the rectory. I'll go back and around through the new construction area, she thought. It's a mess and bumpy, but it will get me past most of this.

Lights and local traffic slowed her progress, but it was still faster than sitting on Mopac. Getting to St. Francis as fast as possible was all that concerned her. Once she turned into the back of the construction site there were no more paved roads. "Go slow or you'll bottom out," she warned herself, resisting the urge to drive faster. "Be careful, pay attention, and keep moving. One wheel turn after another," she muttered. Peering at the road in front of her, she was focused on careful driving to protect her vehicle from damage.

She made her way across a stretch of packed dirt wide enough for one car with scrub brush and twisted, treelike weeds on both sides. Wish they'd pave this damn thing, she thought. The raw, packed earth ran behind the developing housing site. Even driving slow the wheels kicked up clouds of dust and dirt. And she'd just washed it. Oh well, this is more important.

Most of the homes being built here for middle-income residents were framed, but the roads and streets that would serve the community were unfinished. She feared getting stuck and being forced to walk out to a major roadway. There were ravines on both sides, good hiding places for snakes.

This morning, anxiety overrode caution. Weaving over dirt and sand, between big lumps of hard earth, rocks, and potholes, her tension eased as she reached the far side of car-wrecking obstacles. She was approaching the section of road that had a makeshift guardrail running along the side of a deep ravine, at the bottom of which was a dried creek. It was less than a half mile to the paved streets where she would be able to drive faster.

She maneuvered the car over the last section of unpaved road where the ground changed from packed dirt to thousands of pebble-like rocks that would damage her tires or undercarriage if she went any faster. Checking her rearview mirror all she saw were clouds of dirt, sand, pebbles, and rocks skittering up behind her car. She began to relax. Her choice of route paid off.

Her mind returned to Laurette Deene and Jeffrey Scooterman. She was more certain than ever that they were in this together. It made sense. They were both in the medical profession and knew what medications and poisons could be used. It was easy enough for anyone to find out, and even easier for them. She reviewed the information and felt certain that her assumption was reasonable and logical. She looked forward to telling Jake and Father Melvyn about the cell phone number that had led her to this conclusion.

***

Jake Zayas banged the phone down. His wife ran into his office. "What was that about?" she asked. He let out a string of curses. "Jake!" she yelled.

He started toward the front door. "Do me a favor. Call Marv. Tell him to call my cell in five minutes. I'm headed to Saint Francis." Turning, he pecked his wife on the nose. "I'll call you later."

Before he was out of the neighborhood, his cell phone rang. "Marv. I got a call from Sammi," Jake said.

"Who?"

"You know, Mrs. B., the housekeeper at St. Francis. She didn't give me time to ask even one question, just said she was on her way to Saint Francis. I'm going there. She says Deene is here in Austin and involved in this."

"Is that her opinion, or does she have evidence?"

"She hung up before I could ask. Head over to central and wait for my call. That puts you midway between Saint Francis, the Starlight Motel, and the lawyer's office."

"What do you think is happening?"

"I'm not sure," Jake answered, "but she sounded frantic. I have a feeling this thing is going to bust open today. I want to get to the padre. She should be there in about fifteen minutes depending on traffic."

"Will do," Marv said. Once they hung up, Jake tried Sammi's cell phone. No answer. He left a message. "Sammi, I'm on my way to Saint Francis. I don't care if you're driving. Call me when you get this."

***

"Declan, can you come down here, please," Father Melvyn called up the stairs. As if sensing his upset, LaLa sat on the top landing and meowed loudly.

"Sure. What's up, Mel?" the young assistant said on his way down. Before Father Melvyn answered, the phone rang.

Maybe it's her he thought and rushed to the nearest extension. "Mrs. B. is that you?"

"No, padre. It's Detective Zayas. I'm on my way to Saint Francis. You were expecting Mrs. B.?"

"Yes. I received a text from her saying she was on her way...and so were you."

"She's probably stuck in traffic, as am I. If she gets there before me, don't leave. I know you're going to the lawyer's office this morning, but not until I get there," he said and cut off the call.

"What is it, Mel?" Father Declan said, holding LaLa in his arms and stroking her.

"Let's get her fed," Father Melvyn said, pointing to the cat. "Mrs. B. sent me a frantic text. She's on her way. That was Detective Zayas. They're both stuck in traffic. Something is up. Can you be on call all day?"

"Yes. I'll ask Joe—"

"Ask me what?" The question came from the doorway.

"We didn't hear you," Father Melvyn answered. "I've asked Declan to be on duty all day today. I'm not sure, but there's a lot of nervous energy around this Velma case.

Mrs. B. and Detective Zayas are on their way here. Are you teaching? Can you help out?"

"Two classes this morning. Can you hold the fort till I get back around one-ish?" He directed the question to Father Declan.

"Yes. That's fine."

Father Melvyn looked at the time. "Where is she? She texted me a half hour ago." The doorbell interrupted all conversation. Father Joe ran to answer it.

"Martha. What can we do for you?" Father Melvyn heard the question from the kitchen and came out.

"I'm on my way to the hospital. I just wanted to thank you all for your support and prayers."

"How is Chancey?" Father Melvyn asked, walking up behind Father Joe.

"He's doing much better, Father Melvyn. Thank you for asking." Footsteps on the front porch broke into their conversation. The front door was still open, and they saw Detective Zayas approaching.

Martha stepped backward and raised her hands up as if to ward off an attack. "You leave me alone. I won't answer any questions without my lawyer," she cried.

"Calm yourself, Martha. The detective isn't here to talk to you. Go on to the hospital. I'll be there later today." Father Melvyn gently guided Martha out the front door.

Jake Zayas walked in. "You're due at the lawyer's office at ten?"

"Yes. Mrs. B. should be here by then. In fact, she should be here already," he said.

"Do you have any idea what has her so upset? She sounded pretty frantic when she called my house this morning."

Father Melvyn sighed. "She said something about Deene and Scooterman being in this together. I'm worried. It's eight. She texted thirty minutes ago."

Jake called Marv. "This is trouble. Sammi told the padre she thinks Deene and Scooterman are in this together. I'm at Saint Francis. Mrs. B.'s cell phone is off. It's taking too long for her to get here. Have you heard anything? Any calls come into central? Check with the substation in her sector. See if there are any reports of trouble at her address, and check with CTECC."

"What's CTECC?" Father Melvyn asked.

"It's the Combined Transportation, Emergency, and Communication Center. It's one of the best in the country. They provide rapid detection and incident management throughout the city and they handle nine-one-one calls. Their dispatchers are highly trained and very competent."

"I see," said Father Melvyn. "So if Mrs. B. got into trouble and dialed nine-one-one, they'd be the ones to answer?"

"Yes."

From the kitchen, Father Declan called out, "I've made fresh coffee." In the hallway on the way to the kitchen, Jake stumbled. Looking down, there was a blue-gray creature between his feet. She meowed, sounding annoyed.

"Are you okay?" Father Melvyn asked.

"Yes. Someone could have an accident. Does that cat always get between your feet?"

"Meet LaLa," Father Melvyn said. "She is the cat that triggered the latest trouble in the Velma-Martha battle. The day Velma died Martha's dogs spotted LaLa on the sidewalk in front of the church and tried to run after her. They pulled Martha down. In a fit of anger, Martha screamed, 'I'm going to kill that cat,' but she didn't mean it."

Zayas's phone rang. It was Marv Clingman. "No reports in her subsector. Do you want me to come to Saint Francis or wait here?"

"Wait there. I'm coming in."

As soon as he ended the call with Clingman another came in. "Jake Zayas here." He listened intently. "On my way." Turning to the priest he ordered, "Don't leave until you hear from Marv or me." With that, he ran to the front door, flung it wide, and ran down the steps. When the priest reached the front door, he watched Jake maneuver his car out of the driveway, tires squealing; dashboard siren blaring.

49
Rammed

The impact slammed her head against the steering wheel. "Ow," she yelled. For a moment her vision doubled as the car rocked sideways. Struggling to think and to keep the car on the road, she heard a crack come from the right side and the car shuddered. She realized the flimsy wooden guardrails had snapped; splinters flew up. She was headed toward the edge. Turning the wheel hard the screech of metal on wood told her the side of her car was being excoriated from rubbing against what was left of the rail. "What the hell?" She glanced to her right. Something dripped into her eyes. She wiped it away. Her fingers were stained with blood. Heart pounding, she battled to center the car on the horrid road.

Rocks flew up, hitting her undercarriage and careening off her windows. Barely in control, a second impact propelled her forward and to the right again. She hit the brake pedal with both feet, which stopped the tires from turning, sending large plumes of dirt, rocks, and sand up both sides of her car, along with the smell of burning rubber.

Time slowed. Her perception changed. It was like being out of her own body. The nose of the car pointed up like a plane on liftoff and suspended in the early-morning air. She was looking up and out at an overcast sky.

Then, like a ship taking water in the bow, the nose of her car went down. How fast it dropped? She had no idea; she was numb.

A huge boom vibrated underneath her when the car hit the ground. She felt rather than saw the floor of the car buckle. The front wheels appeared to be hanging over the ledge on the other side of the shattered guardrail. The car stopped moving. She found herself peering down at treetops. They looked close.

Sitting behind the steering wheel in shocked disbelief, her hand went to her forehead again. It throbbed from hitting the steering wheel moments before. Feeling detached, she realized she was still bleeding.

Looking into the rearview mirror for the first time, Mrs. B. saw a dark, dirt-covered car behind her, but she didn't see a person. Her right hand groped the passenger seat searching for her handbag. Dazed, she realized her purse had been thrown to the floor, but her cell phone had fallen out and was wedged between the seat and the back, with her scarf half covering it. In a hurry to dial 911, she released her seat belt, reached over and dialed without picking it up. Before she could speak the driver's door was yanked open.

The gun appeared first and then the face. She stared into black, volcanic eyes, accentuated by a fringe of long black eyelashes. Like Chancey's, their anatomical structure was beautiful, but unlike his, they became ugly, filled with hate and rage. She gasped. Fear seized her; these were the eyes that stared at her the night she rescued LaLa. No introduction was necessary. The murderous glare that bore holes into her could belong to no one other than Laurette Deene.

"Get out." Laurette waved the gun at her. Mrs. B.'s pulled the scarf back over the phone as Laurette grabbed her left arm, yanked hard, pulling the housekeeper out of the car in one powerful motion.

Mrs. B.'s legs buckled, and she hit the dirt. Laurette grabbed her hair and wrenched her head backward bringing them face to face, albeit at a bizarre angle. "Where is Charles Maxwell's will," she demanded.

"I gave it to the police."

"Bitch. Get up, or I'll shoot you right here."

Mrs. B. struggled to her feet, never looking away from her assailant. "So you're Laurette Deene," she yelled.

"Yell all you want. There's no one to hear you."

"Am I yelling?" Mrs. B. asked, survival instincts kicking in. "Maybe because my ears are ringing from banging my head," she lied. "How did you know where to find me?"

"Find you? I didn't need to find you. I've been watching you for days. I was coming to pay you a little early morning visit only to see you pull out of your garage at seven thirty. You have been one major pain in my ass, but thanks. Instead of killing you in your bed, I'll have you kill yourself," Laurette said.

The sound of her laugh was chilling. She's insane, Mrs. B. thought. I'm in the clutches of an insane murderer.

"What do you know, and does the nosey priest know Jeffrey and I are together?"

Mrs. B. took no pleasure in the fact the Deene's question confirmed her suspicions. She might have smiled had the situation not been life threatening. Pretending to make a weak effort to loosen Laurette's grip on her hair, she twisted as much as possible so that her voice carried to the cell phone hidden on the passenger seat. Self-preservation brought the lie easily to her lips. "Yes. Father Melvyn knows you and Jeffrey are in it together." Hoping the dispatcher could hear her, Mrs. B. wanted to say something to alert the operator that she was in real danger. "Let me stand up, please," she begged. Holding onto the doorframe facing the car to get on her feet, Mrs. B. said, "Laurette, why don't you put the gun away."

"Sure. We can have tea and chat." Her laugh was high pitched and dangerous, sending new tendrils of fear through the housekeeper. "I don't think so."

Afraid to keep her back to Laurette, Mrs. B. turned and held onto the door. "I can help you. Jake Zayas, the detective in charge of this case is a friend of mine, and he doesn't know about you...Not yet.

"I know Jeffrey and Father Melvyn have an appointment with Velma's lawyer this morning. I'll keep Father Melvyn at the rectory. We'll tell the lawyer an emergency came up and to go ahead with whatever needs to be done. It will give you and Jeffrey time to get away."

"My. Aren't you a kind lady? And why would you do that?"

"Looks like my choices are either letting you and Jeffrey get away with the money or dying. You should be glad for the offer so you won't be forced to add another murder to your crimes."

"Murder is murder. One, two. Won't make much difference if I'm caught, but I am glad to know that the police haven't worked it out yet. Besides, I'm not going to kill you. You're going to have a little car accident, which will keep everyone busy. By the time the cops put it together, if they ever do, Jeffrey and I will have everything, and we'll be gone."

"What's to guarantee he'll share the money once he gets his hands on it?"

"That's why I need that damned will. Insurance. Why else would I put up with that stupid loser? Now, we're done talking. Turn around."

"You're going to kill me?"

"No. We're going to have a picnic."

"If I have to die for this then at least tell me how you poisoned Velma."

"Not hard. An overdose of digitalis with a cup of antifreeze for good measure."

"Antifreeze?"

Laurette laughed. "Antifreeze tastes sweet. I had Jeffrey add it to cover the bitter taste of digitalis and to give Velma an added "kick" on her way out. He poured it in her teakettle because dear old *dead* Auntie Velma loved very strong, very sweet tea. Well, she got it. Damned old bitch. Had the constitution of a horse. A bad stomach ache, dizziness, disorientation. She should never have made it out of her bed, but that cat kept poking her, keeping her awake. I wanted to kill that damned thing.

"Velma wandered outside calling for it, weaving like a drunk; she finally collapsed on church property."

Mrs. B. watched the expression on Laurette Deene's face. My God, she's gone to the dark side.

Laurette continued. "If she had died in her bed none of this would be happening. Now turn around. I'm not going to say it again."

"Why do you hate her so much?"

"Why do you care? Turn around."

The housekeeper pushed the growing panic down. Think! Laurette needs this to look like an accident. She can't shoot. I need to keep her talking. "How did you know about Chancey?"

"Are you kidding? The simpleton came to the funeral mass. One look at those eyes and I knew he was my

278

half-brother. Daddy dearest had strong genes. We both look like him. The rest was easy."

"Laurette," Mrs. B. shouted. "You don't need to do this. I found Velma's journal. She wrote about her revenge on Charles Maxwell. She knew about you and your half-brother. You have a case to challenge Velma's will."

"I suspected you took that journal. I found a bunch of others when Jeffrey and I did another search; I would have liked to have seen that one. Velma was a real bitch, but it's too late.

"If she'd had any self-respect, she would have kicked him out. For all her pretenses, she was no better than the rest of us. She stayed for the money and told me that I would never see a cent. She even called my mother a whore. My mother, who worked hard and raised me alone; she was no whore. Velma was the whore, and the worst kind. Charles was a sadist. He didn't even try to treat her well. He abused and humiliated her, and she let him. For what? Money? Position? What did that make her?"

"You spoke to her?" Mrs. B. was surprised.

"Before I met Jeffrey. She threw me out of her house. That's when I decided she was going to pay." Deene shoved Mrs. B. against the car.

"Enough talk. Turn around."

"You don't have to kill me."

"Look at it this way. Everyone will mourn the well-loved busybody who drove her car off the road. I'll bet Father Melvyn will give a lovely eulogy for you. Now turn around." Laurette pushed Mrs. B.'s shoulder to move her faster.

Mrs. B. had no intention of making it easy. She grabbed the gun, but the younger woman was stronger.

Laurette punched her in the face. Out of desperation, Mrs. B. held the barrel of the gun in a fierce grip. She aimed her other hand at Deene's eyes and raked her assailant's face with her nails.

Laurette screamed, bit Mrs. B.'s fingers, and continued to wrestle the gun out of her hand. "I'd love nothing better than to put a bullet between your eyes."

"Help, help," Mrs. B. screamed, hoping and praying the dispatch operator was hearing everything. Laurette punched the older woman in the stomach. With one final pull, Laurette tore the gun out of her hand and brought it down on Mrs. B.'s forehead above her right eye, just missing the temple.

Sharp pain seared her forehead. Her knees turned to jelly; she fell to the dirt. Semi-conscious her body slacked, but she felt Deene's rough hands pulling her up and pushing her head and torso into the car. She blacked out for a moment. A minute later she was conscious again, with a pain in her chest from the center console pressing into her ribs. Her head and upper torso were on the passenger side of the car. Her arm knocked the cell phone to the floor. She heard the dispatch operator's voice but couldn't make out the words.

***

Laurette didn't bother to push Mrs. B.'s body fully into the car. "This is taking too long," she muttered. One good push, and the nosey bitch and her car would go over the side. Jamming the gun into her waistband, she set her hands on the frame with the driver's door open and pushed. It didn't budge. From behind her a roar sounding like a freight train was approaching fast. She looked back in the direction they'd traveled. A huge dust cloud was churning.

Black and-white vehicles, lights flashing from atop their cars, emerged. The distant sound of sirens approached from the opposite direction. Frantic, she tried again to push the car over the side. She rocked it, and something scraped and squealed underneath. She was about to reposition her hands on the frame of the driver's side and push when gravel flew out and reached her from an oncoming police vehicles.

Without warning, a uniformed officer emerged from the dust storm raised by the vehicles, ran toward her and yelled, "Stop."

Engulfed by rage and no longer rational, Laurette turned, pulled the gun from her belt, pointed, and fired. The officer dove. Sirens, yells, cars, and trucks added to the chaos. Laurette looked around. The officer she'd shot held his arm and scurried behind the door of his police car.

Two officers from the other direction jumped out, drew their guns and positioned themselves behind their doors. "Drop the gun," they ordered, not able to see clearly in the fog of dirt, sand and pebbles. "Drop it, get on your knees, and put your hands behind your head," they commanded again. She noticed an unmarked car join the group.

"You nosey bitch. If I die, you're coming with me. I'm not going to jail," she hissed. Moving fast, Laurette climbed into the car on top of the housekeeper and threw herself over the console into the passenger side. She pushed the barely conscious woman's head up, but she couldn't move her.

"Back off, or I'll shoot her," she screamed at police moving toward the car. "Think I'm kidding?" In a flash, Laurette jumped over Mrs. B., again, dove under the open door, raised herself up behind it, and aimed at the housekeeper. "Give me an excuse to kill her."

A plainclothes detective walked forward. "Hold your fire," he called back to the uniformed officers. Laurette knew they couldn't see clearly enough to take a shot. She recognized the detective by his iron-gray hair and black-rimmed glasses. It was Jake Zayas. She knew from Jeffrey that he was in charge of the investigation.

"Let's talk about this," he said. "We can make a deal."

"No deal. You put that unmarked car up here where I can get in, and she comes with me."

"How are you going to get her out? We can see her feet hanging out of the car. She's unconscious. Put your gun down. C'mon. No need for anyone else to get hurt," he said.

"Really? You want a deal? Here it is. You get that unmarked car up here, motor running. She comes with me and she's not unconscious, she's faking—and she will move, or else." Laurette cocked the hammer.

"Let her go," Jake shouted. "I'll come with you. I'll be your hostage. See, I'm putting my gun on the ground."

Laurette ignored his offer. "You have to the count of five. One – two - three – four - five."

The gunfire was deafening and Jake Zayas was suddenly face down in the dirt.

50
Oh What a Tangled Web We Weave...

The silence following the gunfire was as dramatic as the shootout. Covered in dirt with pebbles imbedded in his skin, Jake picked up his gun and moved forward cautiously. When he reached Laurette, who was face down in a pool of blood, he kicked her weapon away from her body. Reaching down, he felt her neck for a pulse. "She's dead," he called back over his shoulder.

Marv Clingman ran forward. "That dispatch operator was great. She recognized the hostage situation and called for you as soon as she heard your name."

Jake nodded and looked in the car. There was blood all over. Within minutes of Jake's announcement, EMS, CSI, and the fire department were in place.

A firefighter crouched down and looked under the car. "It's not going any place. Caught on a boulder. Leaking plenty good too."

"She's not moving," Jake said, trying to reach Sammi's neck to check for a pulse.

"Let us in here, detectives," EMS said, pushing past Jake and Marv.

"Call Father Melvyn at Saint Francis. Here's what needs to be done." After giving Marv instructions, Jake said, "You go on ahead. I want to wait for a report on Sammi. I'll get a ride back to central. Meet you there."

***

Father Melvyn held his pursed lips between his thumb and forefinger as he paced the long center hall of the rectory. Where is she? He was worried. Mrs. B. should have been here. Even with traffic she should have arrived already. For the tenth time, he checked the time on the text he'd received from her earlier, as if it might have changed: Her text was sent at 7:32 a.m.

Something was wrong. If she'd broken down, she would have texted or called. The phone rang; he flew back to the kitchen. LaLa sat on the counter, staring from him to the phone. "Saint Francis Rectory," he said.

"Father Kronkey, this is Marv Clingman. I'll be there in fifteen minutes."

"What's going on?"

"I'll explain when I get there. We need your help this morning. Will you be able to keep the appointment with Ms. Snellling?"

"Yes. I've arranged for coverage. Mrs. B. hasn't arrived yet. I'm worried and I should be leaving for my appointment with Velma's Lawyer. Have you or Detective Zayas heard from her?"

"Be there shortly," Clingman said and hung up abruptly.

"Declan," Father Melvyn shouted up the stairs.

"Yes, Melvyn?"

"Marv Clingman is Jake Zayas's partner. He's on his

way. He said he'd explain everything when he gets here. I don't know what's going on."

"I know who he is. May I sit in? I'm worried about her too."

"Yes, of course." Father Melvyn looked down when he heard a meow. In one leap, LaLa was in his arms, pressing her head into his armpit. "There, there, LaLa. Everything will be okay… I hope."

A long fifteen minutes later, the front doorbell rang. LaLa jumped down and took her place on the landing.

"Detective Clingman, please come in."

"Are the other priests here?" the detective asked, standing in the entry. Father Declan joined them.

"Father Joe isn't here now. He's teaching this morning. He'll be back later to help out. Please tell us what's happening."

"Let's go into the office," Clingman said. He didn't wait for the pastor to lead the way.

"I've had a call from Jake Zayas," Clingman began. "There's been a shooting."

***

At 9:45 a.m. Jeffrey arrived at the lawyer's office and parked. As Laurette instructed, he checked his cell phone. No messages, but he wasn't comfortable. He hadn't been comfortable since he woke up and found her gone. She'd left his cell phone and a note telling him it was at the bottom of his medical bag. How can that be? I never put it in my medical bag. She must have hidden it from me. Why? Things are getting too bizarre.

He pushed those thoughts out of his mind and called her number. Voice mail picked up. "Laurette, I'm at the lawyer's office. Give me a quick call and confirm that everything is okay. I can't wait much longer. I have to go in."

Jeffrey sat in his car staring at his cell phone, willing it to ring. It remained silent. He was about to leave when he saw Father Melvyn arrive. When the priest got out of the car, Jeffrey called to him. If anything was wrong, he wouldn't be here, Jeffrey thought.

"Are you waiting for someone else, or are you coming in?" Father Melvyn asked.

"I'm coming, of course." Jeffrey got out of his car. He's pale and looks distracted, Jeffrey noted. He should be grateful my aunt left money to the parish. Wonder if I can find a way to contest that. I'll speak to another lawyer when I get back to Dallas. Together, he and the priest entered the building. The lawyer's office was on the second floor.

"Nice weather we're having, and it's only March. Hope this doesn't mean we'll have a scorching summer," Jeffrey stated, keeping the conversation light.

They entered the reception area. The secretary smiled and told them to have a seat. She walked into the Zoe Snelling's conference room. They heard her say, "Jeffrey Scooterman and Father Melvyn Kronkey…" A few minutes later, she emerged and said, "Follow me." She held the door open. Jeffrey walked in first, with Father Melvyn behind him. The secretary stepped out and closed the door.

Putting on his best face, Jeffrey smiled and walked forward with his hand out. "Good morning, Ms. Snelling. Glad to meet you at last." The lawyer stood behind her desk and didn't respond.

"Jeffrey Scooterman." His name was called from behind him. He turned to see Detective Marv Clingman and a uniformed officer. Father Melvyn stepped to the side.

"What…?"

Without preamble, the uniformed officer grabbed his arms and cuffed him.

"What's going on here?" he demanded.

"Jeffrey Scooterman, you are under arrest for the murder of Velma Maxwell and the attempted murder of Chancey Maxwell Johnson."

"What are you talking about? I didn't do anything. This is a mistake. I didn't kill anybody."

Detective Clingman ignored his protests and continued reading him his rights. "You have the right to remain silent. Anything you say can and will be used against you. You have the right to speak to an attorney and to have an attorney present during any questioning. Do you understand the rights I've described to you?"

"This is a mistake. I didn't do anything," Scooterman protested.

"Do you understand the rights I've described to you?" Clingman asked again.

"Yes, yes. I want a lawyer," Scooterman yelled back. "Wait a minute. Ms. Snelling, will you represent me?"

"Sorry, Dr. Scooterman. I don't do criminal law."

"Get him out of here," Clingman said to the uniformed officer. Although it wasn't imperative that they read him his rights immediately, Jake and Marv agreed that it would be done in front of the padre and Velma's lawyer. They already had most of the confrontation between Laurette Deene and Mrs. B., recorded by the astute dispatcher who'd kept the line open while the incident unfolded. Marv dialed his cell phone. "He's on his way. I read him his rights as we discussed. See you shortly."

Clingman turned to Father Melvyn. "We'll talk later, Padre. Jake is waiting. We need to get Scooterman downtown, questioned, and processed."

Father Melvyn rubbed his eyes. "Thank you, Detective." After the police left with Jeffrey Scooterman's shouts of innocence echoing down the halls, Father Melvyn turned to the lawyer. "I never liked that guy, but I never figured him for murder."

The lawyer shook her head. She'd taken care of Velma Maxwell's legal matters for years. "I had no knowledge of a will left by Charles Maxwell. Velma never said a word."

"Where does this leave things?" the priest asked.

"I'll need to look everything over. I think the courts will sort it all out. Does this man, supposedly Charles's illegitimate son have an attorney?"

"Yes. Now that he and his mother will be cleared of any wrongdoing, his attorney, Tom Barbee, will help them sort through this. I'm sure Tom will contact you." The priest and the lawyer shook hands and said goodbye.

Once in his car, Father Melvyn called Saint Francis. Declan picked up immediately. "It's over. Scooterman was arrested. I'm going to meet Zayas."

"This is incredible. I can't believe it," Father Declan said.

"I know. Oh what a tangled web we weave…Thanks for covering. I should be back by dinnertime."

With a heavy heart, Father Melvyn left the lawyer's office and drove to the central station to meet Jake Zayas, who still wanted additional information to "tie up loose ends," he said. After he answered the detective's few remaining questions, he left the police station and made his way to the hospital.

***

Martha and her son smiled when Father Melvyn walked in. Both had tears on their cheeks. "Father Melvyn, Tom is on his way. He said Detective Zayas called him. All charges will be dropped."

"I'm very happy for you, Martha. I'm happy for

both of you," Father Melvyn said. "I saw the detective and he told me that you've been cleared."

From his bed, Chancey said, "You look exhausted, Father Melvyn. Tom told us what happened to Mrs. B. How are you holding up?"

Father Melvyn smiled sadly. "I'm okay, but certainly the day's events are very sad, indeed. Oh what a tangled web we weave, when first we practice to deceive." He said the words a second time, almost to himself.

"But it is a glorious day for both of you. Chancey, you concentrate on recovering. Everything else will fall into place, and Tom will take care of your legal matters. Now I must get back to Saint Francis." Father Melvyn hugged Martha and shook hands with Chancey.

***

It was almost midnight. Father Melvyn sat in the library, breviary in hand. It was time for the last prayers of the day. He looked at the prayer book but knew he couldn't open it and concentrate just yet. The day's events reeled through his head, yet again.

Meow. The plaintive cry came from the floor. LaLa sat at his feet. "Are you waiting for an invitation?" he asked. As soon as she had his attention she jumped up into his lap and nuzzled against his chest. Stroking her head he felt the tension begin to melt away from him. He stopped fighting the natural reaction to shock and allowed the events of the day to replay.

When he returned to the rectory that afternoon there were administrative matters to attend to that Mrs. B. usually took care of. Marv Clingman came by again and there was another call from Jake Zayas. With the case solved, the detectives became more personable and sympathetic. "My wife is contacting Mrs. B.'s family, Jake told Father Melvyn. "Her son and daughter-in-law in Dallas are on their way to Austin. Her daughter, Corinne is making travel arrangements from New York."

"Please let me know when they arrive. I do wish to meet with them privately," he told the detective.

"Will do, Padre. I'll let you know as soon as I hear."

It was past midnight, and still no word. Father Melvyn felt his moustache become damp from the tears on his face. He reached into his pocket and pulled out tissues to wipe his face and clear his glasses.

LaLa didn't move from his lap. "My goodness, LaLa, who is taking care of her cats if her children haven't arrived yet?" he wondered. "If I don't hear anything tomorrow morning, I'll call Jake and tell him I'm willing to go to her house." He thought for a moment. "You know, LaLa, I've never been to her house."

His thoughts turned to the woman who had become dear to him not only as a housekeeper, cook, and administrative assistant but also as a friend. "I haven't been much of a friend to her," he said. He continued to stroke the cat as a deep sadness engulfed him. He lifted himself from his favorite chair, feeling like a very old man. "Let's go upstairs, LaLa."

In his room, Father Melvyn said the last prayers of the day and then a rosary for Mrs. B.

Thursday

The Second Full Week of Lent

51
Tying up Loose Ends

Two days after the shootout with Laurette Deene and Scooterman's arrest, the detectives were clearing paperwork and filling out reports. "Looking forward to this weekend," Clingman said. "Glad to be done with the Maxwell case."

"Wouldn't it be great if we could wrap up every case this fast?" Jake asked from across the desk, where he sat finishing his own reports.

"Yes. This one turned out to be a slam dunk, with a great bonus, although we didn't know that would be the case a few days ago. Scooterman surprised me. Pleading guilty, asking for a bench trial. Of course, he's blaming Laurette Deene for all of it. He decided to give us one of the biggest gambling and drug rings in the Dallas-Austin corridor, the Red Aces, headed by Snake Williams so he could get into the protective custody unit and the witness protection program. As soon as he testifies the Marshall Service will have his new identity and his new life ready.

"His testimony will go a long way toward breaking the back of the drugs moving from Dallas to Austin," Jake agreed. "The Red Aces are deadly. They keep it simple; they don't break knees, they kill and not fast."

The phone rang. "Zayas here." Jake became still. Barely moving, he asked through clenched teeth, "Are you kidding me?" Marv looked up at his partner. "Who had access to him? He was in solitary. What happened?" Jake Zayas slammed the phone back into its cradle hard enough to make everyone in the room turn.

"What?" Clingman asked.

"Scooterman was found dead in his cell an hour ago. No obvious cause. The M.E. will have to determine the cause of death, but it's convenient for the Red Aces, isn't it?" Zayas gave Clingman a knowing look. "So much for the case against Snake Williams."

Marv threw his pen down and ran his fingers through his hair. "These bastards have a long reach."

"It used to be shivs and other sharpened eating utensils. Now they've become sophisticated. How the hell did they get something to him?"

"I'm sure we'll hear from the M.E. soon enough," Zayas said, shaking his head in disgust.

***

Father Melvyn drained his teacup. "Thank you, Martha."

"We *thank you*, Father," Chancey said. "I don't know what we would have done without your help." Martha and Chancey had asked him to stop by. Chancey was almost back to full strength.

"I'm glad things are turning out well for you. Are you going back to Killeen, to your job?"

"Only to tie up loose ends. Mom wants to stay here and there's no reason not to. I've been at the bus company a long time and my pension is secure, but I have no real ties there. I'll find a job here as a mechanic, and I hope to be moved permanently by Easter." He hugged Martha and wiped a tear from her face. "No need to cry. You aren't alone anymore."

Martha smiled. "Once he's settled with a job, more familiar with Austin, and we've sorted out all this stuff about Charles's will, we agree that he needs to have his own apartment, nearby, of course, but his own space. I'd love for him to meet a nice woman and get married."

"Sounds like you two have given everything a lot of thought. I look forward to having you as part of our parish, Chancey."

"You know, Father, Velma was rotten. She knew about Chancey and let me know that she was watching and that my son would never see a penny of Charles's money."

Father Melvyn sighed. If she knew the half of it, she'd really want to stomp on Velma's grave. He hadn't decided if he was going to share the rest of the story from Velma's journal, especially the part about how Velma paid Martha's aunt to persuade the family to force an adoption or how she'd bribed poor old Father Jameson into supporting it.

"Martha, what I'm about to say may seem strange to you, but try not to be bitter toward Velma any more. Count your blessings, and enjoy having your son. You have a lot of time to make up. Don't dwell on the past. I think Velma was a very unhappy woman. Charles humiliated her and she tolerated his behavior because, deep down, I think her standing in the parish and in the city were all she had. She was afraid she'd lose her status if she threw him out."

"And the four million too," Martha said, her tone cold.

Father Melvyn sighed and changed the subject. "Are you going to tell your brother and your aunt? She's very old now, isn't she?"

"Yes. I'll not hide the truth or my son one minute longer. As for my aunt, I don't know how much she understands at this point. She's in a nursing home, you know."

He smiled. "Be patient with them. You know, it may come as a shock and they may not react as warmly as you think they should. Anyway, Chancey stands to inherit quite a bit of money in time. It will probably take a few years to sort it all out. Tom said that Jeffrey's children have a claim too."

Chancey spoke up: "You know, Father, I would love for them to welcome me, mostly for Mom's sake. But if they don't, I won't care. Having found my mother after all these years, and after all we've gone through with Velma's murder then discovering I had a half-sister who was a monster, if it turns out to be Mom and me only that will be fine.

"As for the money, it would be great, right? But it's not going to run or ruin my life. Look what it did to Velma, her nephew, and Laurette Deene."

Father Melvyn smiled. "That's the spirit."

"One more thing," Martha said at the front door. "I understand you've taken Velma's cat." Father Melvyn tensed, waiting for another of Martha's tirades against LaLa. "This seems silly now after all that's happened, but it's bothering me. I never really wanted to kill LaLa. I think the only reason I threatened to do it is I knew Velma loved her, and I wanted to hurt Velma the way she'd hurt me. Think God will forgive me?"

"Yes, Martha. It's understandable, but one of the things we must do in life, in order to be closer to God, is to let go of past sins and bitterness. LaLa is a sweet creature and now belongs to Saint Francis."

On the console table in her front hall Martha reached for a box. "This is for LaLa. It's a cat toy. I hope she enjoys it. It's big and bright, easy to see so no one will trip on it."

Father Melvyn took the box. "This is really nice of you. On LaLa's behalf, I thank you." He looked at his wristwatch. "It's getting late. I have another stop.

"One question, Martha. The night of Velma's murder Father Declan thought he saw you pass Velma's house walking your dogs with someone he didn't recognize. Why were you out so late, and who was with you?"

Chancey stepped up. "It was me. I sometimes visited Mom during the week if I had a late shift the next day."

"Thought so," Father Melvyn said, hugging Martha and shaking hands with Chancey. "You have a good evening."

Walking out of Martha's house Father Melvyn was gratified by her change of heart toward the cat and that she had at least some understanding of Velma's motivations.

52
"In a Cat's Eyes, All Things Belong to the Cat"

When he arrived, he was relieved that there were no other visitors. He'd run into Mrs. B.'s son, John, and his wife, Lisa, as well as Ms. Jenkins, the day before. He was not in the mood to make conversation.

Sitting in an upright chair, he looked around at the beautiful flower arrangements, their fragrance filling the room. He looked at her face, so still, so peaceful. The silence was both comforting and upsetting. He wanted to talk to her, to go over everything that had happened, but he couldn't.

He rose from his chair, opened his breviary and became absorbed in his prayers. His lips moved, and the world disappeared as he prayed the divine office. A sense of peace settled over him. He finished, closed the breviary, and looked away from the book. His heart contracted.

Her eyes were open. She was watching him and smiling.

"When did you wake up?" he asked. "You should have said something."

"You were saying your office. I didn't want to interrupt." Father Melvyn walked over to the bed and looked at Mrs. B.'s face. The stitches on her forehead were covered by a bandage, but the bruising extended down the side of her face. "Looks like I went ten rounds with a heavyweight, right?" she asked. They chuckled. "Doctor said I can go home tomorrow. Other than scaring the hell out of anyone who sees me, there's no reason for me to stay in the hospital. Besides, I miss my cats."

"Your cats are fine, according to your son and daughter-in-law. They've been staying at the house, taking care of Sasha and Ziggy, and Ms. Jenkins said she'll come by every day to help you. I had no idea you two were good friends. She's been here often. She told me about your mutual love of the arts, opera in particular."

"Nancy and I ran into each other at the opera a year ago, and since then we've shared our mutual passion for the arts." She looked at him and decided it was time. "You met John and Lisa. What you don't know is that they're ballet dancers. They dance in a company in Dallas."

"Surprise! They told me. Actually, I asked what they did for a living because I noticed their posture and carriage the first time I met them. It was obvious they didn't sit hunched over a desk all day. I also met your daughter, Corinne. Very smart, very lovely woman; she looks like you."

Her eyes opened wide in surprise. She put her hand to her head holding the stitches under the bandage. "Wow. I'm surprised. You noticed? You asked?"

"And I'm noticing that you are holding your face. Do you have pain?"

"A little."

He nodded. "Back to your children. I'm not completely oblivious," he said.

"I never thought you were. It's just that…" She stopped.

His eyes held the question, "Thought what?"

She shrugged. "I felt badly that they all came running down here when Terri Zayas called them. John and Lisa are going back to Dallas tomorrow, after they get me home from the hospital. They must get back. They have a performance coming up.

"Corinne is going to stay a few extra days, in spite of my protests that she should go back to her children. I'm really in good shape, a lot better than I look.

"Father Joe and I were comparing bruises yesterday. He and Father Declan came by. They said LaLa is causing a commotion in the kitchen, insisting on being fed on the countertop. Wonder who got her into that bad habit?"

"Hmmm." His eyebrows pulled together over his nose. "They didn't tell me they visited." He skipped the question about LaLa's feeding habits, but they both knew he was the one who spoiled her.

Mrs. B. smiled. "I think you are completely smitten. LaLa owns you."

Father Melvyn, always so contained and controlled, blushed. They both knew he was hopelessly attached to LaLa, the flashpoint that ignited the simmering feud between Martha and Velma into much more.

Mrs. B. changed the subject. "Update me on the cast and crew of this drama. How are Chancey and Martha?"

"They're doing well. Some of Martha's sharp edges seem to be softening; she even bought a little toy for LaLa, to make amends, and Chancey is making a big difference. Of course, it's too much to expect her to be completely over her bitter feelings about what happened."

He looked at Mrs. B. expectantly, but she stayed quiet. "Oh, by the way, I told your friend Detective Zayas about the journal. He told me they found several more in Jeffrey's room. He asked to read the one we took. I gave it to him. I have no idea what his reaction will be, but I think under the circumstances, Father Jameson's poor decision is irrelevant.

"Oh, and ahh. Jake called me today with more news. Jeffrey Scooterman died in his prison cell. They're waiting for the medical examiner's report."

"Oh my. That's terrible."

"Your friend Jake turns out to be quite a nice man. He actually smiles. His wife is lovely too. I met them here at the hospital after your ordeal with Laurette."

"Jake and Terri are good people. They were in to see me. I hope I haven't damaged my friendship with them. How he reacts to the journal will tell us a lot.

"As for my ordeal with Laurette, it's foggy. I don't really remember it in detail. What stays with me is the sound of gunfire. Doctors are telling me it's the brain's way of dealing with this type of trauma. I hope it clears up. Horrible as it was, I prefer remembering. I don't like mental blank spots." She shook her head. "It's shocking about Jeffrey Scooterman." She thought for a moment and then continued. "You know, Charles was the architect of this deadly spectacle, but Velma was its engineer. She could have ended it long ago. I wonder what Charles died from?"

Father Melvyn cleared his throat. "Don't go looking for conspiracies," then softened his stern tone, "and try not to think about it now. You need to get well." He felt the strain between them return. It was an awkward moment, something that had never existed until murder made its way into Saint Francis. He lowered his eyes and then pursed his lips and held them between his thumb and forefinger.

She knew that look. Being one to tackle problems head-on, she pulled herself upright in the bed. "OK, why don't we address the elephant in the room right now? Next week, when I return to work, I'll place an ad for a new housekeeper in the bulletin. If you want, I'll work until you've replaced me...or not. Your choice."

Father Melvyn was crestfallen. "So you're determined to leave us?"

"What do you mean, I'm determined?" she asked, her tone sharp; her brows angled down over her nose. "I thought you wanted me to go. You said I'm too nosey. About that, you're right, but you accused me of gossiping and about that you're wrong—dead wrong." Becoming contrite, she added, "After all that's happened, I understand why you want me to go."

Father Melvyn sighed. "No, no, my dear. Sammi..." He cleared his throat and resumed pacing. "I mean, Mrs. B. I regret saying all of that." He stood at the side of her bed, took her hand, and peered into her eyes. He waited a moment. The next words came in a rush. "You know I've come to depend on you. You're an asset to us. You make our work easier. We... I need you." He stood as still as a statue and waited. Tears welled in her eyes. "You're going to cry; I'm upsetting you."

"No, you're not." After a short pause, she said, "Excuse my emotional neediness, but I need to hear you say it."

Without hesitation he replied, "Please don't leave. I want you to stay."

"Good, and thank you. I want to stay... but there is one problem."

"Problem? What problem?"

"LaLa."

Puzzlement was written all over his face. "What's wrong with LaLa?"

She put a hand to her cheek supporting the lopsided smile pulling across her face. "Old English proverb, 'In a cat's eyes, all things belong to the cat.'

"According to Father Joe and Father Declan, LaLa has taken over the rectory, and now I think she has some bad habits, which I shall change."

Joy and relief zinged through the priest's nerve endings. The weight of the world lifted from his shoulders. My assistant and, more importantly, my friend is back, he thought. "Okay, but remember, she is my cat, and if I want to spoil her, I will."

Mischief filled her eyes. "Are you sure?"

"Yes. I am. I think the rectory will settle down into its old routine and LaLa will fit into our lives quite well. Besides, this entire situation was most unusual, an aberration, actually.

"After all, Mrs. B., how many murders can possibly cross the threshold of Saint Francis?" He waited a moment, released her hand and became very formal.

"There is something, however, that I think you need to know. It's my duty to share it with you now because it will have an impact on you." He stared into her eyes and spoke in a quiet tone."

"This sound serious. What is it, Father?"

Looking over his shoulder, checking that no one was within earshot, he whispered, "I'm an addict." He watched as confusion filled her face.

"An addict? What do you mean?" She waited. Nothing more was forthcoming. "I don't understand. What kind of an addict? How can I help you? Have you seen a doctor?" No answer, he sat erect with downcast eyes. Looking at him she demanded: "Please tell me. Addicted to what?"

"Oh my, I've shocked you. I thought you'd have guessed by now."

Her face paled.

He leaned over and whispered in her ear so there was no chance of a passerby hearing.

"The ambrosia of the Italian food gods— your eggplant parmigiana."

***

The hearty laughter coming from Mrs. B.'s room was heard twenty feet away at the nurses' station.

###

Made in the USA
San Bernardino, CA
13 February 2018